Turning Points

Art Williams

THE ART OF WRITING, LLC
PUBLISHERS & AUTHORS

Turning Points

Near dusk on the tenth day out, Andrew greeted his scout, Ray Cooper, who rode up to the circle of wagons. Cooper was pulling a makeshift sled of branches bearing the gutted bodies of two white-tailed deer. The scout dismounted his tired roan mare and slapped his hat across his leather chaps to knock off dust from two days out front on the trail. Some men and women came over to unload the deer and prep the venison for dinner to share with the camp. The fresh meat would be a welcome change from the dry beef jerky they had been eating.

Cooper pulled his bedroll and saddle from the mare and reported washed-out conditions of a section of the trail toward an upcoming gap. His horse shook her head and matted mane and trotted off toward the rope corral to join the other animals, eat some grass, and tell her own stories.

What They are Saying about *Turning Points*

If you don't want to stay up all night, plan to read Art Williams's powerful 'can't put it down' book, *Turning Points*, on the weekend. As you follow Andrew Greene's life, you will encounter how he copes with love, death, escaped slaves, unscrupulous overseers, war, the Oregon Trail, fatherhood, and so much more. This book begs for a sequel, and I can't wait to read it.

—Agnes Alexander—*Sister Circle, Isabella's Baby, Wilma's Outlaw, Nelda's Homecoming, Ulla's Courage, Opal's Faith,* and *Valissa's Home.*

Turning Points by Art Williams provides a vivid, close-up look at an early part of American history from the viewpoint of Andrew Greene, farmer, soldier, and eventually wagon master on a hazardous trip westward. The rich detail in this well-researched book provides an intimate and unflinching view of the realities of life in the first half of the nineteenth century. Andrew survives war, injury, and the deaths of friends and loved ones, with each event molding him into a stronger man.

—Karen McCullough, author of the Market Center Mysteries series

Turning Points

Art Williams

THE ART OF WRITING, LLC
PUBLISHERS & AUTHORS

Copyright © 2025 by: Art Williams
ISBN: 979-8-9936617-0-4

Previously Published by Wings ePress, Inc.
Edited by: Jeanne Smith
Copy Edited by: Michael Embry
Executive Editor: Jeanne Smith
Cover Artist: Trisha FitzGerald-Jung
Images: AI, Pixabay

Published In the United States Of America

The Art of Writing LLC
5302 Candlewick Rd.
Greensboro, NC 27455

Dedication

This book is dedicated to my wonderful wife, Carol.
Thank you for all fifty years of love and support.

One

August, 1824

Early Saturday morning in the cool air, nine-year-old Elizabeth Vining walked to the stables to ride her horse, Grace. She saw low-lying clouds settling around the top of Burge Hill to the north, and buzzards circling closer in. The sun would soon chase the clouds away and bring warmth to the fields of the plantation in Miller's Creek, Tennessee, where slaves tended to crops of sugarcane, cotton, and tobacco.

As she arrived, the young girl could hear, emanating from the clapboard barn, the popping sound of a whip and harsh words from the overseer. She pushed open the rough, hinged door and the words and the whipping stopped.

Charles Loggins, the overseer, tucked his whip into his belt. Eleven-year-old slave Isaiah pulled down his sweat-stained shirt.

"Only two lashes, miss," Loggins said. "It's the best way for him to learn. He won't forget from now on."

Elizabeth said nothing, but she stared at the overseer, her eyes wide. Isaiah grabbed both handles of a wheelbarrow of hay and manure and pushed it out the open, double-back doors, headed toward the gardens. He would turn the mix into a large compost pile, part of his daily routine of cleaning the stables.

Loggins said, "Here's Grace, Miss Elizabeth. All ready for your morning ride. Remember to stay inside the fences."

Elizabeth nodded in agreement, stepped up onto a wooden box, slid her foot into a stirrup, and mounted the English saddle. Loggins handed her the reins and walked the horse out of the barn.

"After your ride, give Grace over to Isaiah. He'll wipe her down and put her away."

Still silent, Elizabeth looked over her shoulder at the man and the whip in his belt, as Grace ambled away. The girl rode past Isaiah, who looked up from the wheelbarrow and nodded. She saw the glistening trace a tear had left below his right eye. She rode on.

At the neighboring farm, in the rising heat, 10-year-old Andrew Greene felt beads of sweat rolling down his neck. While clearing the garden of weeds, he saw a horse and rider trotting down Miller Road and knew who it was.

"I came here, but don't tell anyone," Elizabeth said. She jumped down from her horse.

Andrew stopped weeding and leaned on the handle of his hoe. "I'm glad you came. I was thinking about you. Thought I might bring you some flowers later today."

The girl smiled at him and then frowned.

"I'm not happy with our overseer. I think Mr. Loggins uses his whip too much."

Andrew took Grace's reins and walked the horse and Elizabeth toward the farmhouse. "I don't like him either. I don't think he should use a whip at all."

"He whipped Isaiah this morning, and Isaiah is only eleven."

"You should tell your daddy. He'll do something." Andrew wrapped the reins over a hitching post and held the front gate open for Elizabeth. They could smell freshly baked cookies through an open kitchen window.

"I *will* tell Daddy, and guess what else?" said Elizabeth.

"I don't know. What?"

"Mama said she's with child."

"She's gonna have a baby?"

"And I'll have a new brother or sister."

"When?"

"I'm not sure."

"Which do you want, a brother or a sister?"

"I haven't decided yet."

"Well, I think you need to let your mama know pretty soon."

Seven months later—March, 1825

The season was turning from winter to spring. Buds were on trees across the land and the sight of new blossoms was welcome. Andrew pulled a harness and yoke from a wall in the barn. By now, he had grown accustomed to farm life and understood the need to get the soil ready to hold moisture from upcoming spring rains which would lead to bountiful crops to feed his family and their livestock.

When Andrew prepared to plow shallow furrows in an acre, part of the 500 his father owned, a chilly wind blew in gusts across the field, shaking trees and shrubs and making it difficult for little birds to fly straight.

Andrew began working the field. Eager robins and other birds swooped down to find worms and grubs turned up by the blade of the wooden plow. The boy gave commands behind Hercules, a sturdy gray mule. The strong, patient, plodding animal was easygoing and responded well to Andrew's directions of 'gee' and 'haw' and the light tapping of reins on its backside.

Kicking up little clouds of dust, Isaiah Jordan came running down Miller Road as fast as his skinny legs could carry him. By the time he reached the Greenes' farm, the boy could hardly catch his breath. Andrew stopped plowing when he saw the slave coming.

Exhausted, Isaiah hung over the split-rail fence surrounding the field. "You gotta' come," he yelled. "Master Andrew, you gotta' come." Andrew knew there must be big trouble because a slave leaving a plantation could lead to a thrashing or worse from the overseer.

He halted Hercules, pulled the loop of reins off his shoulders, and ran toward the fence yelling, "What is it, Isaiah?"

"It's Miss Elizabeth. She's cryin' for ya. Her mama's done died trying to bear that baby."

"Oh, no! I gotta get my mother. You better get on back now. Go tell Elizabeth we're on the way."

"Yessir. Yessir. I will. I's just worn out 'bout now."

"All right, of course. I'll fetch my mother. Help me get our buggy ready."

"I'll do that," Isaiah cried, "and that baby boy, he done died too."

Andrew released Hercules and ran to the house, bursting into the kitchen where his mother was putting away dishes. "Mama!"

She turned to him. "Are you hurt?"

He started to cry. "No. Elizabeth's mama died and so did the baby. Isaiah just told me."

Before Andrew got all his words out, his mother grabbed her shawl, a piece of paper, and a pencil. "Now, the buggy is still at the front gate. Daddy's too far away. I'll leave him a note."

Isaiah was waiting at the buggy, holding the horse's reins as Andrew and his mother arrived. "Thank you, Isaiah," she said.

"You best get aboard so we can give you safe passage." She took the reins, popped the buggy whip in the air, and off they went.

When they arrived at the plantation, Isaiah tied the horse and buggy near the main house. Andrew and his mother climbed the steps. Cook and housekeeper Mama Jordan received them. "Thank you for bringin' my boy back safe and sound."

"Of course," Mrs. Greene said. "We've got to take care of our children."

"It's powerful sad," Mama Jordan said. "They's all upstairs. Mr. Vining's beside hisself and little Elizabeth is in a pool of tears. The doctor and midwife are takin' care of things."

Mrs. Greene put a hand on Mama Jordan's shoulder then hugged her. "It's terrible, I know. We just had to come. I know you loved her too. What can we do?"

Andrew looked at both of the women. "I need to see Elizabeth. Can I go up, please? Where is she?"

Mama Jordan put her arm around Andrew. "I need to tell them you're here, sweet boy, so they can gather themselves some. Why don't ya'll sit in the parlor, and I'll see what I can do?"

With tear-stained cheeks, both James Vining and his daughter Elizabeth entered the parlor. Mrs. Greene and Andrew rose from the loveseat. Elizabeth let go of her father's hand and ran to Andrew, crying anew. They hugged each other. Neither could speak. Andrew cried too.

Mrs. Greene spoke first. "James, I hope you'll forgive us for coming at such a time. Robert is away but we heard of your loss. Elizabeth sent word for Andrew to come."

"It's good for her, and me, that you are here, Amelia. Thank you for coming."

"I apologize for comin' empty-handed," she said.

"There's no need for that. We are neighbors and friends for many years now. You *should* be here. Mary Alice would have wanted you here to be with us. She went into labor late last night. Earlier than anticipated, and things turned bad soon after."

Mama Jordan entered the room carrying a silver tray bearing a tea set and a plate of small triangular sandwiches. Mr. Vining thanked her, dismissed her, and turned to Andrew. "Why don't you and Elizabeth go out on the patio? Take some tea and food. The fresh air will do her good."

The children stepped outside and Mr. Vining closed the door behind them. "We are broken, I am sad to say. We are broken today. Thank you for bringing your boy. Elizabeth and he are fast friends. It will distract her some."

"I know you'll be flooded with visitors as soon as the word spreads. We're here for you. Should I ask Mama Jordan how we can best be of help?"

"Mary Alice was so looking forward to this baby. Both of us were."

"I know," Mrs. Greene said.

"I was on the other side of the plantation last evening. I returned as fast as I could."

"She loved you and Elizabeth so."

"We had hoped for even more," Mr. Vining choked. "It was a boy, you know."

"I loved her too. She was so dear."

"A breech baby. A lot of pain."

"I'm sorry."

"So much blood. Neither could be saved."

~ * ~

Outside, Elizabeth and Andrew sat next to each other on the top step of the patio. "I could hear Mama screaming," the girl said.

"I'm sorry."

"The doctor said that always happens when women are having babies—the screaming. Mama said she'd be all right. Just stay with Mama Jordan until it was over, she said."

"It must hurt, having a baby."

"Mama Jordan said it would be all right. She helped me pray about it. It helped some."

Andrew offered her a bite of his sandwich.

"I can't eat. I already threw up."

Andrew put his arm around her as both of them looked out across the yard. "You've got to be sick at your heart. Eat something when you can."

"I would have had a brother."

"I know."

"And now I have no mother."

"I know," he said.

"What will I do?"

"My heart is hurting. I loved your mama too."

She looked into his eyes and put both hands on his wet cheeks. "I love you. You know that?

"Yes, and I love you."

"Just sit with me. Hold me."

Andrew held her hand. The two little people looked out onto the trees and fields that rolled in front of them. Elizabeth put her head on Andrew's shoulder. "You smell like you've been working."

"I was. I was plowing when Isaiah ran over."

Two

A week after the death of her mother and the baby boy who would have been her brother, Elizabeth woke to a commotion outside the mansion and ran to an open window. Still in her night clothes, she heard Mama Jordan screaming and saw her running from the kitchen and down the driveway.

The slave was trying to catch up to a flatbed wagon rumbling toward the road. Snapping a whip over their heads, Loggins drove two brown horses that pulled the wagon. It was hauling a big, iron-barred cage holding four slaves: a girl, two men, and a boy holding onto the bars crying out for his mama. It was Isaiah.

Elizabeth threw on clothes and ran downstairs. By the time she could reach Mama Jordan at the side of the road, the woman was exhausted. She had stumbled onto her hands and knees and cried out, begging for God's help.

"They's took my boy. They's took my Isaiah, Miss Elizabeth."

"Where is Loggins going?" the girl asked.

"The market 'long the Mississippi."

Elizabeth helped Mama Jordan stand. "Why take them?"

"It's a slave market, child. He's gonna sell my boy!"

Elizabeth led Mama Jordan back to the plantation house and the girl ran to her father's room. In his robe, still dealing with his wife's death, the distraught man was looking out his window toward the family cemetery. A glass of whiskey in his hand, he stared unsteadily at the graves where his wife and baby son were buried.

"Daddy, you've got to stop him."

"What's that?" James Vining said, still looking out the window.

"Mr. Loggins."

"Oh. Why's that?"

"Daddy, are you hearing me?"

"Loggins? Yes." Her father turned toward her, and she saw his pale face. His bloodshot eyes stared past her.

"Daddy, he's taking slaves to the market."

"Was that today?"

"So you knew?"

"He said it was time. I've been neglecting my work, seems like for weeks now. I told him to do what's needin' to be done."

"But, Daddy, why did he take slaves away if we need them?"

Her father sipped his drink and turned toward the window again, looking at the cemetery. "We need some new, strong backs, Loggins said. One of the workers died. Maybe you didn't know. Crops are comin' in. Need to harvest."

She reached up and touched his arm. "He took Isaiah, Mama Jordan's Isaiah. Are you understanding me, Daddy?" She could smell the liquor on his breath.

"Well, child, it's not yer business. Sometimes you sell some and buy some. It's just tradin'."

"I want you to stop him and bring Isaiah back. Do you hear me?" Tears ran down her cheeks. "Where are you, Daddy? Daddy, are you listening?"

Her father downed his drink and reached for the half-empty bottle on a table.

~ * ~

From the Greenes' vegetable garden, Andrew saw Elizabeth galloping down the road on Grace. He dropped his basket of just-picked beans, ran across the garden, and jumped the split-rail fence as the girl pulled up.

"I hate him, Andrew. You know I hate him," Elizabeth cried, dropping from her saddle.

"Who?" He started to hold her, but she pushed him away.

"That terrible man Loggins, the overseer, and Daddy isn't behaving right either. I almost hate him. And I really miss my mother."

"Did Loggins whip Isaiah again?"

"Worse. Worse. He drove off with Isaiah in a cage. And other slaves too."

Andrew led Elizabeth into the house where his mother listened to the story and sat the pair down in the dining room. "Drink some of this lemonade, both of you. Try to calm down."

"Someone has to stop that wagon and get Isaiah back. Get them all back," Elizabeth cried.

"What can we do, Mama?" Andrew said.

"There's nothin' we can do, children. I don't like it either. I know Mama Jordan must be sick with grief, and so soon after losin' Mary Alice; they cared about each other so. But we need to get you back home to your father, Elizabeth. I know he'll be lookin' for you and worried."

~ * ~

Two days passed.

Mr. Vining was in the barn saddling his horse when Sheriff Leon Fisher rode up to the big open doors and dismounted.

"Morning, James."

"This is a surprise. What brings you out here?" Vining asked.

The sheriff removed his hat. "Well, first off, I wanted to give you my sympathies a'gin fer yer loss."

"I saw you came to the service. Thank you for that."

"Certainly."

Vining kneed his horse in the side to force out extra air and tightened the cinch under the belly of the animal. "After a week of drinking, I've finally gotten back to work."

"That's good."

"So, what else, Sheriff?"

"I got some bad news, I'm afraid."

"About ..."

The sheriff turned his hat slowly in his hands. "I got a message that yer slave wagon was found empty in a ditch on the way to the market. Horses are gone. Just yer wagon left there with Vining Plantation written on the back of the seat."

"Damn it. I wondered what was holding Loggins up. What'd he say?"

"Well, that's it. There *was* no Loggins. You know, he's well known down that way, having been a slaver for years now. But he's nowhere in sight, and any slaves in that cage are gone."

"What the hell?"

The sheriff moved to mount up. "I'm goin' down there to investigate. Thought I'd let you know first. I'll get yer wagon back to ya."

Mr. Vining looked disgusted. "Abolitionists?"

"Could be. Don't know. Them slaves could'a got out some other way. But I reckon they got help of some kind. Could'a been some thieves wantin' to get slaves fer free. It's a rough business."

"There was four of 'em, just so you know. A girl, two bucks, and that Isaiah boy. He learned how to read and write somehow. Loggins said we needed four more strong backs for harvest. I'm doing a headcount this morning."

"I'll let you know," the sheriff said.

"Reckon I'll need a new overseer, and I'll be busier than ever in the fields. It's bad timing, with a harvest coming up and all. Let me know what you find out when you're able."

The sheriff nodded, mounted up, and headed out. "May be a few days or a week."

~ * ~

After two weeks, Sheriff Fisher returned, leading the Vining Plantation's cage wagon with a new team of horses driven by his nephew, Charles. They stopped in front of the barn where Mr. Vining was applying a curry brush to the back of a horse.

"Leon, I was wondering where you got to," said Mr. Vining.

"Hello, James. It took a while to investigate your missing team and Loggins and all. You remember meetin' my nephew Charles last year, I reckon."

"Charles," Vining said, nodding toward the man.

"How do, Mr. Vining. I'm glad to be of service, and my uncle says you're in need of an overseer."

"Reckon so. What did you all find out about Loggins?"

"Well, that's it, James," the sheriff said. "The last anybody seen of him he was gettin' on a steamboat headed down toward Louisiana. Two different folks saw him. One knew him for sho'."

"So, sounds like he's run off," Vining said.

"That's probly it. Unless he's chasin' some lead on his own, but I doubt that."

Mr. Vining tossed the curry brush into a box. "Well, thank you for looking. Glad to have my wagon back."

"Yeah. You know I ran into Charles down along the Mississippi at the market. Hadn't seen 'im for a couple of months."

"That right?" Vining said.

Charles spoke up from the seat of the wagon. "Yes, sir, Mr. Vining. I was trading down there. If we knew what you wanted in the way of slaves, we could 'a worked it out."

"You don't say."

"Yes, sir. I been overseeing a plantation in Georgia, but I'm lookin' to come on back up here. The rest of my folks are near here. So I'm hopin' you would consider me for the job."

Vining rubbed his chin and looked at the sheriff and then Charles. "Well, maybe. Put the wagon over there and come up to the patio out back. After your trip, I expect you'd like some food and drink, and we can talk more. Leon, let me know what I owe you for the team."

Three

Five years later, June, 1830

Elizabeth Vining enjoyed her breakfast of a five-minute egg, ham biscuits, and a cup of chamomile tea. The warm morning sun greeted her on the front steps. She stopped at the kitchen to thank Mama Jordan for the meal. Before leaving the kitchen, which lay separate from the main house, Elizabeth packed a wicker basket with cheese, slices of ham, six biscuits, and a jar of strawberry jam. Walking through a stand of magnificent, tall magnolias that lined the drive, she strolled toward the stables.

All her young life, Elizabeth had a joy about her. She lost it for a year or so after her mother died, but now, on the day of her sixteenth birthday, she was thinking ahead, expecting a party and a slice of birthday cake before nightfall.

First, she wanted to ride to the Greenes' farm down the lane and visit her boyfriend, Andrew. By the time she would get there, she figured he would be in one of the fields. She liked the way he looked when he was working the farm. His arms were strong and she loved how he smiled when he saw her coming.

Charles Fisher, the overseer, was waiting for the young mistress of the house. Though she could saddle her horse herself, Fisher personally curried and saddled Grace, Elizabeth's eight-year-old chestnut mare.

"Grace is ready for you, Miss Elizabeth," Fisher said. "Fed an' watered an hour ago, so she can run some. She's lookin' bright and beautiful."

"Thank you, Mr. Fisher."

"Are you ridin' alone this mornin'?"

"Yes. I won't be long. Grace needs the exercise. I figured you were down here, so I brought you a ham biscuit," she said, handing him the small cloth-wrapped treat.

At the Greenes' farm, Andrew had stopped planting early, cleaned up, and put on a new shirt. He saw Elizabeth coming and waited until she arrived.

"Hello, sweetheart. This is a nice surprise," he said.

"Really? You are so surprised that you bathed and put on a fresh shirt? You are clever. Anyway, I thought you and I should get together, especially today."

"You been out visiting folks already?"

"Yes. Just dropping off some good food to good people."

Without so much as a mention of her birthday, he smiled at her. "Oh, I'm always glad to see you. You know that, I hope. I've got to finish putting some tools away. Can you go visit with Mama in her garden? I'll be along soon."

She figured he was being secretive in some way about her birthday, so she rode up to the garden and hugged Andrew's mother until he appeared.

Ending a walk at the stone bridge, Elizabeth and Andrew sat on a fallen tree at the edge of Millers Creek, moving their bare feet in the cool water. They had fallen in love with each other long ago. Andrew put his arm around Elizabeth and kissed her.

She kissed him back. The sky was a striking shade of blue with white clouds drifting above the couple.

Andrew tossed a pebble into the water. "You ever feel like you're supposed to do something but you don't know what?"

She put her arm through his. "You mean like maybe you forgot to do something?" She dropped a leaf in the water and watched it float away.

"Yeah, sort of like that, but not really."

"What do you mean?"

"That you're meant to do something or be somewhere, like an adventure."

Elizabeth smiled at him. "Well, Preacher Crawford says life can be an adventure but most of what's going to happen is already planned by God. It's predestined. Predetermined."

"Maybe that's it. I feel like I got some kind of itch that needs scratching, but I don't know what it is."

Elizabeth poked him in his ribs. "You mean like a bug bite?"

"No." He poked her back. "Something else. Something bigger."

"So, do you think *that something* is supposed to happen today?"

"Maybe," he said.

"Like today is somehow special?"

"Well, it's more of what's out there a year or two from now."

Elizabeth could feel her cheeks getting red. "So, not today?"

"No. I don't think so."

She took hold of Andrew's left ear. "Andrew Dale Greene, have you forgotten that today is my birthday?"

Andrew froze with his mouth agape as Elizabeth stared into his eyes. "Maybe my birthday is that something." Letting go of his ear, she turned to get off the log.

"No, that can't be it." He laughed and hopped up and started running up the path toward his father's farm.

Elizabeth ran right behind him. "You're not getting away from me!"

"You know," Andrew said over his shoulder, "one of the things I like about you is your forgiving nature."

"It comes and goes," she said breathlessly. "Stop running, Andrew."

He stopped and turned around. She ran into him. They fell together in a heap laughing.

"I know it's your birthday, my dear. My darling."

"I should hope so. I'm only turning sixteen once, so you better remember."

"I've got a surprise for you," he said, sitting up on one elbow, "back at the farm. Come on." He took her by the hand, pulled her up, and kissed her lips. They stopped and kissed some more.

When the pair burst into the Greenes' farmhouse, they were welcomed with shouts of 'happy birthday' and surrounded by family members and friends. Presents for Elizabeth, wrapped with cloth and ribbons, were waiting to be opened. A garland of flowers was draped across beams in the ceiling and a cake with sixteen candles was being lit by Andrew's mother. A small fire kept a kettle of fragrant cider warm.

"Happy birthday, my dear," Mrs. Greene said, smiling and giving the girl a hug.

Elizabeth laughed. She in turn hugged everyone. "How wonderful! Andrew acted like he had forgotten all about my birthday. He was terrible and sweet all at the same time!"

Andrew's father offered Elizabeth a chair as the guest of honor. "Come have a seat, princess. Then we will bring you cider and cake, and you can open all your presents."

Mrs. Greene said, "To make the wish come true, you must blow out all the candles at once. Andrew, take the cake to Elizabeth and help her."

Andrew picked up the cake and held it in front of Elizabeth. She closed her eyes, made a silent wish, opened her eyes, and blew out all the candles. Everyone cheered. Mrs. Greene sliced the cake and Andrew started passing plates to all the guests.

Mrs. Greene handed a present to Elizabeth. "Open my gift to you first."

The girl admired a colorful bow and string that tied soft paper around the gift.

"Thank you, Mother Greene." Inside she discovered a silver hairbrush. "It's lovely. The silver is beautiful. I can even see my reflection in the back of the brush. And such soft bristles."

"Just the thing for your long hair," said Mrs. Greene.

Andrew teased, "The brush is made with horsehair. Maybe you'll let me brush your hair sometime."

Elizabeth blushed. "Why, Andrew Greene! I never!" Everyone laughed.

There was a bounty of other gifts, including a new spring bonnet, a handmade necklace of wooden beads, and a box of hard candy. Elizabeth opened the candy right away, took one, and passed the box around.

"Everyone must have some, please." Elizabeth looked around the room. "This is all so special, but I don't see Daddy. Where is he?" Just then there was a knock at the door.

Mrs. Greene motioned for Elizabeth to get up. "Maybe you should see who that is at the door, birthday girl."

Elizabeth hurried to the door. Mr. Vining stood there holding the reins to a horse. He hugged his daughter. "Look what I found wandering around in our paddock, and there's a note to go with it."

"Daddy, what have you done?" Elizabeth said. "Come, everyone, look here."

All the partygoers came pouring out of the door and admired the beautiful horse, a young golden palomino with a large pink bow around its neck. Elizabeth removed an envelope from the ribbon.

"Oh, Daddy, I can't believe this," Elizabeth said. She stepped up to the side of the horse and patted its neck.

She opened the envelope. "Listen, everyone, here's what the note says: My dearest daughter, Elizabeth, I am so proud of you on this your sixteenth birthday. I know your mother would be happy to see the woman you have become. Love, Father."

She stopped reading and looked at him. "Oh, Daddy, you're making me cry." She continued, "and wait, everyone, there's a P.S. from the horse: Elizabeth, this is my birthday too. I'm three years old today and ready to give you rides and affection, if you'll give me lots of apples and carrots. But I also need a name."

Elizabeth gave her father another hug and turned to the crowd. "Did ya'll know about this?"

Andrew replied, "Yes, sweetheart. It's not every day that you turn sixteen. Your father and I talked about planning your gifts for the last few months. He had to go to Memphis to find this horse. What will you name it?"

"I'm going to name her Belle!"

That evening, the couple rode their horses to the plantation. After walking Elizabeth to the front porch of the plantation house, Andrew took her by the hand. They sat on white, wooden rockers to say goodnight.

"There is one more gift, maybe two that I have yet to give you," Andrew said.

"Oh, my. But you've been so generous already, Andrew. I don't need another thing. It's not more cake, is it?"

"No. There is one present you've already had for a long time," Andrew said kneeling in front of her. "For years, in fact. And that is my heart."

Tears quickly came to her eyes as Elizabeth replied, "Oh, Andy. I love you too. I think always."

Andrew pulled a ring bearing a small diamond from his pocket. "Elizabeth Vining... "

She started crying softly.

"Will you do me the honor of becoming my wife?"

Andrew kissed her tears away as she nodded. "Yes, my darling. A thousand times yes," she whispered and dabbed her eyes with a linen handkerchief.

"Let's ride to the farm and see my parents. I want to surprise them with the good news."

She agreed right away, hugged and kissed him but then pulled him into the plantation house. "Yes, let's do, but first we need to see Daddy."

Vining gave his daughter a kiss and gave Andrew a firm handshake.

"I thought this would happen one day,". Vining said. "Daughter, I also expect your mother would not have been surprised. You two have been like two peas in a pod it seems forever."

Half an hour later, Andrew's family greeted the couple at the farmhouse door with shouts of joy and hugged them both. Andrew's older brother, Mason, shook his hand, and his older sister, Jeanette, kissed his cheek. His father opened a bottle of wine to celebrate and poured a glass for everyone.

"Young woman, you're only sixteen. Does your father let you drink wine?"

Elizabeth blushed. "I have on occasion."

"Well, this is one special occasion," Mr. Greene said. "It'll be mighty fine to have another daughter in our family."

By the time Andrew returned Elizabeth to her father's plantation, lightning bugs were guiding the way and a cool breeze drifted across the land.

"I won't sleep a wink tonight," Elizabeth said. Andrew kissed her.

"Nor will I. I love you so much I could bust."

Andrew watched Elizabeth step through the front entrance. She turned, waved, and blew him a kiss before closing the door.

Andrew started walking his horse toward the lane leading away from the plantation.

"So you proposed to my daughter," Vining said from the shadows.

Andrew turned, halted by the man's sudden appearance.

"Yes, sir. I'm surprised to see you out."

"She was excited about the ring. An heirloom, I guess."

Andrew dropped the reins to the ground. "Yes, my grandmother's ring. A good night all around. I'm very glad."

Vining crossed his arms. "I expected any young man would have come to me to ask permission to marry her."

Andrew cleared his throat. " ...I did come to see you, sir, but you were in Memphis yesterday, and I couldn't wait."

"I know she loves you."

"I'm sorry I couldn't wait for you, sir. I was too excited. You are right though. Certainly."

"So what should we do?"

"I beg your pardon?"

"About you and me, and permission, and any wedding?"

Andrew had no experience in such matters and found Vining a little mysterious and intimidating, never sure just what his future father-in-law meant sometimes. Vining seemed to like the confusion.

"I'm not sure, Mr. Vining. I've never done this before. I really don't have an answer."

"Mama Jordan said you came by earlier to find me, so I believe you tried."

"I did, sir."

"Elizabeth is young. I think too young to get married right now. And you're young too, at seventeen."

"Yes, sir. Eighteen in July. July first."

"There's some things I think a man needs to do before getting married to any girl."

"I see."

"Andrew, you have no fortune, no career, no prospects."

"Well, I…"

"You won't inherit much, if anything."

"Well, I…"

"So I have a proposal for you."

Andrew looked Mr. Vining in the eye. "Yes, sir."

"Her mother and I didn't raise Elizabeth to leave the life she has enjoyed so far in order to hoe potatoes. You understand?"

"Yes, sir."

"I propose you prove yourself worthy of my daughter by getting established in some way."

"Established?"

"Yes, son. I've known you almost all of your life, and you're smart and strong, and I expect you will do well, but you haven't yet. Not even selected a path, as far as I know. Now, I've heard the Army has a pension of land for soldiers who serve. If you do that, you will be given some land so you can start your own farm. That way, you'll be able to provide a roof over your heads and get started on a road to a bright future."

"Yes, sir."

"So, think about it. Will you do that?"

"I will."

The next morning, Andrew asked around about joining the Army. He met with a local militia officer and found that if he served for two years he could receive 160 acres of land. If he served during a war, the time could be shorter. Later that afternoon, Andrew stepped out of the farmhouse and greeted the sun with a new energy and with a sense of relief and joy combined. But he was also concerned about the future and explaining his plans to Elizabeth.

Four

March, 1832

Elizabeth walked down the marble stairs to greet Andrew in the foyer of the plantation house.

"Hello, sweetheart," he said.

"I've missed you all morning," Elizabeth said, stepping into his embrace.

"I wanted to hold you close ever since I woke up."

"Do you want to stay inside in the parlor?" She gently touched his forelock and kissed his forehead.

"How about outside?"

"I don't know. It's cold, and Daddy said March is coming in like a lion, a windy lion."

"Then the parlor sounds good."

"Mama Jordan said she'd bring hot tea when you arrived. Did she see you?"

"I saw her. She waved from the kitchen window."

"She'll be along soon then."

Sunbeams danced through the leaded glass windows surrounding the parlor. The couple sat on the loveseat and Andrew put his arm around Elizabeth. They kissed and heard the light rattling of cups and saucers coming toward them. Mama Jordan came through the door carrying a silver tea service, china cups and saucers, and little cloth napkins.

"I watched you children grow up all these years," she said. "I guess I better start thinkin' 'bout you as adults since you's gettin' married, though. It's mighty fine y'all bein' in love."

"We are," Elizabeth said.

"Yes we are, and thank you for the tea," Andrew said.

"Master Andrew, I recon' you gonna be here even more now."

"Oh, every possible minute. My parents are glad to see Elizabeth at our farm anytime too."

"They say I'm like another daughter to them," Elizabeth said. "So dear."

"They's a mighty nice family," Mama Jordan said.

"We are in each other's pockets," Elizabeth said.

Mama Jordan turned to go. "I'll leave the pourin' to you, miss." She left the couple alone.

Elizabeth poured. "One lump of sugar for you. Two for me."

"No wonder you're so sweet," Andrew said.

"You do go on." She settled against the back of the loveseat and smiled at Andrew. "Tell me more about how you love me."

"All the stars in the sky."

"I like that, but you seem a little distracted."

"Well, a little," he said.

"Some news?"

"Yes."

"Don't make me pull it out of you." She stirred her cup of tea.

"I don't think there's a good time or a good way."

Elizabeth put her hand to her mouth. "Don't make me cry. Tell me now."

"You know, we talked about my joining the militia."

"And I finally agreed, but I'll hate it."

"I received a letter, a notice, yesterday."

"And you're just telling me now?

"It was late in the day, by rider," he said, setting the cup aside.

"What is it, please."

"I have to report to St. Louis by a week from Friday."

"For what? Why so soon? That's only a few days."

"My father says it has to do with the Black Hawk War."

"A war? You're going right into a war?" Elizabeth started crying. She had trouble breathing between sobs. He held her. "No, no, no," she said, pushing his chest away. "It's not supposed to be like this. I'll die if anything happens to you."

"It will be all right."

"How do you know that?"

"I'll be fine."

Her cries filled the room. A moment later, they heard footsteps coming, and Elizabeth's father appeared at the door to the parlor. Andrew stood.

"How is everyone?" Vining said.

"Daddy, the militia wants him to start right away."

"The Black Hawk War," Andrew said.

"I'm not surprised. Though that's a long way," Mr. Vining said.

"The Missouri militia is lending me and others to the Illinois militia."

"So, you'll be in Illinois and the Michigan territory?"

"I think so."

"Don't you see, Daddy? Off to war in the blink of an eye." Elizabeth continued to cry and wipe her eyes with a napkin.

Vining said, "You have to leave soon?"

"Yes, by Friday-next, for St. Louis, and on from there."

Elizabeth cried and curled up on the loveseat by herself.

~ * ~

When Andrew returned to the Greenes' farm, his father said, "How did your fiancée take the news?"

"Not well. I'm not sure I like it either." Andrew poured himself a cup of water.

"Don't let your mother hear that. She's finally gotten calm about it."

"It's getting very real. The leaving."

"How's your gut?"

"Churning a bit."

"Now what?"

"Pack some things."

"Take whatever weapons you want, just let me know. And plenty of powder and shot and the makings."

"Yes, sir."

"Knives, pistols, rifles, your horse and tack."

"Thank you, of course."

"I think you'll be well-equipped. Be sure you understand the tactics. Look for good men to stand beside you."

Andrew nodded. "I'll go back to have dinner with her tonight, and Mr. Vining."

"Tell your mother. She'll worry the whole time you're up there in Illinois, as will I. Vining will be for you and his daughter's happiness, I'm sure."

"Thanks for all you've done for me."

"You're a good shot and a good man. Do what you need to do out there and come back whole."

"I'll write to all of you as much as I can."

"From what I read, it shouldn't last long. But we'll talk more in the morning."

"Elizabeth wants to set a date for the wedding, so she can let Preacher Crawford know."

"There'll be plenty of time for that once you're back. Your mother and I will help keep your girl's spirits up. We'll have her over here. Your mother could use her help in the garden and the kitchen. But, for now, go see your mother. She'll want to hear it all from you direct."

~ * ~

The next morning his father asked Andrew to meet in a newly plowed field. Andrew figured he wanted to discuss the crop to plant. Instead, when Andrew walked up, without saying anything, his father grabbed him by the neck and threw him down in the dirt.

"What going on?" Andrew sputtered, surprised.

After he got up and regained his footing, his father kicked Andrew's legs out from under him and fell on top of his son. Facedown, Andrew couldn't move.

His father finally said, "What are you gonna do when you have to fight up close?"

"Let me up," Andrew said angrily. "Stop this. You know I've been wrestling Mason for years, but not like this."

Once Andrew got up, his father grabbed an arm and threw his son onto the ground again. Andrew had never fought with his father. They had argued about things like being on time, how to harness the horses, or being more of a help, but they had never wrestled, never fought.

Andrew remembered his father had been in the war of 1812. The man seldom talked about it. Maybe his father wanted to show Andrew what a *real* fight might be like. Andrew had *never* seen his father fight.

"I'd rather wrestle Mason," Andrew said. Five years older, Andrew's brother Mason always won, until Andrew, at fifteen, had pinned him on the ground. Mason had to give up. Andrew recalled it was a strange feeling to finally beat *Mason*. But never his father.

His father said, "The army will be different from tussling with your brother or your friends. In a battle, you don't get to say 'uncle' to your enemy, shake hands, and walk away. You can say 'I surrender,' if you speak their language, and you may be put in prison or tortured for information about your troops, or more likely killed right then and there—no mercy."

"Why are you telling me this, doing this?" Andrew said.

"Because I love you, son, and I want you to know what to do when you fight in a war. I doubt you'll get much training. They'll expect you to know about weapons, and how to protect yourself, your fellow soldiers, and how to take orders, or give 'em."

Mr. Greene started to walk around Andrew in a circle and the young man didn't know what would happen next.

His father said, "There's a dangerous road to travel before you get that acreage, and I want you to come back safe and sound. Now, let's start again."

This time, Andrew grabbed his father first, around the neck. His father swung an elbow into Andrew's stomach. Andrew let go and got pushed to the ground. His father put a knee on his son's chest, pretended one of his fingers was a knife, and dragged it across the young man's throat.

"You're dead," his father said.

His father offered Andrew a hand, then pulled his son up and over his back, throwing Andrew down again. Andrew was getting tired and angry with his strong father.

His father said, "There'll be no quitting during a fight like this—only a bad injury or death. You need to know what to expect and what to do."

"I can't fight you," Andrew said.

"Because you're too weak?"

"No, because you're my father and I don't want to hurt you."

"Let me worry about that. Let's try again, and this time I'll explain what to do."

For the next exhausting hour, Andrew's father won every round. Andrew didn't know when it would end. Each time his father did something different to pin Andrew to the ground, knock him in the head, or kill him with a pretend weapon. After each fight his father explained what he did and what Andrew could have done to protect himself and fight back.

They had never been so physical with each other. That day, even though his father pummeled Andrew, the man showed restraint. Andrew could tell his father didn't want to hurt him; he wanted to teach him, and Andrew wanted to learn. Finally, his father stopped.

"Son, your nose is bleeding. Go get cleaned up. Your mother will have lunch on the table in a few minutes, and we'll do this again tomorrow. Then we'll move on to weapons."

Andrew rubbed his jaw as he stumbled to the well near the garden. He poured water over his head and face then walked toward the house, thinking Mama was not going to like this.

His mother *was* angry but *at his father*. Andrew overheard them talking after lunch. After going to bed that night, he could hear a muffled argument. The next morning Andrew came down for breakfast as usual, but his father was not up yet. A bottle of liniment sat on the kitchen counter.

"He's sleeping in a little this morning," Andrew's mother said. "What's this about you two fighting yesterday?"

"Advanced wrestling. Father figures the militia will do me some good but there won't be much training. What's this liniment for?"

"You wore out your father yesterday. I rubbed that on his back and legs last night. Anyway, I don't like the idea of you going off with the militia. What does Elizabeth think 'bout all this?"

"She was not happy to hear it."

"I bet she cried, didn't she?"

"Yes. I wasn't surprised. Her father seemed pleased and in favor of it. I explained about the land we could get after I serve. She said we may wind up with the plantation years from now anyway, so we don't need the land."

His mother put a plate of eggs, bacon, toast, and potatoes in front of Andrew. "Maybe, after you marry, but I wouldn't count on that plantation. Is there no next of kin in the Vining family?"

"Not that I know of. I don't think so."

"You know, sometimes your father sleeps restlessly and the next morning tells me he re-lived some battle."

"Back in 1812?"

"He was in the Army for two years then."

"Why not the Navy?"

"I think that would have been worse. At sea, with no land in sight. Please, neither one, for goodness sakes. But that's how your daddy was able to expand this farm, add some acres to what your grandfather left him. I was expecting you when your father left. I was nervous the whole time he was away. But I kept working the farm and gardens with some hired help. Every day I didn't know whether I'd be a widow by nightfall with three children to raise. So, it's understandable that Elizabeth and I don't want you to go."

"I may be able to learn about engineering, you know, building a fort or bridges."

"You're a determined young man, no longer a boy, what with your ideas of getting married and settin' up your own home. I guess it's time, whether I want it to be or not. I hope you and Elizabeth can live with it."

"We'll be fine. We'd like to get married in the next year or so. No particular date yet."

His father came into the kitchen. "What's all the debate I'm hearing?"

"Good morning," Andrew said. "I hear your legs needed some attention last night. Should I go get the doctor?"

"You just eat your breakfast, son," his father said. "But yes, I'm a little sore, and I expect you will be too, if you're not already. How's your nose?"

"I think it's a little bent."

His mother walked over, lifted Andrew's chin, and inspected his face. "No. It's a little swollen but not bent any more than usual."

"Thank you, Mama."

"I want you two in different fields today, you hear me?" his mother said.

"We may do a little target practice," his father said.

"You best get some farmwork done while you can. You know those seeds have to get planted and you have to get those vegetables going," she said.

"I'm quite capable, my dear," Greene said as he kissed his wife.

"Mason is already out there milking cows," she said. "You two need to catch up."

After breakfast the men walked toward the barn. His father put an arm around Andrew.

"You're not going to throw me down, are you?" Andrew asked.

"No, my boy, I'm sorry if that was too much for you."

"I *would* like to go hunting again, and you can tell me about weapons and the war."

"We'll see," said his father.

Five

Hunkered down on a tree stump, between bites of his dinner, Andrew wrote his first letter home from the militia's encampment in Illinois. It had been a long twelve-day ride from his home to the Army's position near Rock River. Before sunset, he used a knife to sharpen a pencil and wrote carefully on stationery provided by an officer.

My Darling Elizabeth, May 10, 1832

As I write this letter, I am well and think of you every moment. I did not know it was possible to love you more, but I do with each passing day. I only need to close my eyes to see your face.

The journey from Missouri to Illinois went well. Brownie did start limping as we advanced, but I halted and removed a stone from his hoof. Then re-nailed his shoe and off we rode.

Our militia will be used little, I hear, as this governor will call out almost 2,000 of his own to fight Black Hawk. At this writing, I am resting at a campfire and eating a stew of rice, beans, and venison. The deer was downed by Private James Dobbs yesterday. You may know of his family near Millers Creek. He is the third son of sharecroppers and is eager to claim his own land, as am I for us.

Dobbs and I met on the road to Missouri and have become friends. He too has a loved one whom he misses. As one of nine brothers and sisters, he is homesick already.

Weather here is cool in the evenings and I am glad to have the scarf you knitted to keep my neck warm. Do give my love to my family, and I hope your father's plantation did well with the spring plantings.

I hope this reaches you soon. If you write to me, it may be a long time before the mail is received here, and we may be on the move in the meantime.

I will dream of you tonight. I cannot wait to hold you in my arms again and look into your beautiful eyes.

All my love,
Andrew

Ten days later, at sunrise, cook Frenchie Beauchamp started to make breakfast when he heard a cry from the makeshift corral of horses. He grabbed his musket and ran to the edge of camp in time to see a lone Indian galloping away on a pinto, pulling three horses behind him, too far away in the morning mist to take a shot.

Frenchie knelt next to Private Dobb's body covered in blood, the man's neck sliced from ear to ear.

"He's dead," Beauchamp yelled to two corporals who showed up in their long underwear. "Tell Sergeant Snyder."

Though only five months long, the Black Hawk War in Illinois was deadly for some U.S. soldiers and for hundreds of Native Americans, members of the "British Band" made up of Sauk, Meskwakis, and Kickapoo tribes led by the Sauk Black Hawk. He wanted back land that had already been given to the United States.

On the evening after Dobb's death, Sergeant Snyder addressed newly arrived militia member Andrew Greene.

"Private, you know what happened to Dobbs?"

"Yes, sir," Andrew said, "I helped bury him this afternoon. A good friend."

"Don't let that happen to you, and just say sergeant to me; save the 'sir' for the officers."

"All right, Sergeant."

"It's your turn to stand sentry around the horses tonight, so take the two-to-sunrise duty that Dobbs had. Stay awake and keep your wits about ya'."

"Yes, sir, I mean, Sergeant. Any other instructions?"

"Don't lose any horses, and don't get yourself 'kilt. Stay on your feet, if need be, to stay awake."

That night, thirty horses were tethered to rope lines strung among a patch of oak and maple trees on the south end of the Army camp. Drawing a clear breath was a challenge for Andrew because the air was a heavy mix of campfire smoke, damp ground fog, and the smell of manure. He was surrounded by snoring soldiers, hooting owls, and barking foxes. Shuffling hooves of half-napping horses added to the sounds of the night.

Gauzy clouds rolled by in the sky, pushed by a light breeze, exposing only dim intermittent light from a crescent moon through a gray fog. Andrew slowly paced around the corral, trying to keep alert and awake in the darkness. Armed with a pistol in his belt, a sheath knife, and his reliable musket, he swore to himself he would protect the horses and the camp, light from an oil lantern his only companion.

Downwind of the horses, a Sauk Indian named Ketiwa lay among low shrubs, then rose and stepped through tall grasses. In his beaded leather headband, he wore an eagle feather, bestowed upon him by his chief during a celebration to honor his coup of killing an armed enemy when he killed Dobbs. Staying low and stepping slowly, Ketiwa hoped to earn a second feather for another kill tonight and for the horses he would steal. He knew there would be a celebration upon his return.

The Indian held his sharpened tomahawk, ready to attack. He wanted this kill to be quiet; it would be best if there were no outcry from the tired guard. Touching the hilt of a clay-handled straight knife in his belt, he moved forward, watching the sentry. Ketiwa was worried that it would soon be sunrise, and the brave knew time was running out for him to attack.

Andrew continued to parade around the corral of horses many times. Some of the animals were hobbled; most were tied to the rope line. He repositioned the pistol held in his leather belt and moved his musket from his left shoulder to his right, the gun barrel already rammed and ready, loaded with black powder and a lead ball wrapped in cloth. He rubbed his eyes, drank from his canteen, and had his wits about him. He thought about his dear Elizabeth, his family, and the farm he left behind.

Back home in Tennessee, as a second son, Andrew would not inherit the farm or any fortune. He could have stayed and worked for his older brother Mason, but at eighteen, Andrew was ready for adventure and wanted to seek his destiny. Like many others, serving out his term in the militia meant he would receive a 160-acre tract of land to begin his own farm.

Tired, but continuing to stay on his feet, Andrew listened to sounds in the darkness as he paced the line. Growing up on a farm, he knew animals well, especially horses. He helped birth foals and raised the young animals to maturity. When he was old enough, he mounted three- and four-year-old horses to break them for riding and for sale. He knew their whinnies and neighs and how skittish some could be.

The young private had brought his own horse into the Army. He knew the animal's personality well from hunting back home, and he knew the gelding would stay steady under the sounds and flashes of gunfire.

Andrew tensed when his horse pawed at the ground.

Ketiwa, twenty yards away, ran toward Andrew's back, throwing his sharp tomahawk and raising his hunting knife. Already alerted by his horse, Andrew heard the footfalls approaching from behind and ducked. He heard the thud of a tomahawk cutting into the trunk of an oak tree above him. He wheeled around.

In the breaking morning light, he saw the Sauk racing toward him. The edge of Ketiwa's hunting knife reflected an early sunbeam, piercing through branches. Andrew swung his musket forward and fired a ball of lead into the Indian's chest. The force of the shot entering his body stunned Ketiwa, and he fell to his knees five yards away. As smoke from the musket fire faded away, Andrew pulled his pistol and fired another shot into the staggering Indian's body, then ran up and hit Ketiwa in the face with the butt of his musket. Once, twice, and the Indian fell on his back—still.

Sleepy soldiers came running in response to the gunfire.

"Better make sure he's dead," said Frenchie as he slid to a stop. "Be careful."

Andrew bent over Ketiwa's motionless body. With a sudden burst of energy, the dying Indian swung a stone knife toward the soldier's face, cutting Andrew's cheek. Surprised and angry, Andrew kicked Ketiwa and clubbed his head until there was a muddy pool of blood and an eye on the ground. He felt a rush of revenge for his friend Dobb's death.

It was Ketiwa's last effort to steal horses for his tribe. There would be no celebration for the brave today. It was Andrew's first time killing a man. He felt blood running down his face as Frenchie led him back to camp.

Andrew breathed heavily with tears in his eyes from pain and exhaustion. The terrible fight had drained his energy. He described the attack for the camp doctor who treated his face wound. Andrew winced and moaned as the sawbones swabbed his cheek with alcohol and sewed in stitches to close the cut.

"Listen, Private, we are born and live and die. It is the middle part, the living part that matters most. We don't get to choose the beginning or the end, but we like to think we control our lives until destiny intervenes. You were lucky *you* didn't lose an eye today."

It was not Andrew's time to die. He was still shaking when two corporals led him back to a campfire and sat him down on a log. Frenchie gave him a cup of coffee with a splash of whiskey.

The cook described the fight to Sergeant Snyder—the bravery that Andrew displayed, along with the young private's carelessness over a wounded enemy, but a victory nonetheless. It proved Andrew capable in combat and able to help protect the regiment.

To Andrew it meant a scar, a promotion, and a haunting memory.

Six

With a cool morning breeze at his back, newly promoted Corporal Andrew Greene rode his horse toward the rising sun. His militia had elected him to be their captain, once they found out he could read and write, and after he killed the Indian. The position of captain was a title of leadership within the patrol, but not a military rank. They had just watered their mounts along the Rock River, and he was a hundred yards out front of his six-man patrol.

In a blooming field that led toward woods of oaks, elms, and maples, Andrew passed a groundhog relaxing in the tall grass on its haunches while it chewed on a stolen potato. Then he heard screams.

A young girl burst out of the woods. She ran toward him. Her long blonde hair flew behind her narrow shoulders. She wore a plain ragged dress and an apron stained blue from berry picking.

Andrew quickly dismounted. The frightened girl jumped into his outstretched arms. A Sauk Indian galloped out of the trees and raised a spear. Andrew drew his pistol. He fired three times. Two bullets found their mark. The Indian fell to the ground dead. His horse, covered in war paint, turned back into the woods.

The scouting patrol quickly closed the distance, guns drawn.

Andrew held the girl at arm's length. "Where's your home, child?"

The girl stopped crying long enough to point back toward the woods and then buried her face in Andrew's shoulder. He waved his men forward. "Search those woods," he said. "Then let's find her family."

The patrol rode into the woods while Andrew held back with the girl. A minute later, one of the men emerged. "It's clear, Cap'n, and there's smoke up ahead."

When Andrew rode up to a farmhouse with the girl, he saw a dead Indian near a well and a farmer pushing through the gathered patrol at the front door. The farmer carried a shotgun across his arm. The weeping girl pushed away from Andrew and ran into her father's arms. A chicken coop glowed with fire.

Andrew yelled an order, "You men put out that fire, for gosh sakes." Four of the patrol ran past the house while others stood guard.

"There's a trough out back and buckets," the farmer yelled, then turned to Andrew. "Where's my son? Where's Jimmy?"

"Is he in the house?" Andrew said.

"No. The two of them was fetchin' water when the injuns come. My wife and other kids are safe, hidin' in the root cellar."

Andrew heard an echoing cry. "Let's check the well." They ran to the surrounding stone edge. The farmer put his head below a wood awning and ducked under a pole used as a bucket crank. A taut rope hung down into the darkness.

"Jimmy, Jimmy, is you down thar?" the farmer yelled.

"Papa, Papa."

"I'll get you out, boy. Ride that bucket up here. Hold on to that rope," the farmer said.

Andrew tried to turn the crank. "It's too much weight. We've got to pull the rope up by hand." Both men grabbed the rope. Finally, a seven-year-old, wet, tow-headed, squinting boy popped up. He clung to the bucket with his legs and hugged the rope until his father peeled him off.

One of the patrolmen appeared from behind the cabin. "The fire's out, Cap'n. Two dead chickens. Five live ones."

The farmer said, "We had ten. Them injuns must'o took some."

"Or they's in the woods somewhere," one of the men said.

"My thanks to ya'," the farmer said to Andrew. "You and yer men. I don't know how to repay ya'."

"I'm glad we got here in time to help. It's what we're supposed to do. We're part of the militia trying to clear out those Indians."

The farmer's wife and other children came out of the cabin.

"We got this sack of potatoes for ya'," the woman said.

"Oh, no, ma'am," Andrew said. "You feed those to your family, but that's mighty nice of you."

"Well, here now," she said. She opened the sack and handed a potato to each man. "I won't have it any other way, and you take one of them dead chickens too."

The patrol helped the farmer bury the dead Indian and went back to the meadow. The body of the other Indian had disappeared. The grass was red with blood where he had lain.

"I expect they came and took him while we were at the cabin," Andrew said. "Let's patrol the area for a while then move on."

Back at camp that night, Andrew wrote a report for the officers. He described how the patrol helped the farmer save his family and property. In his tent after his chicken dinner, Andrew folded a blanket across his body and laid his head on a pillow made from a rolled up jacket. He closed his eyes, listened to the sounds of the night, and fell asleep with a new understanding of his purpose in the militia.

Two days passed before Andrew wrote another letter to his fiancée.

My Dearest Elizabeth, June 2, 1832

I am sending you all my love and enclosing a kiss in this letter for your lips, or at least in my mind, and I know I will dream of you tonight. It is with the aid of a calendar that I even know what day it is here as time drags by. I would so rather be by your side.

My schooling has been a benefit. The militia has chosen me to read our orders, lead them on some patrols, and write about our progress. I have also helped some of the men write letters to their families, and officers have noticed my work as well. Indeed I was pleased to receive a promotion to the rank of corporal in light of my service.

Our cook, name of Frenchie Beauchamp, surprised us with a strawberry shortcake yesterday evening. A farmer, whose house and family we saved, brought a basket of the berries to the camp and Frenchie grabbed some for our little militia. I told the men that I would consider the dessert an early birthday cake, what with July 1st soon upon us. They received that comment with humor.

I have met several good men from Illinois, including an intelligent and thoughtful man named Abe Lincoln. He is also serving to receive his own land. He too has helped some of the men with writing letters home. He's a tall man, taller than my six feet, and the best wrestler in camp.

Though I have written to them recently, do give my love to my family. I know Mama will be glad to have your company any time, and say hello to your father for me. I miss you all.

The Army is making progress against Black Hawk and his marauding Indians. Some say the war will be over before fall. If so, I look forward to holding you in my arms and setting the date for our wedding.

All my love,
Andrew

A month had passed since Andrew left Tennessee and reported for duty in Illinois. Back home, Elizabeth tried to keep busy. She received his first letter, but worries about his safety gave her many restless nights. Just as she would forever miss the love and advice of her mother, now she also missed Andrew's affection and support.

She found solace thinking of Andrew's abiding love for her and re-read his first letter. His physical presence had helped sustain her for years. She remembered holding his hand at her mother's funeral. Andrew had shed tears with her, for Andrew had known Elizabeth's kind mother most of his life.

During Andrew's absence and with her frequent visits to the Greenes' farm, Elizabeth grew closer to Andrew's mother. Amelia Greene, known for her hugs and kisses, gave them freely to her family members and to Elizabeth. The girl was always welcome to help in the kitchen and share a meal.

"I'll show you how to fix one of Andrew's favorite recipes each time you come," Mrs. Greene said. "You can fix him something special after he gets back from the war."

"He'll be so surprised," Elizabeth said.

"Let's start with cornbread."

As the weeks dragged by waiting for news from Andrew, Elizabeth found that caring for others helped fill the void created by his absence. She liked baking and visiting friends and neighbors, especially those less fortunate. The visits gave her a chance to learn about the world outside the comfort of her father's plantation. She had a natural way with children who basked in the attention they received from such a lovely young woman.

Having accepted Andrew's proposal of marriage, Elizabeth knew her destiny and looked forward to being a wife and mother. She learned much about how to run a household from Mrs. Greene, and she nurtured many friendships in the community.

With the help of the plantation cook, Mama Jordan, Elizabeth learned how to make cookies, cakes, and bread. She took her finished pastries to local tenant-farmers, widow ladies, and poor families. After packing a lunch, she often wound up giving it to children in the homes she would visit.

This morning she led her golden palomino Belle out of the stables and began walking the horse slowly down the drive past the stone pillars that marked the lane leading to the plantation house. She carried a basket of freshly made baked goods to take to some friends. She saw her father coming.

"Daughter," James Vining said, as he rode up from the fields and stopped. "Are you going to ride Belle or walk her forever?"

"Good morning, Father," she said.

"I've been watching you mope around for weeks."

"You know very well what it is," Elizabeth said. She mounted Belle.

"I guess I'd have to be deaf and blind not to know," he said. "I've heard your sobs at night and have seen your red eyes most days."

"I'm worried sick about Andrew. I wish he hadn't joined the militia. Will I ever see him again?"

"I wish your mother was still with us. She'd know what to say."

"You know I love Andrew. I always have. But, Daddy, he's been gone a month. It's forever."

"Child, he'll be fine," her father said, "and if not, there are at least ten young men around here who are eager to call on you. All you have to do is choose one."

"*Daddy*! How can you say that? You know I'm engaged to Andrew. Mother would tell me to follow my heart and comfort me. That was a terrible thing to say."

Vining knew he had made a mistake and tried to recover. "He'll be fine. The Army is good experience, and after the service he'll be out and back with the rights to some land to start a farm for y'all."

"That's what I pray for every night, Daddy. Not for the land but for Andrew's safe return."

"Well, your young soldier will never be a plantation owner, my darling. He's a farmer at best, and you deserve a better life than that. He has no fortune; that's why he joined the Army. Maybe that's what's meant to be."

Elizabeth began to ride away; her cheeks grew red with anger. She yelled over her shoulder, "He could be hurt or lying dead, God knows where right now, and there's nothing I can do."

While her palomino trotted along the side of one of her father's cotton fields, Elizabeth smelled the fragrance of honeysuckle and started to calm down. A few of their slaves stopped tending the cotton plants, looked around for the overseer, and shyly raised their hands in greeting before returning to their work. Elizabeth gently waved back and continued on. If she were to ride all 50 miles of trails through the 1,500 acres of the plantation, it would take most of the day, but she was on a specific mission to homes of friends and then on to Millers Creek, before returning to study with her tutor.

Before noon, the front door of a modest log cabin flew open, pulled by an energetic five-year-old girl who ran out into the waiting arms of Elizabeth.

"Miss Elizabeth! Miss Elizabeth!" the girl shouted in her high-pitched voice.

"Hello, my darling Gwen. It's so nice to see you," Elizabeth said, as she kissed the girl's round pink cheeks and leaned in through the doorway. "Mother Donaldson, may I come in?"

"Of course, come in, come in, and welcome," Mrs. Donaldson said from her chair where she held a young baby.

"Yes, yes," little Gwendolyn said as she took Elizabeth by the hand. The child pulled her in and helped carry a basket of bread and jam to the rough-hewn dining table.

"I baked loaves of bread this morning and wanted to bring them over." Elizabeth set the basket on the table in front of the woman who was expecting again.

"You are too good to be true, Elizabeth. You shouldn't have."

"Oh, I wanted to. You've been good to me for so long, and I've eaten plenty of your pies and cakes." Elizabeth sat down, dropped a light shawl from her shoulders, and picked up Gwen, already halfway into her lap.

"This is my fifth time being with child," Mrs. Donaldson said. "We lost one daughter to the flu last winter, as you know, but I'll soon have four dear ones again. Little Charlie's out with his father bringing in some wood for the cook stove. The tyke can only carry a few sticks, but even at three he loves to help out."

"You know, I'll come by to sit again whenever you need me," Elizabeth said. "I love all your children."

"So, what's the news? I'm so busy with these sweet babies I seldom get a chance to find out the latest gossip."

"Well, even though the heat is upon us some days, I do welcome the blossoming flowers. And fruits and vegetables are coming in now. The peaches are coming in and ready for picking and putting up. Let's see, now. If you haven't been to Memphis lately, I hear a new theater opened. I heard they've got plays and wonderful music. I hope to go there sometime this summer."

"How wonderful. And what about you? What have you heard from your Andrew?"

"Thank you for asking. That's a concern. I haven't heard from him lately. He wrote he's in Illinois in part of the Black Hawk War. I'm beside myself with worry, and I'm ready for him to come home to me."

"Of course you are, my darling. I'm sorry I asked," Mrs. Donaldson said.

"No, of course you want to know, as do I. I hope to receive more mail soon, and I'll come to share it with you when I do."

Gwen jumped out of Elizabeth's lap and held up her little hands. "Let's play patty cake, Miss Elizabeth."

After a quick game with Gwen and hugs all around, Elizabeth said her goodbyes.

Her next stop was one of charity and friendship at Widow Rankin's small house.

"I thought that was you. Come on in, my dear girl," Mrs. Rankin said as she opened the door. "I've knitted some mittens, and I want you to give them to Andrew when you see him next."

"Hello, Mrs. Rankin. I brought you some fresh-baked bread and a jar of jam," Elizabeth said. She bent down to kiss the cheek of the short, gray-haired woman. "Thank you so much for the mittens. I know Andrew will be able to use them, especially on cold nights in the fall. But you shouldn't worry about Andrew. I think I'm doing enough of that already," she said with tears welling up in her eyes. "He's only been gone a little over a month, but it seems like a lifetime. Waiting is terrible."

"Have you heard anything from him?" Mrs. Rankin asked as she poured a cup of tea for Elizabeth. They sat down on a sofa in the main room of the little house.

"Only one letter came. He said his militia made it to Illinois. That's all I know. And, of course, he wrote how much he loved me and missed me."

Mrs. Rankin put a hand on Elizabeth's arm. "It is hard, sweetheart. My William, in the Army from 1812 to 1814, saw the Navy Yard burn. Back then, I only knew what happened by reading the newspaper, and by the time I received the paper, it was old news to boot. He came back to me finally—wounded in his right leg, you know. He recovered all right. Had a limp ever after. But he didn't let it slow him down none. He got out there and plowed, and baled hay, and took care of the livestock. He even added a room onto this old house with his own hands."

"I remember Mr. Rankin. So good to you, and he helped me with my saddle one time. He always had something to say about the weather."

"Been gone now three years. You never know how much time you'll have with your loved ones. And you can't stop a man from being a man, darling."

Later, Elizabeth dismounted Belle at the stone bridge over Millers Creek. The heat of the day would reach its height soon. She dropped the reins so Belle could graze on tall grasses. The bridge marked the spot where Elizabeth and Andrew had lingered hundreds of times, exchanging sweet words, holding hands, and sharing their thoughts of the future. The creek marked the northern boundary of the plantation with the Greenes' farm beyond.

She stepped past tall magnolias, a stand of redbuds and dogwoods, and was delighted by a cooling breeze passing through her sun-streaked hair. She watched the pink and blue ribbons on her sleeves flutter like the wings of newly emerged butterflies that populated the meadows.

The young woman approached a fallen oak log where she and Andrew used to sit, her back warmed by the sun. The log was their favorite spot. As young children they had stopped there on the first day after school and, years later, that's where they shared their first real kiss.

She dangled her bare feet in the creek's cool waters, remembering how Andrew said he loved her for the first time. She had cried then from joy, just as she did now but out of sadness at his absence.

When Andrew had left for the Army she waved to him as he rode away. Now she sat and watched her tears drop into the water. She had made him promise to be careful, and he had given her a locket on a red ribbon along with a vow that he would return to her before the end of the year. She reached up and felt the locket she wore around her neck every day.

Belle stopped grazing when Elizabeth returned. The girl put on her shoes and mounted the horse for the ride home.

Seven

June 23, 1832

In the evening, Andrew sat by a campfire after dinner. During the day, his militia had snared four rabbits and shot a wild boar. Andrew appreciated his new friend Frenchie Beauchamp, out of New Orleans, who made a stew from the boar, along with a meal of biscuits, rice, and gravy. In the distance, as darkness enveloped the land, Andrew could hear hoots of owls.

By this point, his experience in the Black Hawk War had affected a change in his outlook on life. With the death of his friend Dobbs and having to kill the enemy, a new reality was forced upon him. His thoughts were both of his home and the war while he performed mundane tasks.

Frenchie scraped out a Dutch oven with a spatula and looked toward Andrew. "*Mon ami*, you did good gettin' this game."

"Plow, plant, pick ... plow, plant, pick ...," Andrew said, rubbing dirt on tin plates to clean them. He dropped them into a metal bucket of boiling water.

"What's that now?" Frenchie said.

Andrew moved out of the way of plumes of smoke from the fire. "I guess that by the time I was eighteen, I figured I had done enough farming—ready for adventure—doing anything, anything else besides plow, plant and pick."

"I see."

"I hope it never happens, of course, but when my father dies I'll be lucky to get a gold pocket watch while my older brother Mason inherits the farm."

"But you say you are finished with farmin', yes?" Frenchie said.

"I'm just complaining. Everybody kept telling me growing up that second sons have to make their own way—that's the law—go seek your fortune. I figure there's gotta be a lot of bellyaching second-, third-, or whatever-sons out there."

"But you want to leave the militia with some land of your own, my friend," Frenchie said. They stopped talking to listen to a fox barking and some soldiers laughing in the distance.

"My father is a good man, a hard worker in the fields. The more war I see, the more I think a plow is better than a sword. It's all hard to do, and you can't be sure of anything."

"Like it says in the good book, 'beat your swords into plowshares,' yes."

"My father fought the British in 1812. His unit saw the Capitol burn. Now he sure likes farming. He knows the seasons, the weather, and the land. He can grow everything."

"A good man," Frenchie said. He added some sticks to the campfire.

"My brother says when the time comes I'll be able to stay at the farm as long as I want. I keep that in the back of my mind. But the front of my mind is still thinking plow, plant, pick ... plow, plant, pick, so that's why I joined the militia. That's how I wound up here."

"It will be different, will it not, when you have your own land and with a new wife. That will be good."

"Yes. I really miss Elizabeth. I know she's bound to be worried."

"Plannin' a weddin'?"

"Oh yes. She's busy doing all that. Just not sure of the date."

Sergeant Snyder walked by. "Frenchie, you got any coffee in that pot?"

"Help yourself, Sergeant. Need a cup?"

"Brought my own. Thank ye. And you, Corporal, how you gettin' along?"

"He's grumblin'," Frenchie said.

"Some of us are," Andrew said.

Sergeant Snyder said, "I'm ready for this to be over, 'specially after Stillman's Run. We lost twelve soldiers. No more than five Indians kilt." He took a sip of coffee. "Didn't mean to interrupt you. Thanks for the drink."

"Any time," Frenchie said.

"I'm thinkin' it's about time for me to turn in," Snyder said, and he walked toward his tent.

They watched Snyder disappear into the shadows.

"Andrew, did you write to your girl today?"

"No, but I will tomorrow."

They listened to the crackling of the fire.

"What's it like in Tennessee?"

"Well, there's some good, rolling land, and it's fertile enough when you mix in manure and all, but a lot of clay. Our farm isn't far from the Mississippi. We sell some timber and raise cattle and horses. We grow our own food." Andrew used tongs to fish hot plates out of the boiling water and toss them on a table made of lashed sticks.

"There's lots of game around home," Andrew continued. "Growing up, I hunted with my father and Mason—shot rabbits and deer and one bear—skinned them all and ate 'em. I figured that was fair because those animals stole our crops and killed our livestock. It's just the way of the world, like those inheritance laws."

"So, I'm glad you are a good shot," Frenchie said.

"How long have you been a cook?"

"I learned to cook in my mother's kitchen," Frenchie said. "But I've been an Army cook now goin' on four years. I started out as a regular soldier at the age of seventeen out of Louisiana, but I saw too much killin', scalps, and all. So, I asked to be a cook and the men liked the food, so it stuck. All told, I've been in eight years now. I shoot straight and know how to survive."

"We've had to bury too many settlers in the last few weeks," Andrew said.

"It's not good."

"You know, sitting here by the fire gives me time to think, and I figure I didn't do anything much wrong as a boy. I was a good kid and a decent student. The best thing to come out of all those years of schooling, though, was Elizabeth."

"What do they say; you are over the moon, yes?"

"Yes. I met her when I was in the second grade. She was a year younger and it was her first day. She stood in the doorway like a scared little kitten, wide-eyed, missing some baby teeth, and she stared at me. When she smiled in my direction, I pointed to an empty desk next to me."

"Love at first sight, yes?"

"Maybe so. Over the years, I don't know how many times I walked her home, held her hand, teased her, got teased back, kissed her, and held her in my arms, but on her sixteenth birthday, I knelt in front of her and proposed.

"A fine moment," Frenchie said. He poured a final cup of coffee for himself.

"So, like an idiot, I joined the militia for the land, really. I didn't know I'd be this far away. I'll get those acres and can start my own farm. Somehow, when I own the land, when I'm building my *own* future—my fortune—I think the plowing, and planting, and picking will be all right."

"I 'spect so."

"Feels like rain may be coming in tonight," Andrew said. "I'll leave you to it, Frenchie. Thanks for letting me bend your ear."

"Any time, *mon ami*."

At the end of the war in August, Andrew collected his weapons, his bounty of land, and mounted his horse to return to his family and take his fiancée into his arms.

By the age of 19, he had seen combat and destruction. He had to kill or be killed. His training, strength and cunning had served him well. His experience as a hunter on his father's farm had given him a keen eye and an understanding of weapons. He was shocked at being able to convert his hunting ability to the battlefield to attack and repel an enemy. He followed the orders of his superiors and learned how to take defensive and offensive positions. He understood the importance of completing a mission, leadership, and how the stench of war could penetrate and linger in his nostrils.

With the end of the Black Hawk War that summer, Andrew returned as a tested and different man but eager to find Elizabeth, his long-time love. Riding toward her father's plantation, he was overjoyed when he saw her. He laughed at her screams of delight as she ran to greet him. He dismounted and jumped over fence rails to reach her. She fell into his waiting arms and her sunbonnet blew off. Her long brunette hair bounced on her shoulders. She was as beautiful as he remembered, and her sweetness enveloped him like the fragrance of honeysuckle that hung in the air. She placed her hands on his face and cried as she kissed his lips and the scar on his left cheek.

Having grown up together as neighbors and classmates, she already knew his heart well, and friendship had long ago been taken over by an abiding love. The engaged couple walked arm-in-arm and talked about their future. They set a date for a spring wedding.

At the Greenes' farm that evening, a dinner party welcomed home the warrior and celebrated the reunion. Mr. Vining arrived with an appetite and a bottle of whiskey to add to the festivities. Though Andrew was not as well off as his future father-in-law would have preferred, the man gave his blessing to the pending union, glad to know his young daughter would marry a man who loved her and who was developing good prospects.

Andrew received the acreage he expected near his father's farm in Millers Creek. With his family's help, he set to work building a five-room house with timber from the land. The acreage would need to be farmed properly to make it productive enough to sustain the couple. But Andrew also had ambitions to advance his rank in the Army and acquire more land to create a fortune they could rely on.

Eight

Spring, 1833

The invitations, hand-delivered in double envelopes to the households of recipients, were printed in black script on creamy, embossed stationery, featuring a floral border and the text:

James Vining and the late Mary Alice Vining
request the honor of your presence
at the marriage of their daughter,
Elizabeth Anne Vining
To
Andrew Dale Greene
son of Robert and Amelia Greene,
on Wednesday, the fifteenth day of May,
Eighteen-hundred and thirty-three,
at noon at the Vining Plantation
290 Emory Lane
Millers Creek, Tennessee
Feast and merriment immediately following the ceremony.

Elizabeth entered her father's study. "Thank you for what you have done to help invite everyone. There are a few extra invitations, in case we need them—if for nothing else than a wedding memory book to show your grandchildren."

"I'm glad you like them, my dear. The printer did a good job. I know your mother would have been so happy to see you on your wedding day. My heart hurts since she didn't live to see it."

Elizabeth's eyes filled with tears. "Mine too, Daddy."

"I count twenty-four folks to come, at most. It's up to you to choose what dishes you want prepared. Tell Mama Jordan what you want and plan the flowers. Maybe talk to Mrs. Greene about what else you may need to do."

"Father, I have been talking to my future mother-in-law since Andrew proposed. She and I are in agreement about the plans. You know Andrew and I have already given the date to everyone, but I so like these invitations. The style is so special. You know Andrew's brother, Mason, and his sister, Jeanette, and their families will be attending and, of course, Andrew's parents. I think you've met all of the adults before, but not all the Greenes' grandchildren."

"We will be greatly outnumbered," Mr. Vining said, smiling.

"It will be a happy day—my most happy day. We will have music, and you will dance with me, won't you, after I first dance with Andrew?"

"Whatever you want, my dear child, but it's been years since I danced."

~ * ~

Though he thought of her all day, it was five o'clock before Andrew arrived at the plantation. Having risen at sunup, and after a day of work with animals, he had bathed and put on clean clothes. At the plantation, a house servant opened the double doors, and Andrew found Elizabeth approaching when he entered the gracious marble foyer.

"Hello to the future Mrs. Andrew Greene," he said, waving one of the wedding invitations. "It looks so official. I guess we'll have to do it for sure, now."

Elizabeth raised an eyebrow. "Oh my! Here's a handsome young man who just missed out on a kiss. Don't be too smart, Andrew."

She laughed. He pulled her into an alcove for some privacy.

"You know I'm teasing, of course. It's a month away, but I wish it was tomorrow," he whispered. "Or even right now."

She pushed a hand onto his chest. "I will be wearing my new dress. You can't see it yet. It must be a surprise."

He stepped toward her. She extended both her arms. They held hands and kissed and kissed again.

"Should we practice the ceremony?" he said. "The part where we kiss at the end?"

"You are here for mischief I believe, sir."

"I thought about you all day."

"While you were feeding the hogs?"

"Well, maybe not then, but all the rest of the time. I wanted to come see you." He leaned in to give her another kiss.

"I'm afraid you will wear out my lips, but I'm glad you came." She pulled him out of the alcove. "Let's sit a spell in the parlor. I expected you, and had Mama Jordan put out those little ham biscuits you like and tea."

Andrew put his arm around her waist as they walked. When they sat down he pulled out an envelope.

"I wanted to show you the house plans for our farm like we discussed." He spread out a sheet of paper revealing a simple drawing. "It's just a sketch, but I figured you'd want to see."

"Oh, Andrew," she said, putting her arms around his neck. "It looks wonderful." She held on until they heard footsteps approaching.

"Do I hear a groom somewhere?" Mr. Vining asked.

"We are in here, Daddy," Elizabeth said.

"Ah, I saw you ride up from my window, but now I see you are too busy to visit with your future father-in-law."

"Hello, Mr. Vining," Andrew said. "How are you?"

"I think you may call me James in private, Andrew."

"Thank you."

"Daddy, Andrew was just dropping by to talk about the wedding a little."

"And, I dare say, steal a kiss or three," Mr. Vining said.

"Don't try to make me blush, Daddy."

Mr. Vining helped himself to one of the ham biscuits. "So what does our newest farm owner have to say?"

"I plowed half an acre today and planted corn. Fed the animals. Trying to get seeds and plants in the ground."

"If you want to borrow some of our hands, just let overseer Fisher know."

"I'm doing all right by myself. I'm arranging to sell some standing timber, and I talked to a possible tenant farmer. He and his wife and their children can help when I'm away ..."

Mr. Vining looked at his pocket watch. "Yes. That's a good idea. Elizabeth can't do all the work. No one can. I best be gettin' on. Time to check on my cotton fields before sundown. Aiming for a bumper crop. Those boys added another five acres."

The couple watched the man leave then sat on a loveseat to share the biscuits and tea.

Andrew said, "I don't think he likes the idea of you working on a farm."

"Don't worry about that. I *like* to get my hands in the soil, and I love working with the animals, especially the horses. Not the pigs, though. They're a smelly bunch."

"We can change out to something else if you like. We've got five piglets ready for market soon. Maybe change to goats and making cheese."

"I can learn all about making bacon and sausage, if need be."

"The tenant farmer's wife said she knows all about that."

"So, where will those folks stay?"

"When that timber is cut, we'll get back wood from the lumber mill and can build a cabin on the cleared land. It'll be well away from our house and barn. Father and Mason said they'd help."

"There's so much to do."

"I've got it all mapped out and we'll start soon. All *you* need to do now is get ready to get married and love me for the rest of your life."

Andrew found it hard to leave Elizabeth's side, but he returned to his parents' farm. "I thought I'd bring in some wood." Andrew entered the farmhouse and set down three logs on the hearth.

"Thanks," his father said. "We just need one more log. Headed to bed soon. How was your visit?"

"Wonderful. She liked the sketch. She said it will be cozy. Of course, it's no plantation house. And though he said hello for a minute, I didn't show it to Mr. Vining."

"It's a good start. You can add on if you need to. You know Mr. Vining inherited the plantation, so most of it was already in place. He keeps it running well. But don't sell yourself short. I expect he'd be glad to help you and be interested for his daughter's sake, if not yours."

"I've got plenty of time before the wedding or before we start to build. I didn't mean to keep you up."

"I just wanted to share some things with you without your mother around."

"About the wedding?"

His father pulled the cork from a bottle of brandy and poured the drink into two small glasses.

"When you get married, it's forever, and it's important to talk to each other every day. Tell your wife that you love her. You'll like to hear those words too." Mr. Greene set his glass of brandy on the table.

"Elizabeth and I do that all the time. It's easy to say." Andrew put a log on the fire. He used a poker to position it over the hot coals and still-flaming wood.

"Your mother and I work together as a good team."

"Oh, yes. I see that," he said and took a sip of the brandy.

"We had to figure that out, though," his father said. "So early on we talked about what both of us expected from our lives together."

"Hopes and dreams?"

"That, but more practical matters too—how we'd handle our chores, how to manage the farm. She'd have to make decisions sometimes when I wasn't around."

"Like at market or traveling."

"Or at war ... I handle all the finances and banking, but I keep her informed, so she knows what's going on and where the money is. It helps ease her mind from worry to know we're okay. That way, she doesn't have to ask, but if she has any questions it makes it easier to talk. It's part of sharing how we run the place. It also eases my mind to let her know."

"And Mama taught you how to cook, I guess."

His father peered at Andrew over a pair of bifocals.

"Very funny. No. Only if you like bread and water and burnt squirrel. I bring home the game and your mother takes over from there. She is in charge of what we eat and how we eat it. We did the best we could teaching you children manners and all. But we both helped with your lessons and with discipline. When you have children you'll understand more."

"That will be good."

"The main thing is to talk to each other. It helps relieve your minds. And if you continue with your Army career, Elizabeth may need to run the farm without you around."

"While I'm on active duty?"

"Or wounded or dead on a battlefield."

"Damn, Dad!"

The two men finished their brandy.

"I haven't heard anything from the Army for a while. I don't know when they'll need me next."

"Things are pretty quiet from what I read, but seems like Texas wants to break away from Mexico in the coming years."

His father held up an envelope. "Your mother and I liked the invitations."

"Elizabeth is planning a floral archway."

"Plenty of food too, I'm sure, and it will be good to see your sister and her brood. It's been a while."

"One day I plan to bring you another grandchild."

"Or two, or three, or six?" Mr. Greene said.

"Ha. It will all be good. You'll see."

~ * ~

The month passed slowly and finally the families gathered on the wedding day. Leading up to the ceremony in the parlor of the plantation home, the church choir director, Emily Crawford, played hymns on the family piano. Those in attendance were dressed well. Children were bathed and instructed to be on their best behavior. Andrew's older sister, Jeanette, three months pregnant, sat next to her husband. She held her two-year-old son close, talking in whispers.

Next to Jeanette, to keep their three children occupied, Mason held one son in his lap and his wife, Julia, held their new baby boy in her arms. In awe of the ceremony, their four-year-old daughter sat in an armchair next to her mother.

To get the ceremony underway, Preacher Crawford stood before the families. Andrew, with his father as best man, strode to the front of the room to the left side of the minister. Stepping through a floral archway arm-in-arm, Mr. Vining entered with Elizabeth. She was dressed in a new pink gown. The father and daughter walked to the right of Preacher Crawford. Mr. Vining kissed Elizabeth on the cheek and took a seat nearby.

Mrs. Crawford continued to play the piano quietly as the Greenes' family members settled into their seats. Preacher Crawford cleared his throat and the music stopped.

"Let us bow our heads and pray. Dear Lord, we come before You today in fellowship and in wonder at the good fortune You have provided us. We bring two families together to celebrate the marriage, love, and commitment between Elizabeth and Andrew. We ask that You bless their union with bountiful happiness and all the good things life has to offer. We beseech You to watch over this fine couple in all the days ahead. In Your name, we pray. Amen."

Everyone else said 'amen.' The young children squirmed in their seats. Mason's young daughter ran up to the bride and groom. She handed Elizabeth a bouquet of spring flowers tied together with pink ribbons.

The girl said, "I'm sorry. I forgot to give these to you, 'Lizbeth."

Elizabeth reached for the flowers. "Thank you." The child stood there unsure of what would happen next. Elizabeth smiled and kissed the girl's cheek. "Sweetheart, you can go sit down now."

As the little girl returned to her chair, Preacher Crawford smiled and began. "We are gathered here in the sight of God and these witnesses to join Elizabeth and Andrew as they commit their lives to each other in holy matrimony. This ceremony is an outward expression of the love and devotion they have for each other."

The preacher added some of his own thoughts. "It's an honor and a privilege to be here today. I can't help but think back over the last several years. I've learned to know and to love these two fine people. I remember baptizing Andrew when he was ten and Elizabeth a year later. After leaving the seminary, I had just joined the church as an associate pastor, serving beside the Reverend Macintyre before he went home to the Lord.

"So, this is a day of remembrance for me, as well as celebration, and I'm sure it is for all those gathered here. It's a day of happiness and special meaning. I know that Elizabeth's mother, Mary Alice, is also looking down from heaven and smiling, because she knows the joy of this occasion.

"These young people have been in love ever since I have known them, and this is a blessed day. Elizabeth and Andrew, I would ask you to join your hands, but I see you have already done so.

" ...Andrew Dale Greene, will you have Elizabeth to be your wife; to live together in the holy covenant of marriage? If so, answer, I will."

"I will," said Andrew.

"Will you love her, comfort her and keep her in sickness and in health, for richer or poorer, forsaking all others, till death you do part?"

"I will," said Andrew.

"Elizabeth Anne Vining, will you have Andrew as your husband; to live together in the holy covenant of marriage?"

"I will," said Elizabeth. She looked into Andrew's eyes.

"Elizabeth, will you love and obey him, comfort him and keep him in sickness and in health, for richer or poorer, forsaking all others, till death do you part? If so, answer, I will."

"I will," said Elizabeth.

The preacher addressed the gathering. "Elizabeth and Andrew have other marriage vows of their own to add. Andrew."

Andrew gave a slight cough and cleared his throat. He spoke in a soft voice. "Elizabeth, I love you with..."

One of the children said, "Speak up, Andrew. I can't hear you," and everyone laughed.

Andrew tried again, louder and more relaxed. "Elizabeth, I love you with all of my heart. I promise to work beside you as a partner in life to create a home for you and our children and to protect you and support you in your hopes and dreams throughout our lives."

"Elizabeth," said Preacher Crawford.

"Andrew, I love you with all of my heart. I promise to care for you and support you and your dreams, and, just as I will plant seeds in our gardens and nourish them, I will nourish you all the days of our lives, love you, and create a home for us."

Preacher Crawford said, "Andrew will present Elizabeth with a ring now. The ring is made of precious metal and symbolizes the union that is to be cherished. Andrew, please present her ring to Elizabeth."

Andrew pulled a gold band from his vest pocket. Elizabeth held out her left hand, and Andrew gently slid the band onto her ring finger, saying, "With this ring, I thee wed." Tears of joy filled her eyes.

Preacher Crawford said, "By the authority vested in me by the state of Tennessee, I now pronounce you husband and wife."

The preacher then said, "Let us pray. Our heavenly Father, bless this union between Elizabeth and Andrew. Keep them safe. Help them to grow their love. Remind them to talk to each other openly and honestly about their hopes, fears, and challenges in life. Help their families and friends to give support to this young couple now and throughout their lives together. Amen."

He looked at Andrew. "You may kiss your bride."

After the ceremony, a fine feast awaited the gathering of three generations. Mama Jordan, Mrs. Greene, and the house servants had prepared a long dining table set with fine china and silverware on a white linen tablecloth. Lighted candles in polished silver candlesticks graced the table.

Mr. Vining sat at the head of the table and an empty chair was placed at the foot of the table in remembrance of where his deceased wife would have been. The plantation owner rose to speak. "What a wonderful day this is. I am not one to always thank people in our lives as I should or to let you know how important you are to us, but I look out upon this group with thanks and happiness for your friendship and for caring for Elizabeth and me.

"Millers Creek is a small community but it is full of fine folks and it's wonderful to have you all here today. Mrs. Crawford, thank you for your talent to provide the lovely music. Preacher Crawford, that was a fine ceremony—heartfelt and well done. Thank you, Preacher, for being here today. Will you please bless this table and the food we are to enjoy?"

Preacher Crawford nodded and stood. "Dear Lord. Our hearts are full of hope and joy today for Andrew and Elizabeth. Please bless this couple and the households they represent as they go forward in life. Please bless those who prepared the food set before us. May it provide nourishment to keep us strong, healthy, and ready to go forth and do God's work. Keep us safe in the days ahead and protect us on this journey of life. We ask in Your name. Amen."

After the meal, musicians performed in the large parlor near the dining room. The furniture had been rearranged against the walls for seating and a rug had been removed from the hardwood floor to create room for dancing. Elizabeth and Andrew danced the first waltz by themselves and bowed to applause from their families. Then, Elizabeth and her father, and Andrew and his mother danced. Then everyone joined in around the room. Servants offered glasses of champagne to the adults and lemonade to the children. Some of the mothers stepped out to tend to their babies.

With her arm through his, Elizabeth said, "Daddy, thank you again for all this. The ceremony was just as I wanted, and your dancing is just right too."

"I am pleased for you, my dear. Everyone is dressed so well. The food tastes so good, and I was surprised at the number of babes in arms, and on the way as well."

"Wonderful children."

"Shall I invite the men now to enjoy some tobacco and whiskey on the patio?"

"Oh, please wait a little longer. I so want to dance more with Andrew."

"All right, my dear. It is your day, of course, and I would not separate you from your husband."

Nine

On the night of their marriage, they were both shy but eager to share their bodies. They lay together in a bed for the first time. Andrew found his love for Elizabeth had a deeper meaning when he touched her skin and she held his hands to her breasts.

"I love you with all of my heart," he said.

"You are my heart, Andrew. You will be always."

Elizabeth held him close. He kissed her lips and neck and she helped him remove her nightgown, then she lay on her stomach.

"What are you doing?" he asked.

"I don't know if I'm ready, if I'm pretty enough for you."

"If you're not ready, I understand. We have our whole lives ahead of us. But so you know, I think you are a beautiful woman and I have dreamed of this night for a long time."

She laughed.

Andrew kissed her back and shoulders, then the nape of her neck.

"Oh, Andrew, you're making me feel all tingly. Is that good?"

He felt her back getting warm. "Yes, it is all good."

Elizabeth rolled over and Andrew gently lay on top of her, kissing every part of her body he could get to.

"It tickles," she said. Then she admired his strong arms, touched his chest, and looked up into his eyes.

A moment later, she moaned when he made love to her. Tears of emotion and happiness filled her eyes. They lay in the bed for another hour just holding each other.

~ * ~

Though they knew Andrew might be called back to military duty at any time, the first year of their marriage unfolded with joy-filled months together.

Andrew and Elizabeth lived at his family's farm for a while, but with the help of his father and Mason, Andrew built a comfortable house on his nearby farm. He turned trees cut from his acreage into lumber and by fall the new five-room home was finished. They painted it white, to match a picket fence in front of the house. Next they built a small house for future tenant farmers.

Elizabeth set to decorating her new home with the help of her father and in-laws. Mr. Vining delivered her bedroom suite from the plantation house. Andrew's parents furnished a second bedroom with all of Andrew's old furniture, including a dresser, mirror, washstand, and another full-size bed.

A happy wife, Elizabeth planted an herb garden behind the picket fence in front of the house, after turning over soil with a shovel and chopping out weeds. She also tried her hand at plowing and learned more recipes from Andrew's mother and Mama Jordan.

Then in December of 1835, after Andrew brought in more wood for a fire, he found Elizabeth holding an envelope addressed to him.

"Is this from the Army?" she asked.

"It was delivered yesterday. I was going to tell you tonight." He opened it and handed the paper to Elizabeth to read.

"Must you leave again? It's so soon, and all the way to Florida?"

"I know, but I need to report. The Seminoles have to be moved to a different reservation west of the Mississippi. It will be good for my efforts to advance. Did you see where they approved my commission as a second lieutenant?"

"That is good. An officer. I know you wanted it. I am proud of you, of course, but I wish you would stop the Army. Can't you end it, Andrew? It's not safe and there's so much you need to do here."

"I know. I know. But it means more land for us, and I'll be all right. It will be all right."

Elizabeth started crying.

Andrew put his arms around her. "The sooner I get this done, the sooner I can get back to you. Let's have a good time tonight at my folks'. Mama is fixing a special dinner for us."

"So you already told them?"

"I saw Father late yesterday and he said he expected something like this because of the news. He said to come over tonight."

Andrew could tell Elizabeth was more upset. "Maybe you can tell your *wife* first in the future."

"I'm sorry, sweetheart. I ran into him at the general store just after I got the orders. I wasn't thinking."

She cradled his face in her hands. "I worry so much when you're away. But you know I'll continue on here." His eyes met hers. "I was going to surprise you tonight with an announcement of my own, but I see it can't wait. Andrew, I'm going to have your first child."

"What?"

"I thought I might be expecting."

He laughed again with joy and put his arms around her. "This is wonderful. My darling wife, pregnant." He kissed her lips and whispered in her ear. "I love you so much."

"So it's good news?"

"Of course. It's wonderful news. Everyone will be so pleased."

"Yes, and the doc said I'm almost two months along."

He counted the months in his head. "So, I'll be a father in ..."

"... July I think."

~ * ~

Andrew continued his career in the Army but came back from his Florida tour of duty for the birth of their son. They agreed to name him Thomas. The boy was healthy and strong. But complications injured Elizabeth and meant no more children. The health and well-being of his darling wife was the most important thing to Andrew. They hoped the disappointment they faced with no more children would be overcome as they watched Thomas grow.

A week after Thomas was born, Andrew returned to his regiment. He realized the transition from loving husband and father at home to officer and warrior in the field was starting to make him weary.

However, he carried on. He led men into battle and faced death many times. He called on his soldiers to be courageous and called on God to protect them all. He trained men to kill and had to bury too many comrades.

Even when there were nights at home with Elizabeth, he often slept poorly and woke in a sweat from a battle nightmare. He thought he heard gunfire in the distance, only to realize it was rumbling thunder. Other mornings before waking in a tent, Andrew dreamed he was in a storm only to find his camp under attack.

He and Elizabeth wrote letters to each other, eventually to be delivered through the developing mail system. In his letters to his wife, there was no mention of war. He only described his love for her and Thomas. He wrote of his thoughts of her smiling face and of his plans to return as soon as possible. In her letters, she wrote about the latest harvest, her love for Andrew, and how Thomas was learning to ride.

Ten

Spring, 1836

During a visit home, Andrew talked with his father and Elizabeth about the reasons for the Seminole War. The South wanted control of Florida because escaped slaves found a haven among the Seminoles outside the U.S. boundary. Many American settlers in the peninsula wanted protection. Both factors furthered tensions and arguments between the U.S. government and Spain, which claimed the territory.

Back on the battlefield, Andrew led troops to help rout thousands of Seminoles from Florida. The troops burned Seminole villages to the ground and battled fierce Indians to the death. One day during the mission, Andrew got separated from his fellow soldiers. A bullet from a Seminole rifle hit his left arm and he fell from his horse—knocked unconscious.

When Andrew came to, he discovered his childhood friend Isaiah was standing over him.

"Mr. Andrew, Mr. Andrew, I know that's you? It's me. Isaiah, Mama Jordan's boy."

Still dizzy from the wound and fall, Andrew realized he was on a bed inside a log cabin.

"I found you, Mr. Andrew. I knew it was you. Drink some of this water."

Andrew took a sip from a clay cup.

"What are you doing here, Isaiah? Our army is all around you."

"They done moved on. This house is out by itself in amongst these trees. Away from the village. Never saw us. That bullet went on through your arm. We patched you up. How you feelin'?"

Andrew looked at the bandage on his wound. "It hurts for sure, but the bleeding's stopped. I can't believe you're here. Thank you for helping me. I reckon my troop took me for dead and moved on, but I've got to get back to them."

"I got your horse out in the shed, still saddled up. Maybe you strong enough to ride now."

"How long have I been out?"

"'Bout two hours, I reckon."

Andrew looked around the small cabin. A pregnant woman was wiping her hands on a towel near a cabinet and a little girl was hiding behind the woman's apron.

"Mr. Andrew this here's my wife, Morning Star, and our girl, Lilly."

Andrew sat up on the edge of the bed. "Thank you for what you've done to get my arm right."

The woman smiled and nodded.

Isaiah said, "I done told her 'bout how you and me growed up in Tennessee before I got away from that plantation."

"I didn't know what happened to you. When you disappeared, I was too young to go looking for you."

"It was abolitionists stopped old Loggins and freed us on the way to the slave market. They helped me get cross Georgia and to the Seminoles down hea'."

"And now our Army is after you and all the others."

"Looks bad, don't it?"

"They'll be back. I'm sure of it. Isaiah, you have to get yourself and your family out of here. Go west now along the panhandle. Just keep going as fast as you can."

"Well, I don't know 'bout that, Mr. Andrew."

"It's for sure they'll come back looking for me and any other fallen soldiers before the sun goes down. See if they can save us or bury us. You have got to go now. Have you got a horse?"

"We got one mare and a mule and we got yours too."

"I can't give up my horse, Isaiah. I'll give you some money and try to delay the troops. Lead them in a different direction for a bit, but that's all I can do. So, get your things together. They'll find your house soon enough and burn it to the ground. You don't want to be in it."

"Yes, sir. I reckon we'll go then. I hear what you sayin'. If you see my mama, you tell her we all right."

The controversial Second Seminole War continued until 1842. Andrew served in the Army for two years before returning to his home and family in Tennessee. He was glad to be able to farm again, lie beside his wonderful Elizabeth, and help rear his growing boy.

Eleven

Nine years later, April, 1846

"Father, we're going to war with Mexico," Andrew said.

"I thought as much, after that annexation. I'm not surprised."

"I've been called back. This time with the rank of captain." Andrew put a commission document on the table. His father slipped a pair of eyeglasses on and read the papers by the fireplace.

"It's about time," his father said. "You deserve it. I'm proud of you." The man had lost weight recently, was pale, and leaned back in his chair after a cough.

"I took the long way around," Andrew said. "Should have gone to the Academy in the first place, I guess."

"If you had, I think there would not have been any land for you." His father took a sip of coffee.

"I guess it may have come, but much later," Andrew said.

"I don't have to tell you to stop guessing, do I?" his father said. "You've proven yourself for years. Go with the confidence you need to have. If you don't act certain, your men will see it in your face, the way you sit in your saddle, and the way you give them orders. Do I need to take you out in the field and fight with you again?"

Andrew laughed. "I'm just thinking back, and I don't need another demonstration." He smiled at his father. "Are you feeling all right? Mama said you're taking a day out of the fields."

"I'll be fine, just a little cold. It's all about the future now. Growing this country. Texas territory is important as we grow westward."

"It's part of the Manifest Destiny idea, isn't it?" Andrew said.

His father coughed. "I believe it. We're a young country with growing pains. I think Polk is right to push for it. Take it from Mexico when we can."

"Some are for it and others against it. A point about slavery and a way of life."

"It's been determined, son. Let the government fight that kind of fight," he said with another cough. "You've got your orders, so go be a soldier and a leader, but come back to me and your mother. We'll keep up with Thomas and Elizabeth. I know they'll write to you. I hear Thomas could be bound for the Academy. Maybe he wants to follow in your footsteps."

"I'm glad of the way he's growing up," said Andrew.

"You leave this week?"

"Yes. Report as soon as I can."

"Talk to your mother."

"Yes. I will."

"Come here and let me hold you." They wrapped their arms around each other. "I love you, son. Be a good man and be careful."

~ * ~

By May in Texas, Andrew had led a charge of American Dragoons at the Battle of Resaca de la Palma. He received shrapnel wounds to his back from artillery and had to convalesce near Fort Brown in Texas for a week before rejoining his forces. It was then he received a letter from his mother. As he read the heartbreaking message of his father's death, tears fell from his eyes to join ones already on the paper. Then he was called to return to the battle on the way to Mexico City.

His father had died of pneumonia, and it had taken a month for the message to reach Andrew at Fort Texas. Upon his eventual return to Tennessee, once the war was won, his mother gave him the gold pocket watch that had been his grandfather's, then his father's and now his.

Andrew's year tour of duty ended in April, 1847. He began the long ride home from Texas. He gladly resigned his commission and was happy to return to life on his farm. It was early spring when he mustered out and became a civilian. He thought about the many years of separation from his family and from Elizabeth.

As he rode into Millers Creek, a trailing dust cloud followed Andrew's six-year-old Appaloosa, Noah. The horse turned up the lane to the little white farmhouse, but no one ran to greet Andrew. The sky was an overcast gray, and a chill found its way inside his coat. Windswept dead leaves scurried across his path in swirling circles.

Andrew dismounted and threw Noah's reins over a hitching post. An empty, black, one-horse buggy stood at the gate—the animal tethered to the picket fence. Andrew knew it belonged to the doctor.

Entering the house, Andrew paused at the hearth in the main room and barely felt the warmth of a low fire. He could hear someone crying and a quiet, muffled conversation. Throwing off his coat, he climbed the stairs two at a time. He threw open the door to the master bedroom, startling his son, the doctor, and the housekeeper. They surrounded the bed bearing the still body of Elizabeth. She had died within the hour from diphtheria.

When Thomas saw his father, the boy stopped crying and angrily demanded, "Where were you?" Sobbing, Andrew fell to his knees beside the boy and pulled his son to him. The doctor gave his condolences and warned the disease was contagious and the household would have to be quarantined. Andrew rose and asked the housekeeper to take Thomas from the room.

Crying, Andrew knelt beside the bed. He touched Elizabeth's hands and face. His tears would not stop. The doctor explained Elizabeth must have caught the disease while helping poor tenants. She often got up early to make loaves of bread to drop off to needy families. Her kindness had led to her end. The doctor would oversee a swift and safe removal of her body and the plans for her funeral. He would tell neighbors about her death and the quarantine, and he posted a warning sign on the front door.

After Andrew and Thomas partially ate a dinner left on the stoop by friends, the exhausted boy went upstairs to sleep. A distraught and depressed Andrew sat alone in front of a fire, a bottle of whiskey on a table by his side. His heart ached with the loss of the only woman he had ever loved, his life companion, and an overwhelming guilt settled into his mind and body. The whiskey bottle was empty by morning.

A small, somber, family-only funeral was completed within a few days. Once the quarantine was lifted, Thomas returned to school. He was soon surrounded by the love of his friends and cousins. With Andrew's Army career ended and his wife dead, he avoided any social engagements and let weeds take over the fields. Being absent during the loss of both his father and beloved wife overwhelmed him.

Later, with little interest, he worked the farm by day, and by night he relied on bourbon to get settled and fall asleep in a chair.

Thomas spent more time and more nights with his cousins at Mason and Julia's house. Andrew found it hard to focus on anything, including caring for his son.

The night drinking turned into day drinking as well, and after two months, Mason came to call.

"I know her passing has turned your life upside down. Elizabeth ran this place most of the time, and I loved her too," Mason began. "But it's time for you to think about what's best for Thomas and yourself."

"I'm sick, I think," Andrew said, "sick at heart, Mason. She was my rock, my anchor. Without her, I'm adrift. I think I could have saved her, had I been here. It's my fault and I hate myself for it. I've wasted all those years. I lost all that time."

Mason put his hand on his brother's shoulder and nodded in sympathy. "Listen. I've talked this over with Julia and the boys, and we think the best thing for Thomas is he comes to live with us for a while. Our boys and Thomas get along fine, and he needs a place where he can get regular meals and be around people who can take care of him."

"No, he's my son."

"Let us do this. It'll give you time to figure out what's best for you to do next and give Thomas a good place to stay. The boys even help each other with their studies."

"I don't know," Andrew said.

"Thomas says he wants to go to the Academy at West Point. Giving him a steady home life will help him get ready for a good future. He admires and loves you, so let us help him and you."

After a few more protests, it was finally agreed, and Thomas moved to his aunt and uncle's house. Mason tried to spend more time with Andrew to keep him busy working on the farm and to reduce his drinking. Andrew began searching for a purpose, something important and big to which he could devote his life. But the whiskey kept calling.

Guilt for not saving his dead wife and nightmares of battles drove Andrew to drink—first at home by the fire then at the Bluff Bar where he drank himself under the table, until Molly MacAskill dug him out and dragged him upstairs to her room.

Andrew was drunk when he found Molly, or she found him. She was drunk too. They were both lonely and sad. Elizabeth had been ripped out of his life and he blamed himself for her death. Had he been there by her side, as a better husband would have been, perhaps he could have done something to save her. Maybe he would have noticed her health was different, her energy slowly draining, her chest congestion, the tone of her skin. Something a good husband would have noticed—had he been there instead of serving in the Army.

Molly had been lost for a long time when she first met Andrew. She too was lost at the bottom of a bottle of whiskey, drowning her sorrows at her life's twists and turns, and her desperation led her to work upstairs at the Bluff Bar. She missed her parents; both had died too young when she was little. She hated the orphanage and the nuns who beat her for just chewing her fingernails, so she ran away when she was fifteen. She was hungry—hungry for affection, for belonging, for being wanted by someone. She was still sad, five years later, at how she made her living, but determined to carry on.

So, when their paths crossed, they were ready. The good of their relationship would outweigh the bad. It wasn't just business for her. It was the closeness, a look, and a touch brought them together at a round wooden table in the dim bar on the edge of town. They were both looking for something they somehow found in each other. It would lead them upstairs to Molly's room. It would be different for many reasons. The sadness brought them together. The guilt of past acts made him stay and his desperate hunger for affection and need for whiskey would make him return. He needed repairing. She needed caring. It would be good for a while.

A month later, bartender and owner Ben Harrington looked across the room full of patrons and could see the expression on Andrew Greene's face. "I tol' him and tol' him," he said loudly to his helper. "Darren, get Molly afore he tears up the place again. I can see where this is headed."

Darren ran up the barroom stairs and knocked on Molly's door.

From behind the door, Molly said, "I'm busy."

"Ben said to get you," Darren hollered.

The door opened enough for Molly to stick out her head. Darren could see a man beyond her, sitting on the edge of the bed, buttoning his shirt.

"Sorry, Molly, but Captain Greene's down there drunk as a skunk and startin' to get wild-eyed again. Ben said to ..."

"All right. All right. Go on. I'll be down shortly."

Darren nodded and said, "Sorry, Sheriff," to the man on the bed.

A minute later, downstairs, Molly put her hand gently on Andrew's drinking arm. "Captain, sweetheart, how are you doin'?"

Andrew used both elbows to prop himself up on the card table and was staring at an empty bottle and a losing hand. Molly took his cards and laid them on the table. "He folds, ya'll." The other players nodded. "It's best he come with me."

Andrew rolled his eyes up to her. "I ain't goin' nowhere."

"Andrew, it's me, Molly. It's time to come up now."

"I'm waitin' right here. I know Elizabeth's comin' to see me."

"Well, you know she can't come. Not anymore," Molly said.

"Don't tell me what to do." Andrew pounded the table with his fist.

The dealer and the other players pushed back their chairs.

The dealer said, "Didn't she die months ago ..."

Ben and Darren grabbed Andrew as he lunged for the dealer saying, "I'll tear yer head off ..."

Molly stepped in front of Andrew. "Ya'll hush up now." She took his hand, and with the help of Darren, led the drunken warrior up the stairs to her room.

Andrew said, "I can see her. Elizabeth is comin' through the arch, up to me."

"I know, I know," Molly said.

Darren let go of the retired soldier at Molly's door and retreated to the bar.

Andrew kept slurring and talking. "She's all dressed in pink. Purty as can be ..."

"Come here to me," Molly said. She held him to her breast and stroked his head until he fell asleep. He would lie there until morning.

By the end of the next week, with the help of Mason, Andrew began to drink less. He stayed sober during the week and worked his farm again. Sweating in the fields felt good. His body was recovering from his bout with whiskey. He did lapse on the weekends but his drinking was reserved for Saturday nights—still at the Bluff Bar. In early August, feeling like a farmer again, Andrew put up meadow grass for his small herd of cattle and pure orchard grass for his horses.

One night after dinner, he found an old copy of *United States Magazine and Democratic Review* and re-read with great interest a column by John O'Sullivan titled *Annexation*. More than once, Andrew read the article advocating annexation of The Republic of Texas as part of America's 'Manifest Destiny' to expand across the continent.

The idea of expansion swept throughout the Oregon Country to the Pacific Ocean. Opening up the territory would make it possible for millions of new immigrants to populate the land and grow the country from coast to coast. It was the big purpose and opportunity Andrew needed and wanted. He just wasn't sure how to be part of it, but he agreed with O'Sullivan who wrote 'the United States had a divine mandate' to expand across North

America. But Andrew didn't like the fact Texas would be a slave state.

Within a few days of Andrew's reading the 'Manifest Destiny' article, there was a knock on his front door. He opened it to find two area preachers smiling at him. He recognized Preacher Crawford from Elizabeth's funeral and from attending church with his family. He did not know the other man.

"Captain Greene, you know me, of course, and this is my new associate, Reverend William Bowen. We would like to talk to you about a proposition and wondered if this was a good time. Or should we make an appointment?"

Andrew received them and the reverends explained a sizable group of their congregants were interested in forming an expedition to explore and re-settle in the West, to find a more healthy environment and more fertile lands on which to raise their families. The congregants were not in favor of slavery, were worried about catching malaria common to the local climate, and wanted to build a better future. The interested families were made up of peace-loving farmers and craftsmen. Some were former soldiers.

The more the reverends talked about plans for leading a wagon train to Oregon, the more interested Andrew became. He realized he could be part of the big movement to the West. It would be nation-building. The enthusiasm of the two reverends was obvious as they spelled out their proposal.

"The wagon train wants to leave as soon as possible, hopefully by March next year," Preacher Crawford said.

Reverend Bowen added, "That gives us, and you, if you agree, time to get to St. Joseph and pick up the Oregon Trail."

Andrew rubbed his beard, saying, "It will require a lot of organizing and manpower."

"We already have enough families for eighteen wagons. Maybe close to a hundred souls to populate the West and establish a new church when we get there," Crawford said.

"What we don't have ..." Bowen began.

Crawford added, "... and this is where we need you ..."

"... is a leader and good protection for the train, guards, if you will," Reverend Bowen concluded.

Preacher Crawford said, "Because we'll be making such a long journey, I understand close to six months, we figure a lot can happen where we'll need a man of your background and capabilities to keep us safe ..."

Reverend Bowen said, "... possible trouble from outside the group and maybe within ..."

"So, please consider this seriously and let us know what you would need to join us," said Crawford.

"Most folks have already committed to the plan and paid their thousand-dollar fees," said Bowen.

Preacher Crawford handed Andrew a pouch. "Here's a list of the travelers, what they've paid and what's due, and their skills for you to look over. We'll need it back soon. You know most of these folks already."

"It will be a moving community until they get settled and establish a permanent community as part of the Oregon territory," Reverend Bowen said.

Andrew said, "With so many people, a lot can happen. And with the outside hostiles, outlaws, and threats from Mother Nature, you'll need more than one man for protection."

"See what you think of the people on the list," said Reverend Bowen.

"We know each other and have lived in this area for a long time, a pretty well-behaved bunch," Crawford said. "But, of course, there will be problems. The wagon master we need is a combination sheriff and military leader. Why don't you think about it? See what's missing from this list as far as you can tell. My wife Emily and I will be part of the train, while Reverend Bowen takes over my ministry here."

"May we meet with you again on Friday to hear your thoughts?" Reverend Bowen asked.

Andrew agreed to consider their proposal and during their next meeting, he described his concerns about the timing and requirements for such a trip.

"Pastors, what you and some of your congregation want to do is certainly worthwhile, and I am interested in being a part of settling the West," Andrew began.

"Wonderful," both preachers said at the same time.

"However, there is not much time to gather the people and resources needed for such an excursion."

"What do you think is missing?" Preacher Crawford said.

"Though I've been in some of the lands west of the Mississippi, I have not been past the Platte River in the Nebraska area, so there is much of the trail I don't know. We would need time to find a guide who could keep us on the Oregon Trail, be out front of the wagon train, and understand the pitfalls and peoples we may encounter," Andrew said. "I have led men in battles with Mexicans, Indians, and outlaws, and know we will need qualified and experienced men who can defend the expedition—men who can shoot straight and handle themselves in an attack. On the list you gave me, I saw few men who would qualify."

"We agree with you," Reverend Bowen said, "and we have already heard back from an experienced mountain man who knows the territory. His name is Ray Cooper, and he has agreed to be our scout. Do you know of this man?"

"Well, yes," Andrew said, surprised, as he began to tamp tobacco into his clay pipe. "I met him once in Missouri—a powerful mountain of a man."

"He was recommended by some of our parishioners," said Reverend Bowen. "They are former Missouri militiamen, Anderson and Pike, who are now eager to go West with their families. They were on the list. Like you, they fought in the

Indian Wars and they know Cooper to be a capable man, a reliable scout who has led wagon trains to the West already along the trail we will follow."

Preacher Crawford said, "We wrote to Cooper some months ago and he has promised to be our scout if we can get our group to St. Joseph by the end of March. We should have told you earlier. My apologies."

Andrew lit his pipe and puffed a smoke ring into the air. He tossed the burnt match into the fireplace and looked at the flaming logs. "So, gentlemen, I mean reverends, that will leave assembling a security detail as the remaining need."

"We will rely on your expertise to find the best men, ones who will be trustworthy and reliable for the whole journey and able to defend us when needed, and able to meet us in St. Joseph or before."

~ * ~

In early September, Andrew awoke upstairs one more time in the Bluff Bar. Molly laid her head on his bare chest and pulled the bedcovers over her exposed shoulder to ward off an early morning chill. Even though his eyes were closed she knew he was awake, thinking about the day ahead, and getting on the trail.

"I don't want you to go. I really hate it," she said.

"It'll be a long while, you know," he said, as he rolled to the edge of the mattress to put on his pants and boots. "Cooper and I got to get to Oregon and back as soon as possible. We're mapping locations along the trail for all sorts of reasons."

Molly wrapped her arms around him from behind. "I'll just miss you, is all. It's nice havin' you round. It'll be Christmas before I see you again."

"I told you. I won't be coming back by then. The pass in the Rockies will be closed with snow." He lifted suspenders over his shoulders. "It'll be about March when we get back and that'll be to St. Joseph, not here. It's where I'm meeting the others."

Molly got out of the rumpled bed, stepped onto the creaking wood floor, and held a sheet across her naked front. "You know, Andrew, there ain't no reason I can't go west with you," she said.

Andrew buckled his holster and checked to make sure his new Colt Walker pistol was loaded. "It can't happen. I won't be able to take a woman along, even if I wanted to."

"So, you sayin' you ain't sure you want me along?"

"No, Molly. I am sure. It's time for me to move on. I'm leaving my life here behind me."

"But, Andrew, you mean a lot to me."

"It's been good to be with you these months, no doubt, but I got to get a new start."

"I'm the only woman you lain with except your Elizabeth, God rest her soul."

"I'll not have you speak of her."

"You told me so the first night. The first time you came to my bed. I'm the only other woman you've been with. You said so."

"I was drunk and so were you. You know I loved Elizabeth with all my heart. Since I was a kid. It's different."

"And she's gone now, and I'm right here."

"I said that's a whole different thing."

"Well, I might just get on a horse and follow your damn wagon train all the way to Oregon."

"I haven't got time to parley with you. I got to get on now," Andrew said. He put on his wide-brimmed hat.

"But, Andrew, I'll salute you and everything, all along the way." She tried to smile as tears ran down her cheeks, and she gave Andrew a salute.

"Goodbye, Molly," he said. Andrew marched out of her room and out of her life. He closed the door behind him. He walked away and could hear Molly cursing. The sound of glass crashing against the walls of her room echoed down the hall.

With the death of his wife, Andrew drank his way to the bottom of many a bottle of whiskey trying to forget the guilt he felt and to get numb for a while. He blamed himself for all those missed months and years he could have spent at the side of Elizabeth and the time he could have been a better father to Thomas. By agreeing to lead the wagon train, Andrew had found a new purpose. He felt it was his destiny to help the country grow. If he had to make sacrifices, so be it.

Twelve

1847

Andrew set a ribbon-wrapped bouquet in front of Elizabeth's gravestone in the plantation cemetery. "I picked these wildflowers you like down near Millers Creek. I know I haven't been here for a while now, my darling, and I'm sorry. I love you so much still. I think the aching in my heart and my head will never stop. But I'm leaving today to go out West. By spring, I'll be leading a wagon train. I'm here to say goodbye."

"You think she hears you?"

Andrew recognized the voice behind him and turned. "Mama Jordan, I didn't hear you coming."

They hugged without hesitation and the fingers of her black hand intertwined with Andrew's.

"I know you were lost in your thoughts sayin' goodbye to her," Mama Jordan said.

"It's been a while since I came."

"I pass here every mornin', every evnin'. She's restin' peaceful."

"I'm afraid my heart will never heal."

"I've known you since you was a little boy. You got a strong heart. Elizabeth would want you to carry on. Do good things. Take care of other folks too."

"You know I gave Thomas to Mason to raise," Andrew said with tears in his eyes. "He's made it to the Academy now."

"For the best then, I reckon. It was good for him to be with those other good boys and get some caring for himself from Mason's family. He'll be all right."

"It's been so hard. It's part of why I'm leaving. I've got to get right."

"It's a good thing."

"Have you heard from Isaiah?" he asked.

"I did. He says I got three grandbabies. Ain't that somethin'? A grandmother three times over."

"I'm glad for you."

"Reckon I'll never see their sweet little faces, but still ..."

"I'm glad he could get a message to you."

"Said you saved his life down in Florida. You boys was close. Wouldn't tell me where he was, but there's sunshine, he said, and freedom."

"That's good. And he saved my life too."

"Reckon I'll never see freedom neither," she said.

They stood silently for a moment. Andrew put his arm around her shoulder. "Where's Mr. Vining these days?"

"Hole up in his room upstairs mostly. Can hardly walk. Just sittin'. Ready to join his wife and family down here."

She placed her right hand flat on Andrew's face just below his scar. "But that ain't you, Andrew. There's lots of life left in you. Jest like my boy. You s'pose to keep on livin' out all your life."

"I'm starting to see that."

"You got lots of good things to do, but I gotta get back in the kitchen now. You go on. Get back to where you was, all strong and smart. And when you get to that place, be glad you can come back to Millers Creek. Maybe get your son and see your family." Mama Jordan turned quietly away.

Andrew closed his eyes, knelt, and put a hand on Elizabeth's gravestone. He said a prayer and asked for guidance and forgiveness. He was lost in thought when he heard the slow tapping of a cane behind him on the flat flagstones leading up to the cemetery.

"Andrew, my heart has been broken too many times." Mr. Vining coughed. "My Mary Alice, my baby boy, and then my sweet Elizabeth."

"There's dampness in the air. Are you warm enough?" Andrew said.

"My bones are hurtin', and I can't ride these days. My back keeps me inside most of the time. I'm just waitin' to join my loved ones here, next to Mary Alice. We had so many plans."

"Elizabeth and I wanted more children, but it wasn't meant to be."

"I saw Thomas riding with Mason and his brood a while back. It's good you gave me a grandson to love."

The two men stood quietly as the sun broke through gray clouds.

Vining said, "I hear you're leaving us."

"Yes. Today. going west to map the Oregon Trail. Back to St. Joseph by spring to lead a wagon train."

"You leaving behind some sadness, I expect."

"Yes, I am."

"I loved Mary Alice so much I couldn't consider finding another wife, another mother for Elizabeth."

"It's hard."

"Probably should have."

"Every man's life is different. I think you're married to this plantation."

"That I am, and I wish you good luck. Don't expect I'll see you again, but it will be good to get a letter now and then to know where you are."

Andrew mounted his horse, and pulling a pack mule, headed toward the Mississippi River. He would meet up with Ray Cooper in St. Joseph and ride west to the Pacific before the winter snows made the South Gap in the Rockies impassable. They would mark a map for water holes, forts, trading posts, and tribal lands of friendly Indians. It would take forty days by horseback to reach the Portland area and the Willamette Valley where the two men would have to winter before returning to St. Joseph to meet the wagon train they would lead west.

Thirteen

In May 1848, the Crawford Company wagon train, named for Preacher Horatio Crawford, took two weeks to get organized to depart from St. Joseph. It gave Andrew enough time to get everybody lined up, collect any remaining fees, and inspect each wagon. A former Army officer, he knew what was needed on the trail and how to give orders and get cooperation.

Though the travelers from Tennessee were skilled farmers, hunters, or tradesmen, a few more people were needed to make the train safer and more profitable. Andrew wanted to add experienced ex-soldiers for protection and maybe one or two other qualified people with specific skills. But the pickings were slim.

He didn't accept everybody who wanted to go. He ruled out people who didn't have camping experience, like a city dandy from Boston who somehow made it to Missouri but would be a problem to nurse all along the way. Andrew suggested those folks try getting on with a different train. He also ruled out people who didn't seem healthy enough to make the grueling six-month trip. And he ruled out the poor folks and the men with alcohol on their breath, not that he was a teetotaler, of course.

There was already a good mix of farm families on the trip who wanted to settle out West, start a new church, and become part of a community. Some of the farmers had special skills. There was a blacksmith and a cobbler. A herdsman and two drovers were pushing a herd of thirty cattle which would travel some distance behind the train. All the folks owned wagons covered with white canvas and pulled by teams of oxen or mules. People called the wagons prairie schooners because they looked like ships sailing across the plains.

Preacher Crawford and his wife, Emily, only had a buckboard with a tent pitched over the bed of the wagon and a pack mule tethered behind. Fortunately, a young, childless couple agreed to carry extra supplies for them in their prairie schooner. Otherwise, Andrew would not have allowed the buckboard. It would not have been able to haul the typical thousand or so pounds of supplies needed for such a long journey.

Some of the cattle in the traveling herd were for food along the trail or for trade, and some would be used for setting up a ranch in the Oregon territory which stretched from the Rocky Mountains to the Pacific Ocean. It had been acquired from the British in 1846, allowing the U.S. to expand across the continent.

One night, with folks gathered in a local hall in St. Joseph, Andrew stood in front of the crowd. He wore his usual buckskins, old Army boots, and bushy mustache.

"It's good to see all you folks. And I know you are excited about getting this wagon train underway." He was interrupted by whooping, feet stomping, and applause.

Andrew waved to the crowd to quiet down. "Now, as I've told you all, this trip will not be easy. There will be times we have to rely on each other for help fixing a broken axle, righting an overturned wagon, or for protection against hostiles. It will take us about six months to get to Oregon. Five if we're lucky."

Some of the folks moaned at such a timetable, and a baby in her mother's arms began to cry and everyone laughed, thinking the child didn't want to travel any six months either. The mother gave her baby a corn cob to suck and the child was suddenly happy and quiet.

"All right. All right." Andrew calmed the people and smiled at the woman and child. "We'll be crossing some rough landscape, and there's no general store along the way, maybe a trading post here and there and some forts. So you need to be sure you have more than enough supplies to get you where you're going. As a reminder, we're passing out a printed-up list of what you'll need in your wagons. If you take all this, the weight of your belongings and the supplies will add up to about two thousand pounds. It's a lot for any draft team to pull.

"So, you need a healthy, strong team of animals for your wagons. By now, you know using oxen or mules is best. The oxen can eat prairie grass when other animals won't. The beasts are slow-moving animals but will get you there. And they're not bad eating in a pinch... just don't tell them I said so." People laughed.

"When you signed up, we wrote down all the rules for our journey. To help us get organized, the reverend and I formed a company and we'll be keeping records as we go along. I chose the name for our wagon train. It is The Crawford Company, in honor of the man who has been major in making this possible." There were cheers and some people shouted, "Hooray for The Crawford Company."

"We leave at seven o'clock in the morning this Friday. You are welcome to gather your wagons ahead of time just to the west of town by the lake where my lead wagon will be located. See me now if you got any questions."

Having spent many years in the Army living outdoors, Andrew knew the hardships the settlers would face on the six-month journey. He collected a few remaining fees and confirmed the names of each of the travelers inked into a ledger. He figured he'd also find out if he made a good decision to seek his destiny in the dust of the Oregon Trail. It was better, Andrew knew, to weed out anyone who wasn't ready to go. At St. Joseph it wasn't too late to turn back. Go back to the old farms where the parents or grandparents waited. But no one left. They were all committed to getting to Oregon, to get free new fertile land, and grow crops and their families.

In town, creaking wooden planks formed the sidewalk beneath his dust-covered boots as Andrew stepped from storefront to storefront. He requested permission to post a circular about the wagon train's plans. "GUARDS NEEDED" read the message, which described a five or six-month commitment.

He stomped dust from his boots before entering the sheriff's office where he was greeted by the soles of the sheriff's boots propped on a cluttered desk. Andrew's eyes followed the boots to the legs and up to the clean-shaven sheriff's closed eyes. A slight wheezing snore was being emitted from his lips. Andrew banged the door shut.

Waking up, the sheriff looked past his boots. "Howdy, mister. What can I do for you today?"

"Sheriff, I'm glad you're in. I'm Captain Andrew Greene, and I'm leading a wagon train to Oregon."

"I'm Sheriff Tate," he said, shaking Andrew's hand. "Seems to be a lot of that goin' on—wagon trains, that is. I don't envy you the trip. I got headed west once in a posse, saw nothing, I mean nothing, and turned back around. I'm happy here."

"There is some flat, uninviting land between here and the Rockies, but afterward, things are much better."

"Been out there, huh?"

"Yes. My scout and I already rode the trail and marked good places to camp. We've got about eighty folks planning on farming for the most part."

"Can I pour you a cup of coffee—made this mornin'?"

"Thank you. And then I want to get back to Lake Browning where we're setting up. I'd like to post this notice for security guards on your board."

"Yeah, there's room up there. Tack away. Why don't you put it next to the Dan Barton wanted poster."

"Wanted dead or alive. That's what he looks like, eh?"

"Pretty much. It's a good likeness. I hear he's got a bad temper. He'd just as soon shoot ya' as look at ya'."

On the way out, Andrew glanced at ten WANTED posters tacked to a board on the wall. By the look of it, several posters were yellowed with age, while three looked recently printed.

He said, "Any of these been captured?"

The sheriff walked up to the board. "Oh, yeah, I need to change some. One killed. Two captured, one of 'um up in Independence. Just got the messages this week. These three new ones went up last month."

"A thousand dollars is a good size reward."

"Yep. Dead or alive for Barton."

Andrew tacked his notice on the board. "You can remove this later. I don't expect to be back through."

"Sure 'nough. Now if you run across any of these fellas, they may be part of a gang. So, be careful."

After getting a response to his posted flier, Andrew accepted four former soldiers into the wagon train, partly because he wanted their firepower and because he figured they could handle trail life after fighting in the Mexican-American War. The war had just ended in February with the Treaty of Guadalupe Hidalgo. The soldiers had left the Army when the fighting stopped last fall and were eager to explore the West and the possibility of finding gold in California. In addition to food and low pay, they were provided wagons and draft animals.

A former sergeant, Eric McFarland, was the brains of the foursome. Based on word-of-mouth rumors gold had been discovered in California, the men figured on searching for a fortune together upon reaching the Pacific coast. McFarland's wagon partner was Donald Quinn, his childhood friend and fellow warrior. Quinn was missing two fingers from his left hand from a combat wound but he was still fully capable of firing a rifle. As it turned out later, being able to hold his liquor was to be his larger problem.

As the days rolled by, Andrew would find out that Peter Duff and Connor Shaughnessy had quick tempers, especially after a few drinks. The two managed their own prairie schooner all right, but arguing seemed to be one of the few ways they communicated. They argued about former battles, about who had conquered the most women, and whether there was enough liquor.

Before leaving Tennessee, the travelers winnowed down their possessions to essentials. They brought furniture, clothing, tools, and livestock to Missouri. Once in St. Joseph, all the pioneer families gathered near Browning Lake, four miles outside of town. They all knew each other. They had grown up together and attended the same church. They had been part of each other's weddings, tended to each other's babies, and shared lives and deaths back home. Now they were determined and invested in a long, difficult trip along the Oregon Trail to a better life. They left behind one or two generations of family, poor soil, and unhealthy swamp land.

The party had confidence in the men who would lead the congregation across the country. The Right Reverend Horatio Crawford had preached to them every week, held their hands in times of trouble, and enjoyed many a meal at their homes. Their wagon master, Andrew Greene, had grown up amongst them. An Army officer with fifteen years of experience, Andrew knew what was needed on the trail. He instructed each family to make sure they and their livestock were healthy enough to begin the six-month trek to the West.

Reverend Crawford had been inspired by the enthusiasm of the faithful, younger generation of families to pursue the journey and to create a community of Christians in Oregon. He was also answering his sense of adventure and the feeling of a divine calling. He felt the Lord was calling him and the immigrant families to help settle the West and save souls. His wife, Emily, would contribute her medical knowledge and experience as a nurse and midwife. Now middle-aged, the older couple planned to help guide the young congregant families to a better life. The pioneers had made quick work of crossing the Mississippi and were eager to get the wagon train underway, cross the Missouri River, and roll into Kansas.

Outside the general store, a young man tapped Andrew on the shoulder.

"I thought that was you, Captain. Remember me? Billy Armstrong. I know it's been almost two years."

Andrew turned around. "What in the world? Billy, what a nice surprise."

"It's good to see you." They shook hands.

"I just read your poster," Billy said.

"I thought you were in Tennessee plowing up your farm."

"I was, I was, but it wasn't for me. I tried it for a year then sold it off."

"Too much work?"

"Not really. I may try again someday, but I still got a hankering for adventure of some kind."

"I last saw you in Texas. I'm glad you made it out."

It was a good reunion. Billy told his former captain he was ready to seek his fortune out West and told Andrew he wanted to join the train. Billy figured he could use the pay and company on the trip to Oregon. Andrew figured he could use an experienced soldier and teamster as a right-hand man. Plus, Billy could play a bugle.

When Andrew and Billy rode out to the campsite, they saw some eager pioneers had already written 'Portland or Bust' or 'Oregon Trail' on the sides of their white canvas covers. Over a year ago, younger couples had come to Preacher Crawford to explain their eagerness to explore the West, find richer farmland, and escape the scourge of malaria and cholera which had sickened so many in southwest Tennessee. Based on what started as a seed of an idea, there was a lot of enthusiasm as the train was finally getting underway.

That night, sitting by a campfire, Andrew thought about his life, and realized by the time he'd reached the age of 37 he'd been a farmer, a soldier, a husband, a father, a widower, and a drunk. He'd dealt with beatings, stabbings, shootings, losing, and winning. One of the things he knew he couldn't cope with was the loss of his lifelong love, Elizabeth. His dreams were filled with scenes of terror from battlefields and sadness from memories of losing Elizabeth. After those nightmares, he would welcome the end of his sleep.

The next morning, he woke up at 6:15 and heard a wagon creaking to a halt nearby. He slid his wide-brimmed hat from across his face and took a breath of fresh air. He smelled the coffee the train's cook, Frenchie Beauchamp, already brewed and he felt a chill in the air. When he heard the footfalls of someone approaching, Andrew opened his eyes to see a woman walking up to Frenchie.

"I'm here to see Captain Greene. Are you he?"

Andrew saw Frenchie poke a stick into the fire and look up toward the tall woman standing on the other side. Her hands were on her hips and Andrew could see her jaw was tightly set.

"Nope. He's not up yet. Though it's best to wait till he has his coffee before engaging him."

"Well, I'm here and ready to meet. I've got to get on with a wagon train, and I saw this bulletin at the general store. This yours?" The woman thrust a piece of paper toward Frenchie, who looked at it but didn't take it.

"Yep."

She tilted her head toward the lead wagon and saw Andrew stirring. "Is that Greene under there?"

Andrew knew Frenchie wasn't in the habit of answering questions posed by strangers, especially early in the morning, and especially from what he saw as a rude woman; nor did Frenchie like to repeat himself.

"Best to wait till he's had some coffee," Frenchie repeated.

The woman stepped over to the lead wagon, bent down, and stuck her head under the sideboard.

"Captain Greene, I'm Mrs. Rachel Richards, and I got a loaded prairie schooner out here. I just need to hook up with your wagon train."

Andrew blinked to get a clearer view of the visitor, a somewhat pleasant-looking woman with a bit of a shrill voice.

He said, "If you will, please wait in your wagon. I'll be with you shortly."

"That's all I'm asking," she said.

Mrs. Richards righted herself, left silently past Frenchie, and returned to her wagon where she was greeted by another woman and a young boy. Andrew put on his boots, stepped away to some shrubs on the other side of his wagon to relieve his bladder then went over to the fire. Frenchie handed him a tin cup of coffee. Andrew looked at him sideways.

"Looks like we got an early riser," he said, taking a sip, "on a mission."

"She may need a bag of patience," Frenchie said. "Got a bee in her bonnet."

Andrew finished the last of his coffee, thinking there was nothing like a determined woman. He stretched for the first time, felt some of his muscles straighten out, and rubbed his handlebar mustache. He reached the waiting wagon where four donkeys were hitched.

"Thank you for meeting with us, Captain," Mrs. Richards said, with a little honey on her tongue. "Permit me to introduce my sister, Claudine Lafayette. We are all descendants of the late Marquis de Lafayette."

Claudine gestured from the wagon seat. "*Bonjour*, Captain. We have just arrived from New Orleans on yesterday."

Andrew recognized a French accent from both women, similar to the soldiers he had commanded from Louisiana. He knew of the exploits of the marquis and had studied the battles of the American Revolution which included the Frenchman.

Mrs. Richards continued. "And this is my son, Daniel."

"Morning, boy," Andrew said.

"I'm eight," Daniel replied.

Andrew looked at the trio. "Well, our wagons are pretty well set for this trip."

Mrs. Richards stepped down from the wagon seat. "We've got everything we need for the trip, and it says on this paper you're going to leave Friday. Plenty of time to add one more wagon, don't you think?"

"Where are your menfolk?"

"There are none with us right now," she said, with her eyes looking to the side. She spoke quietly to Andrew. "We lost our father last year to malaria. However, my husband is waiting for us along the Oregon Trail. And we can take care of ourselves."

She looked Andrew in the eye. "We had been running our family restaurant in the Latin Quarter but sold it a few months ago. We can make the pay."

Andrew walked around their wagon with Mrs. Richards and Daniel trailing behind him.

"This is Bessie," Daniel said, as they got to a milk cow tied to the back of the wagon. "And we got three laying chickens for eggs. And I've been sleeping outdoors for ten days."

Andrew looked down at the boy and then the bed of the wagon. He saw bags of flour, cornmeal, and rice.

"You got bacon, coffee and all?" he said to the woman.

Mrs. Richards said, "Yes. With the wagon, the whole load is over eighteen hundred pounds."

"Why my wagon train?" Andrew asked.

"What do you mean?"

"I mean your good planning would mean you would have already signed on with a company going west before leaving New Orleans. Otherwise, you could wait a long time here wandering around."

"We did have plans but they fell through. We were headed to St. Louis when we heard about the terrible cholera outbreak there. So, we came here, but we were a little late, and then the other wagon master didn't like we had no men. All his other travelers were men and he saw nothing but trouble ahead."

Well, she was right and honest about that, Andrew thought. He looked down at Daniel who was staring right back at him.

"What about you, boy? You help out your ma and your aunt?"

"Yes, sir. I make the fires, feed the animals, clean up, and behave myself."

"You do?"

"Yes, sir."

Andrew knew there were a good number of women among the travelers in the Crawford Company, but they were all wives with husbands. He was looking for ways to rule out this trio.

"I'd be concerned about your safety, Mrs. Richards. There are all sorts of problems on this kind of trip—Indians, outlaws, wild animals. Who knows what else? Can you shoot?"

"Captain, I have a letter here from my husband. He's a surveyor and travels around the country. He will join us in Nebraska. He sent me some of the money we needed for supplies, the wagon, and fees." Rachel handed the letter in an envelope to Andrew.

He took the envelope and looked at Rachel, Claudine, and Daniel.

Mrs. Richards continued. "So, you see, it is our destiny to go, and I need your help."

Two women and a little boy, Andrew thought. *Was it meant by some higher power for our paths to cross and I would be the one to help them meet their destiny while I sought my own?*

He walked around the wagon again. This time he wrote notes on the back of the company flier: Animals, wagon bed, weapons, experience, shoes, canvas.

"We may be attacked by hostiles or need you to help hunt for game," he said. "What kind of weapons do you have? I can't have anyone on the train who can't defend themselves, or all of us, if need be."

Mrs. Richards looked Andrew in the eye. He noticed her pink lips turned into a little smile. She stepped to the back of the wagon and pointed to a flat wooden trunk.

"Take a look," she said.

Andrew removed a cow horn peg from a leather strap holding the trunk closed and lifted the lid. What he saw surprised him: two shotguns, a musket, a carbine, two small pistols, and a derringer, plus boxes and bags of bullets, shot, wads, and other shooting supplies.

She said, "Until two years ago, our father took us hunting. When he died we kept his chest of guns and added the pistols and derringer. We sleep with those at night."

Andrew was pondering how to convince Mrs. Richards she shouldn't go. The letter from her husband wouldn't help his case much. It would only take thirty days to reach the new Fort Childs in Nebraska, he pondered, and at least then she would have her man on board.

"Can you and your sister shoot?" he said, unwilling to let go of the point.

Rachel Richards summoned Claudine and Daniel. She chose the musket, Claudine took the carbine, and Andrew escorted them toward a fallen tree. He placed some empty bottles on the log.

Walking off thirty paces, he asked them to demonstrate their marksmanship. The women loaded their rifles. Mrs. Richards fired twice, hitting a bottle each time. Her sister Claudine fired twice, hitting a bottle and the log. Mrs. Richards passed her rifle to Daniel and the eight-year-old loaded it and fired once, hitting the bottle Claudine had missed. The demonstration more than satisfied Andrew, much to his chagrin. He had to figure whether they were hunting game or defending the camp they could do their part.

Upon further discussion, Mrs. Richards explained she was 29 and married Carl Richards when she was 19. She asked Andrew to read the letter. He opened the envelope and pulled out a handwritten letter in which her husband told her to bring their child to join him and to bring Claudine too. So, all four would go to Portland where Carl had already acquired land for a farm.

As further evidence they were prepared for the trip, Mrs. Richards showed Andrew a bag of gold coins to pay the necessary fees to join the train. She talked further, trying to relieve any concerns the wagon master may have had.

She explained while she had been running the family restaurant and raising Daniel, Claudine, now twenty, had spent the last two years caring for their ailing father who died from complications from malaria. Their mother had died many years earlier during the birth of Claudine.

Andrew listened to the story and learned that, without their mother's guidance, their father saw to it both his daughters were well-educated and spoke French and English. Because the women had followed their father on hunting trips and helped cook and clean at the family restaurant, Andrew saw how they could be a help on the trip.

With fair skin, dark hair, and blue eyes, Claudine Lafayette was a natural beauty. When she spoke English it was with a French accent. Andrew knew Billy Armstrong would notice that right away, as would every other man in the camp. He figured Billy would be eager to provide Claudine with any assistance needed during the journey. Mrs. Richards, with dark eyes and a sweet smile, was almost as pretty as Claudine and wore her brunette hair in a high bun with long curls toward the front.

"Here's the thing, Mrs. Richardson," Andrew said.

"It's Richards, Captain."

He nodded. "We leave Friday morning early. But there's a lot you'd have to do before then."

"Whatever it takes," she said.

"I don't know who sold this rig to you, but it will never make it like it is."

Mrs. Richards' eyes looked down at the ground and back at Andrew. She raised one eyebrow.

"Biggest thing is your animals," he said. "These donkeys can't pull this wagon. Before long they'll wear out and your wagon will come to a halt. So, I can't allow you, unless you switch out your draft animals to either oxen or mules."

"I see."

"Then there's the wagon. It's not close to being an acceptable prairie schooner. If you look under it, there's no tar on the underside of the bed. You need to get the underside sealed with tar."

"Why tar?"

"You got to cross creeks and rivers. Some will be deep. If the boards aren't sealed, your wagon won't float. It'll leak or sink and all will be ruined or lost."

"So, I'll get it sealed. I'm sure someone can do it."

"Those fancy shoes you're wearing. You know you'll be walking ten or twelve miles every day. Those aren't right."

"I have other shoes. We all have boots. They're broken in. We've been walking everywhere to get here."

"Your chickens won't last long either. The ride's too bumpy and the weather's too rough for them," he said, handing her his written notes. "Here's what you'll need, including adding linseed oil for the canvas to make it shed water. You'll need to get a water barrel, bear grease, and add iron rims onto those wooden wheels, or maybe get yourself a whole new wagon."

Mrs. Richards took the paper. Her eyes widened as she looked over it, and her mouth opened slightly as she inhaled and let out a sigh.

Andrew said, "We leave Friday morning. If you can be back here with the entire list taken care of by Thursday before dinnertime for me to inspect it, then you can go as far as Fort Childs. There you can connect up with your husband. Then you can all continue on. I suggest you start with the blacksmith at the far end of Main Street. Tell him I sent you."

"Thank you, Captain," Mrs. Richards said. "I'll see you. We'll all see you Thursday."

Andrew returned to the campfire where Frenchie had a second cup of coffee poured for him.

"Did you get the bee out of her bonnet?" Frenchie said.

"There was a lot of buzz'n. I doubt she can do it. We'll see," he said. "Got any biscuits?"

Fourteen

May 18, 1848

By Thursday afternoon, outside of St. Joseph, eighteen covered wagons and one buckboard formed a circle. It created a corral full of oxen, horses, cows, and mules. Some of the men and boys were throwing out fishing lines tied to bamboo poles, hoping to catch some largemouth bass in Browning Lake for dinner.

Tents were pitched around the perimeter of the wagons and children were gathering brush, sticks, and branches to help feed cook fires. Women and older girls were kneading balls of dough. They would make loaves of bread in metal ovens once the stoves heated up. Large burlap bags leaned against wagon wheels while cooks scooped out cups of beans and rice to prepare for the evening meal.

When Andrew heard somebody banging on a pan he looked toward the noise and saw little Daniel Richards standing on the seat of an approaching covered wagon. The boy was beating on the pot with a wooden spoon to announce his arrival. Mrs. Rachel Richards and Miss Claudine Lafayette were walking beside the wagon goading four oxen.

"We have arrived, Captain." Mrs. Richards smiled. "With a full wagon, and new oxen, and we addressed all the other items on your list."

Andrew couldn't help but laugh and shake his head. He looked at Frenchie, who raised both arms as if surrendering.

"Well, I declare, if it isn't the Richards-Lafayette wagon," Andrew said. "Very impressive."

"Would you like to inspect our new entry, Captain?" Mrs. Richards said. The women halted the oxen.

Daniel put down his pan gong, jumped to the ground, and ran up to Andrew. "We did everything, Captain. Everything. Come take a look." Not shy at all, the boy grabbed Andrew by the hand and pulled him toward the new wagon.

"Daniel, do not drag the captain so," Mrs. Richards said. "My apologies, Captain. Daniel can be excited."

Andrew looked around and anyone in the camp who could see was watching the new folks' arrival. How could he turn them away? "Well, let's take a look. I guess you found the blacksmith in town to be helpful."

"Yes," Mrs. Richards said, "thank you for your recommendation. He exchanged the ox teams for our donkeys and some money. He even showed us, including Daniel, how to put the yokes on the animals. We've got a strong pair at the front of the wagon and a younger pair at the lead position as directed."

Andrew looked under the wagon for waterproofing, ran his hand over the canvas cover to feel for linseed oil, and checked the wagon wheels for metal rims. He peeked in the back and saw bags of grains, a butter churn, and a barrel containing a salted ham.

"I must say I didn't think I'd see you all again, but the wagon looks shipshape."

Mrs. Richards handed Andrew a pouch of currency and gold coins. "I trust you will accept this for payment of our fee."

"Yes," he said, feeling the weight of the bag.

"And will you provide a receipt?"

"I'll be glad to." Andrew counted the money to confirm the $1,000 amount and wrote his signature on a note to confirm payment. "Now you need to work your wagon into this circle, put your animals inside the corral, including Bessie, pitch a tent, and get settled in. I see you still have your chickens."

Daniel and Claudine walked toward the wagon and Rachel called over her shoulder, "Sure do. They'll either lay eggs or get fried in a pan."

Late Friday, at the end of the first day of travel, Andrew and Rachel moved slowly around the camp. "So, Captain, were you in the Army for a long time?" Rachel asked. Andrew was introducing Rachel to the other travelers. Claudine and Daniel were either cooking or caring for their livestock.

"Yes, I joined when I was eighteen and resigned my commission about a year ago. Have you met the Crawfords yet?"

"Just Mrs. Crawford, for a few minutes."

When Andrew and Rachel arrived at their wagon, the Reverend and Mrs. Crawford were cooking dinner. Their buckboard was part of the circle of prairie schooners, and Preacher Crawford had just put their animals in the corral. Emily Crawford was adding beans to a pot of boiling water over the campfire.

"Good evening, Reverend, Mrs. Crawford," Andrew said, nodding and touching the brim of his hat. "Let me introduce Mrs. Rachel Richards of New Orleans, a last-minute addition to our company."

They all exchanged greetings.

"Reverend, I look forward to your Sunday sermon," Rachel said. "Perhaps on sin and salvation or brotherly love. Both would be welcome."

"I will be speaking from the heart, as usual, and reading from the Bible," the reverend said.

Andrew continued, "Mrs. Richard's son, Daniel, and her sister, Miss Claudine Lafayette, also of New Orleans make up their party."

"And where is your husband, if I may ask?" said Reverend Crawford.

"We will meet up with him at Fort Childs, if not before," Rachel said. "He is a surveyor for the government and will await our arrival there. In the meantime, I rely on Claudine and Daniel to share in all our duties along the trail."

~ * ~

The wagon train pulled out of St. Joseph without incident and on the third day on the trail Andrew rode into the middle of the camp as folks were waking up.

"Indians!" Andrew shouted from atop his stallion, Noah. He had ridden the Appaloosa around the camp perimeter that morning. "Indians!"

"Indians!" Billy Armstrong yelled as he ran past every tent and wagon.

Everyone started yelling and screaming for their family members and rummaging through their wagons or tents to find their firearms and ammunition. Those with single-shot muskets hunted for their ram rods, caps or gun powder horns and started loading their weapons. Men checked their six-cylinder pistols and slid bullets into the chambers.

Crying mothers and children climbed into their wagons and laid down behind the sideboards or bags of food for protection.

Andrew rode up to the wagons of the four ex-soldiers he had added to the troupe and found them fumbling with their carbines and boxes of shells, spilling the bullets on the ground.

It was chaotic.

Only a few wagons had animals hitched up and were able to move to tighten the circle to cut off open spaces where marauding Indians could cross into the camp.

After three minutes, Andrew had Billy blow a trumpet for assembly. People were confused. Were they to prepare for battle or gather for a meeting?

Andrew rode in, reared Noah up then settled down.

"I'm here to tell you I was testing you," he shouted. "There is no attack. There are no Indians on the warpath."

All of the travelers shouted complaints. Some booed or turned their backs on Andrew and stood there grumbling.

"This was a surprise drill, and most of you were not ready to protect yourselves and your families or this wagon train," Andrew continued.

"It is better to find out now than during a real attack. Ask yourself if you were prepared. Were your weapons ready and at your sides? Could you find all your children? Did you panic? You be the judge. Now, load up your wagons, hitch your teams, and let's get moving."

Andrew rode out in front of the lead wagon goaded by Billy, and they all headed west.

Near dusk on the tenth day, Andrew greeted his scout Ray Cooper, who rode up to the circle of wagons. Cooper was pulling a makeshift sled of branches bearing the gutted bodies of two white-tailed deer. The scout dismounted his tired roan mare and slapped his hat across his leather chaps to knock off dust from two days out front on the trail. Some men and women came over to unload the deer and prep the venison for dinner to share with the camp. The fresh meat would be a welcome change from the dry beef jerky they had been eating.

Cooper pulled his bedroll and saddle from the mare and reported washed-out conditions of a section of the trail toward an upcoming gap. His horse shook her head and matted mane and trotted off toward the rope corral to join the other animals, eat some grass, and tell her own stories.

A few minutes later, scout Cooper took off his boots and jumped into a cool nearby creek, clothes and all. It was his first bath in ten days. Then he shaved before dinner. In the setting sun, you could still see his weathered skin and the wrinkles across his face. Billy had already heard how Cooper started out scouting at age eighteen and twenty years later still didn't want to do anything else. Andrew said Cooper was never married but had women friends here and there.

Frenchie Beauchamp was at the lead wagon campsite fixing dinner. The cook was busy when Cooper arrived with the deer. Like other cooks in the camp, he was making biscuits and a pot of beans. Frenchie was a hard worker, getting up before the rest of the camp every morning to start breakfast and pack up for the day's journey. When Billy or Andrew asked Frenchie 'What's for supper,' he always scratched his gray-and-black beard and mumbled something about 'same as yesterday, beans, coffee, biscuits and whatever you caught.' Today it would be deer.

Before dinner, Reverend Crawford led everyone in prayer and asked the Lord to bless and protect all the pioneers in the days ahead. After dinner they sat around campfires, swapping tall tales, laughing at jokes or singing. One man played fiddle and another played a tune on his harmonica. When everyone heard coyotes howling in the distance, they knew it would disturb the livestock, so extra men volunteered to stand guard till morning along with the usual two sentries. Nobody wanted a stampede or to lose any livestock to preying animals.

After other folks turned in, Ray, Andrew, and Billy leaned back against the lead wagon. They watched their fire burn down to glowing red embers and followed the path of a few sparks as they rose into the night sky. Billy asked the scout if he wanted a drink of whiskey. The men laughed as Cooper said he could take or leave liquor.

"Yep, I can take a full bottle and leave an empty one," he said.

Billy uncorked a small flask and passed it around. Before it was empty, the scout explained what he had seen the day before. He had shot a mountain lion not far from the trail and traded food and some tobacco with a small hunting party of Indians. He had met that group of Cherokees on previous trips. They were only armed with spears and bows and arrows and were friendly, and Cooper wanted to keep it that way.

The Indians complained about the number of wagons passing across their land and they reminded Cooper the train should keep moving to the West. When they all came across a group of white-tailed deer, Cooper said he took three shots with his Sharps rifle and dropped three of the animals from 100 to 200 yards. Cooper said he thought it was smart to let the Indians see he was a good shot. He left one deer for the Indians. By dawn, Cooper was already back on the trail.

"Mornin'," Frenchie said, as Andrew stepped up to the campfire and stretched his six-foot frame, reaching his hands and arms toward the sky. "Is that how you got your height—stretching?"

"If stretching worked to make me taller, I reckon I'd be several feet higher up. But it gets some of the soreness out and wakes up my muscles. Don't you stretch?"

"Afore I get vertical I do. It helps me get out of the bedroll."

"I reckon you've got some kind of internal alarm clock to wake up before everybody else."

"After dark I usually drift off before everybody else to make up for it."

Andrew dropped his arms back to his sides and sniffed at the dampness in the air. "I think it's going to rain." He made three clicking sounds with his tongue and Noah trotted over to the edge of the corral of wagons.

Frenchie said, "I'm up. 'Bout all I can say, 'cept coffee's ready and biscuits will be soon."

"What do you think the day's going to be?" Andrew asked. He led Noah past the wagons, smoothed the hair along the horse's spine, and carefully positioned a blanket.

"Smells a bit like rain. My joints are forecasting rain too," Frenchie said. He handed a tin cup of coffee to Andrew.

"Where's our bugle boy?"

"The camp's awake already. Do we need him to play?"

"Maybe we got them trained."

"Yep." Frenchie raised the lid of the Dutch oven just enough to check on the progress of the biscuits. "I could hear you talking in your sleep last night."

"You know I tend to do that. Did it wake you?"

"Naw. I was stirring anyway."

"I dream a lot these days. Could you decipher anything?"

"You were unsettled. Something about you being sorry."

"I was dreaming about Elizabeth. I could see her face. There was no expression."

"I know you miss her."

"All the time."

Frenchie sipped his coffee. "Wish I'd had a chance to meet her, but we never crossed paths. I've only been east of the Mississippi a few times."

"I should have invited you to the farm, my friend. My apologies."

"No, I didn't mean it that way. It's just one of those things. What's it been now? Two years?"

"Just over a year," Andrew said after draining the cup of coffee.

"For me, I dream about life in the Army and making stew."

"As I recall, your cooking gave me a few bad dreams early on, but I've gotten used to it now, or you've gotten better." Andrew hoisted his saddle onto Noah and cinched it.

Frenchie raised an eyebrow and looked at Andrew over the top of his eyeglasses. "That reminds me. It'd be good to pick some dandelion greens when you see 'em. Need to make a tea or a salad to help our guts later. Some of the folks have been complaining."

"Will do. Maybe I'll ask Daniel to do it."

"*Oui*," the Frenchman said.

Billy rolled out from under the cook wagon, scratching his head. "Captain! Sorry, I had sentry duty last night, you know. Hard to wake up."

"It's all right."

"Should I still play reveille?"

"Best to form the habit for everyone. When you're ready."

Billy stepped away from the wagon and put his bugle to his lips.

"Point your horn away from me," Frenchie said.

"Oh, yeah," Billy said.

He played reveille toward the sky and one of the nearest men said, 'I guess it's six o'clock somewheres and other folks laughed.

"Better late than never," said another.

"Wake my baby and it's yours," said a woman with a sleeping baby across her shoulder.

A few minutes later, the wind started to pick up and slap tent flaps around. Dark clouds started rolling to the north of the trail.

"Better get packed and hitched up if we're going to make any progress today," Andrew said. He stowed his hammock and bedroll in the lead wagon and climbed aboard Noah. "Roll 'em up," he yelled as he rode around the perimeter of the camp.

Frenchie scraped the done biscuits into a tin pot and covered them. He poured the rest of the coffee on the fire and broke down the hot iron tripod which still needed to cool before being stowed on the back of the cook wagon.

"Hey, I wanted a cup," Billy whined.

"Sorry. You can have two cups tomorrow," Frenchie said. "You gonna saddle up and help your boss?"

Across the camp, at the newest wagon in the train, the women were packing. "Sister, we better get going," Rachel said to Claudine. "Daniel's already hitched up the team."

"I'll put away the tent and things. Do we need to milk Bessie?" Claudine asked as she got busy.

"Yes, please do. The poor cow's udder is about to burst. Let's make some butter today too. Just get the churn ready and prop it up in the wagon. Emily said the shaking ride will get us halfway to butter before the end of the day."

Andrew rode up. "Ladies, I can see you're getting ready. I want to let you know we're heading into a section of the country where some heavy storms can happen pretty quickly. So, let's head out soon. Probably best to eat lunch as we're traveling. I expect there won't be any time to stop before we reach the next campsite. Need any assistance?"

"No, Captain," Rachel said. "You know we're independent, and we expect to be ready before seven. Do you think Frenchie could use some milk?"

"I'm sure he'd be grateful, Mrs. Richards. As would I, if you've got some to spare."

"I'll see to it," Rachel said.

"By the way, do you think Daniel can pick a bunch of dandelion greens today and tomorrow? The tea's good for the gut, or you can make a salad."

"I'll ask him to pick some. He knows what to do."

"Thank you," Andrew said and rode off.

Just after noon, Ray came back to the wagon train, riding his horse quickly. He pulled up next to Andrew, stirring up a small cloud of dust.

"We need to take a detour up ahead, Andrew," Ray said. "If we keep going straight up the trail, there's a mess of wagons and no living souls. Bodies scattered all over the place."

"Damn. Our people don't need to see that."

"Right. Looks like a hurricane hit maybe two days ago. There's too many bodies to bury. Lots of vultures. We can get around it by taking the trail to the right."

"And let's hope that's clear," Andrew said. "Don't alarm the folks. Get Billy to help. Just spread the word the main trail is washed out. It's the reason for the detour. It's all they need to know."

"Will do. But then I need to get ahead of everyone on the detour."

"Have you ridden it before?"

"It's been a long time. I know there's some Indians along there. I'll meet up with them. Shouldn't be anything to worry about."

Andrew nodded once and Ray headed toward Billy.

On the detour, as the wagons entered a wide canyon around noon, one of the herdsmen returned from rounding up a stray. He told Billy he heard a couple of rifle shots in the distance. Billy caught up with Andrew to let him know. The captain said with the echoes in the canyon it may be hard to tell what's what, and the shots could be mountain men doing some hunting. Billy looked to the horizon and saw vultures circling in the distance. He was still unsure.

A few minutes later, while Andrew took his turn guiding the lead wagon oxen, Billy walked his horse to the front of the train. Looking ahead, he saw a horse and rider coming. As they got closer, the rider fell off his horse, and Billy realized it was Cooper. He yelled to the captain, mounted up, and rode out fast.

When Billy got there, the scout's mare stood next to Cooper. An arrow was sticking out of the man's back. He had passed out but was still breathing. Andrew pulled up in the buckboard. They brought Cooper around with some water before he passed out again.

Billy looked at Cooper's wound. "The blood's still pretty fresh, and his rifle's missing."

As they picked up Cooper and laid him in the wagon, Andrew said, "Looks like a Cheyenne arrow, so the Indians can't be far away. You take the buckboard, leave the arrow in him, and get him to the preacher's wife. She'll know what to do." He looked ahead to the horizon. "I'll get these horses."

When he got back to the wagon train, Andrew brought everyone to a halt and ordered them to circle the wagons and break out their weapons. The women put their children in the wagons, telling them to lie down behind the sideboards. Loading their rifles and pistols, all of the men, and a few women, stood beside their wagons or crawled below them.

And they waited.

It was a hot dry day, and after two hours the travelers were getting restless. The sun bore down on the people and the livestock, creating a thirst made worse by the tension before a battle. People drank from canteens, or bladder bags, or ladled water from barrels on the sides of their wagons. They set buckets of water in front of the draft animals, still hitched to wagon tongues. The settlers knew a sick or dying animal could stop their journey altogether and, if they had to run from the Indians, there would be no time to hitch up a team. A few cook fires burned inside the circle, because dinnertime would come, whether or not the Indians did.

Andrew opened the face of his gold pocket watch: five o'clock. Two hours had passed since the wagons were drawn into a protective circle, after the wounded Cooper returned with an arrow in his back. Andrew expected an attack by the Cheyenne would have happened by now.

Before moving around the camp, he handed his telescope to Frenchie, so the older army cook could pan it across the horizon. Frenchie pointed toward the ridges running up the sides of the valley, "This ain't the best place for a fight, Andrew. We'll be givin' up the high ground if Indians get up there."

Extending the telescope for himself, Andrew aimed it at the rocky hills, sparsely covered with scrub oaks or cottonwoods. "I know what you mean, Frenchie. But sometimes you don't get to choose where you fight. It'll be better here than further into the valley where it appears to narrow."

Because he might need to mount up at any moment, Andrew kept Noah close and saddled. He walked the Appaloosa around the inside perimeter of the camp from wagon to wagon, checking with each group—any sightings, guns ready, any questions. They were all still waiting. No Indians in sight.

The preacher's wife, Emily, had fixed Cooper up. The only way she could remove the embedded arrow was to push it out through the front of the man's shoulder, cut off the arrowhead, and pull the broken shaft out his back. She poured alcohol on Cooper's torn flesh and cauterized the back entry wound with a red hot knife. She sewed his damaged chest closed and applied clean bandages. Cooper was laid out on a blanket beneath the wagon, his left arm in a sling and his head resting on a saddle. The scout was still unconscious when Andrew knelt beside him.

"How's he doing, Emily?"

"Seems to be good. I cleaned the wound and patched him up. Poor man."

After seeing Cooper's condition, Andrew considered asking Billy to ride out, but he didn't want to risk anyone else. Billy knew he might need to fill in for Cooper as the scout, at least temporarily. It could be several days before Ray regained his strength and longer before he could ride point. Hopefully, with care a deadly infection could be avoided.

Andrew bent beside Mrs. Crawford as she cared for the unconscious Cooper.

Preacher Crawford walked over. "Looks like you and Billy did a good job. I want to thank you for saving Cooper's life."

"I think he'll be all right," Emily said. "I'm watching out for any fever and trying to keep him cooler with wet cloths. You think the Indians are really coming, Andrew?"

"I expect so. And everybody seems ready."

Preacher Crawford set his rifle against the wagon. "Mrs. Crawford and I are worried about something else, though." Andrew turned his head toward the minister. "The Anderson's teenage daughter doesn't seem well. We couldn't help but hear her getting sick the last few mornings. I don't want her to have anything catchin', you know."

At the back of the circle, the Anderson's wagon faced east. Andrew dropped the reins of his Appaloosa as he neared Jeremiah Anderson. Anderson had his shotgun by his side and sipped water from a canteen while looking down the trail.

Andrew said, "I expect the Indians will come from the west up the trail, but you never know."

"Andrew," Anderson said, nodding his head in agreement. "I've been looking just the same, but ain't seen anything moving yet."

"I hear tell your daughter isn't well."

"Oh, Ella is fine. Just an upset stomach."

"Been going on for a few days?"

"Yes, sir. But don't you worry about it." Anderson said, turning his attention back down the trail.

"What's going on?" Andrew said.

Ada Anderson heard the conversation and stepped down from the back of the wagon where their daughter lay sleeping. "Jeremiah, you may as well tell him. It won't be long before everybody knows anyway."

Jeremiah wiped his brow with a bandana and squinted into the sun. "Well, our girl's gotten in the family way. She's about two months pregnant. She's only sixteen. Her ma and I are sick about it."

Ada said, "She's known the James Kincaid boy for almost a year. She's been crying for him every day."

"He's a no-account boy," Jeremiah said. "No prospects, and I made sure he stayed behind in St. Joseph. I turned him over to the sheriff for being a vagrant the day we left."

Andrew shook his head. "I'm sorry to hear about your troubles. I expect Ella's lucky she has a ma and pa to take care of her."

Though Andrew wanted to help in some other way, he figured he couldn't tell people how to run their lives. He was just trying to get them to the other end of the Oregon Trail in one piece. Lifting his telescope to his right eye, Andrew turned his attention back to the East. "There is someone coming fast way out there." He adjusted the focus of the eyepiece. "Looks like a lone rider ... not an Indian."

He passed the telescope to Anderson who took a look and then spoke quietly to his wife, "Thunderation, Ma, it's the Kincaid boy. I don't know how he could 'a made it out here."

The couple looked at each other in disbelief. Having awakened, Ella overheard them talking. She jumped down from the back of the wagon and started screaming as she ran down the trail toward James. Mr. Anderson ran after her. Other settlers hurried over to see about the commotion. Andrew mounted his horse and set out down the trail. If the hostile Indians were watching, the sudden distraction would expose a vulnerable breach in the circle. Andrew knew he had to round up everybody.

James Kincaid jumped off the skinny mule, ran to Ella, and wrapped his arms around her as she collapsed into him. Andrew herded everyone back to the wagons.

With her folks beside her and James' arm around her, Ella continued to cry as Andrew talked to the boy, asking if he'd seen any Indians. James said there were no Indians down the trail and he had been riding long days to catch up to the train after getting out of jail. He said he hadn't done anything wrong except love

Ella, and he didn't think it a sin. He wanted to marry her and be a good papa to their baby. Mr. Anderson just shook his head.

Andrew looked at all of them. "Y'all know starting out with a new baby ain't the easiest thing for a young couple, but I hope you can open your hearts. Otherwise, I guess Ella will be a mother without a father for the baby. Maybe two people getting hitched ain't such a bad idea. But we got other things to worry about. Tell me this, boy, how come we didn't see you until just now?"

James pointed to the south. "I came up the dry gulch over there where I couldn't be seen, and then I climbed out onto the trail when I realized I was close. If I hadn't seen the footprints and wagon ruts turning off the main trail, I would have missed you altogether."

With a longer look, Andrew saw where the land dropped off to the south along a line of scrub brush and then picked back up leading to the hills.

"I'm going to put you to work right now, boy," Andrew said, "and later you can stay with me up front if the Andersons won't have you."

Andrew signaled for Billy and told him to take James and sneak out of the camp on foot and get to the edge of the winding gulch. The boy and Billy carried carbines and stayed low and quiet. As they neared the gulch, the pair laid down behind a pile of rocks. Billy saw a fallen handmade cross of sticks beside the rocks and realized it was a grave. He whispered to James to stay there and to only shoot if they were attacked.

With his carbine cradled in his arms, Billy crawled on his belly toward the edge of the deep, meandering gully, and from behind some brush, he peered up the line. In the distance, he saw Indians coming slowly toward him. He counted fifteen braves on foot, armed with bows and arrows and one mounted chieftain carrying a rifle.

When back safely at the wagons, Billy reported what he'd seen. Andrew had already moved the four former soldiers to take up positions around the wagons closest to the gulch.

Frenchie shouted, "Captain, we got company."

Andrew rode his horse back to the lead wagon with Billy and James running behind.

From the head of the trail, three Indians on horseback were approaching the circle of wagons. One wore the feathered headdress of a chief. The other two had bows slung across their chests and quivers of arrows on their backs, riding pinto ponies. One of the braves led a horse bearing a large roll of buffalo hides.

The chief saw Andrew and raised both arms above his head, Plains sign language for peace. Andrew knew enough Cheyenne and sign language to talk to the chief. If he could avoid people getting killed, he would.

Frenchie said, "I don't trust 'em."

Andrew told Billy and Frenchie to cover him. As he led Noah out of the circle, the wagon master turned toward Frenchie, smiled, and whispered, "If they put an arrow in me, kill 'em all."

By the time Andrew walked up to the chief, a brave had spread a buffalo hide on the ground. Andrew signed a greeting toward the chief and they both sat down cross-legged on the hide. The chief explained he came in peace. His people were hungry, because hunting was poor. The buffalo hides and extra horse were for trading for some of the livestock. But there was more.

The braves rolled out all the hides and one bore the dead body of a white man. The man's face was marked with war paint. He was shirtless. His sunburned chest had a bullet wound, he was wearing torn blue pants, and Army boots.

The chief explained his braves discovered the horse and body on the trail next to a bow and arrow and a small camp.

Andrew left his Appaloosa with the chief as a sign of trust and went back to the wagon train. He came back leading a steer on a rope. James followed carrying sacks of rice and cornmeal.

Andrew told the chief about the injured Cooper and thanked him for the meeting. He said the chief could keep the dead man's horse but asked if the braves had found a rifle along with the body.

The chief did not answer the question but said it was a good day to trade and to keep peace in the valley. The Indians left the buffalo hides behind and rode back up the trail, leading the steer behind them. Billy snuck out to the edge of the gulch again and saw the group of braves walking away.

As Billy went back past the grave of stones, he looked up and saw the mounted chieftain ride up the side of the gulch and come toward him. The Indian held up his hands in peace, then handed Billy a Sharp's rifle. Billy took it and saw the letters RC carved into the butt of the gun. It was Ray Cooper's.

Fifteen

During the early days on the trail, Andrew noticed Mrs. Richard's son, Daniel, was an energetic boy who did well at camp life. He gathered wood and dried grass or buffalo chips and built cook fires. He fed and watered the oxen, helped cook and clean, and churned butter made with milk from their cow, Bessie. The animal would spend the whole trip trailing along behind their wagon.

Rachel watched over Daniel the best she could while goading the team of oxen. She also encouraged him to be independent but aware of potential dangers on the trip. When he wasn't playing chase or tag games with other children, Daniel hiked alongside the wagon with his aunt, Claudine. Sometimes he even rode Bessie.

During Billy's regular rounds of visiting each wagon, he found a little extra time at the sisters' wagon to say hello to Claudine and Rachel and play a brief game with Daniel. Andrew had noticed Billy's interest in Claudine from day one. Late in the day, after trading a steer to keep the peace with the Cheyenne chief, Andrew pulled Billy aside.

"Billy, we talked about you and the women folk."

"Oh, yes, Captain. I'm aware," said Billy.

"The point is, don't be getting women upset, no broken hearts. We got almost six months of travel ahead of us."

"I understand," Billy said. The young man also knew what was coming next, due to Ray's injuries.

"Now, with Cooper still recovering from his wound, I need you to be our scout for the next few weeks. So, plan on heading out in the morning. Ride out a day and back a day. Mark any hazards, gather any information you can, and plan the best way forward. And if we need to take any more detours, tell me about it. You think you can do that?"

"Yes, sir. Similar to our Army days." Billy sighed.

There was a brief silence between the two before Andrew spoke again. He packed some loose tobacco into a clay pipe, lit it with a stick from their fire and puffed on it, thoughtfully blowing smoke into the air.

"So, you and Claudine are about the same age, I reckon."

"Yeah. I'm a little older. She said she's almost twenty."

"Well, maybe your absence will make her heart grow fonder, as they say."

"Right, Captain. And you know I'll do what you want, but I'm wondering about something else."

"What's that?"

"It's when you asked me to go out and find the gulch with James. I don't think he has any combat experience, you see, and I'm not sure what good he'd uh been if those Cheyenne had started something."

Andrew thought for a moment.

"I get your point, but I had just let that boy into the camp and he knew about the gulch, so it made sense at the time.

Besides, I've seen you take on three men at once and you were the last one standing."

"True. But I reckon one of the ex-soldiers would have been better protection."

Andrew raised an eyebrow. "I hear what you're saying, Billy. I ain't perfect."

With the body of Cooper's attacker on his hands, Andrew asked Billy to organize a burial. Billy asked Preacher Crawford for his help, then 'volunteered' two of the former-soldiers to dig a shallow grave. An hour later, most of the travelers came to the service and piled stones on top of the body which had been wrapped in linen and laid in the shallow grave.

Andrew addressed the group. "Friends, we are safe tonight from an Indian attack. The Cheyenne came in peace, and I know we are all thankful for that. I think the Indians understand we are just passing through their valley and we mean them no harm.

"Now, we are gathered here to pay respects to a man we need to bury this evening. We don't know his name or where he's from. We do know he shot our scout in the back with an arrow and was wearing Indian war paint. Cooper ended this man's life in self-defense. I think the man was an Army deserter and desperate. Many people have their demon moments and their angel moments, and I figure this man was no different. May God have mercy on his soul." Andrew sprinkled a handful of dirt on the stones.

"My thanks to those who dug this grave and thank all those who carried stones to the site."

At the end, Billy planted a cross of sticks on the pile of rocks. Then, Preacher Crawford read from the scriptures and led the people in singing, "God's Word Is Our Great Heritage." After a final prayer everyone returned to the circle of wagons to get ready for dinner. Billy escorted Claudine back to her wagon. Rachel trailed behind with Daniel.

Billy tried to speak a little French, but mainly he just wanted to listen to Claudine speak English with her French accent. He didn't really care what she said. The two were close enough for Billy to catch the fragrance of lavender in Claudine's hair.

Claudine and the older lead wagon cook, Frenchie Beauchamp, had also struck up a friendship, based on speaking French, sharing recipes and being from New Orleans. She offered to help Frenchie make a cobbler and in the evening brought rhubarb and a crock of butter, along with Rachel and Daniel, to the wagon master's campfire. Billy carried Claudine's Dutch oven and handed the heavy covered pot to Frenchie. Daniel helped cut the rhubarb and rolled out the dough Frenchie gave him.

It was twilight and Andrew wanted to check on Ray Cooper's condition while dinner was being prepared. He invited Rachel to walk with him to meet Mrs. Crawford, the preacher's wife who had tended to Cooper's wounds. He figured the two women would enjoy each other's company.

As they neared the preacher's wagon, Rachel said, "I want to thank you for protecting us from the Indians."

"Well, that worked out better than I expected. I think the Indians just wanted to exact some kind of toll for us crossing through their land. So, now I owe the cattleman for a steer. He knows we'll settle up at the first trading post."

"And the deserter posing as an Indian."

They arrived at the preacher's wagon where Cooper was just waking up on his bedroll beneath the preacher's buckboard.

"I just fed him some broth," Mrs. Crawford said, holding an empty bowl. "He seems to be coming around okay."

Though the women had already met, they were glad to see each other again, especially after such a long day. They listened as Andrew talked to Cooper.

"You should be fine now the arrow is out," Andrew said. "Mrs. Crawford knows what she's doing. So, you behave, and do what she says, which is nothing. You hear?"

"Hey, Andrew," Cooper said, holding out his good right hand to clasp Andrew's. "I'd like to get back out there as soon as I can."

"You're fine. Just get some rest. Billy will pitch in until you recover more. Then, I'll put you back to work. And, by the way, we ain't gonna have any problems with the Indians. Their chief brought us the body of the man who shot you. Turned out to be an Army deserter, pretending to be an Indian with war paint on, but his Army boots gave him away. Plus, your bullet in his chest."

Cooper shook his head and looked at Andrew. "He weren't no deserter. It was a Cheyenne brave shot me in the back. I turned and fired my rifle in time to kill him. Hit him in the face. He was wearing buckskins and no shoes."

~ * ~

During the next morning, the Crawfords kept Cooper resting on the bed of the buckboard. A rain shower dampened the usual clouds of dust along the trail. As the day wound down, the wagons were formed into a circle with the livestock corralled in the middle while the people set up tents around the perimeter. Everyone cooked and ate their dinners. Later, two musicians were entertaining a gathering of folks. Another light rain began to fall, canceling the show.

James Kincaid ran up to the lead wagon to find Andrew and Billy. "There's a fight," he yelled. "You'd better come quick. It's them old soldiers again—but worse."

Frustrated, Andrew grabbed a bullwhip. He and Billy ran around the camp toward the soldiers' wagons and heard cursing. They saw all four men were in a fistfight: Peter Duff fighting Connor Shaughnessy, Eric McFarland fighting Donald Quinn. Smelling alcohol in the air, even before seeing empty bottles of whiskey, Andrew knew there had been drinking. It had been a long, tiring day on the trail. With everyone exhausted, the combination of fatigue and gulps of liquor made for shorter tempers and dumber decisions.

The next thing, Andrew saw Duff picking up a fat, flaming stick from the campfire and starting to swing it. The wagon master uncoiled his whip, slapped it around the burning stick, and popped it out of Duff's hand. The drunken Duff stumbled and turned toward Andrew, surprised to see him. Billy grabbed Duff from behind and threw him to the ground. Since his opponent had been removed, Shaughnessy sat down on a rock, rubbing his jaw and stopped fighting.

Andrew turned his attention to the other pair of soldiers. "That's enough. McFarland, you and Quinn stop it right now."

"Aww, Greene, we were just messin'," McFarland spit back at the captain, just as Quinn landed a knockout blow to McFarland's jaw.

A few minutes later when the drunken McFarland came to, he discovered he was hog-tied to a front wheel of his wagon with Quinn tied up next to him. Duff and Shaughnessy were hog-tied to a back wheel.

Before he and Billy walked away, Andrew said, "You men may not be able to understand this right now, but your fighting puts the rest of the camp in danger. Tomorrow morning we'll discuss this again."

It rained all night, creating mud puddles throughout the camp. In the morning, during a brief break in the weather, Andrew took his first sip of hot coffee when he heard a small voice behind him. "Captain, are we in Oregon yet?" He turned slowly and looked down to see towheaded Daniel looking up at him.

"Well, good morning to you, little soldier," Andrew said. He put his hand on the boy's shoulder. "No, we aren't in Oregon, but we are on the trail to get there. It's the way we'll eventually get there; we've got a long way to go."

Walking quickly toward the lead wagon, Rachel Richards stepped up next to her son. "I'm sorry, Captain. I didn't know Daniel would come to see you so early. He woke me up with a question, and I just said we would have to ask the captain and next thing I knew he took off.”

Andrew smiled down at the boy. “Well, it’s a perfectly good question, Daniel. And let me show you where we are right now on a map.” Andrew opened a wooden box under the driver’s seat and produced a pouch. He pulled out a rolled-up leather map and spread it on the food table folded down from the back of the wagon.

“Do you know where we started from?” he asked Daniel, as he lifted the boy onto the table.

“Yes sir. St. Joseph.”

“Can you find it on the map?”

Daniel looked across the map, found Missouri and put his finger on the town of St. Joseph.

“Very good,” Andrew said. “Now we are headed west and, by the end of today, we should make it to a fort near Childs, Nebraska. Can you find the town of Kearny? The fort’s near there.”

A moment or two later, Daniel pointed to the middle of Nebraska. “There,” Daniel said. “And it looks like it’s near a river.”

“Yes, the North Platte River. We’ll rest at the fort for at least one day, switch out some livestock, buy some more food, and I may take a nap in my hammock. But we’ve got to get underway now for everything to happen. So, go on back and ready your wagon.”

A few minutes later, Andrew and Billy appeared before the bound soldiers who were thoroughly wet and muddy from a night in the rain. “So, you men may be wondering why you’re tied to a wagon wheel.”

“I got to pee,” Duff said.

“All of us do,” McFarland said.

Billy and Andrew untied the ropes to free the men while Andrew summarized the results of the fight. “The next time you all get into a brawl, you will face harsh consequences. Is that clear?" They probably heard Andrew, but there was no response, as the men were already out watering some of the prairie grass.

~ * ~

The four security soldiers had convinced Andrew to allow a horse race. Andrew's objections regarding safety and the expected gambling were overcome after a bottle of whiskey was emptied. Andrew liked the idea of pitting his Appaloosa against Quinn's black stallion. Billy wanted to race too. The event had been talked about during the last three days. The winner would get bragging rights and a purse, based on the riders' entry fees, and maybe a secret side bet.

On the day of the race, Billy adjusted the cinch on his saddle a little tighter than usual. He applied his knee to his horse's side to force out any extra air in its lungs and tied off the cinch.

"Billy, I wish you luck for this contest," Claudine said as she came over.

"Well, hello. I expect I'll need some, going up against the captain and Quinn on Jit. You think it'll be all right with the captain if I win?"

"Of course. He will make happy for you, *mon cheri*."

She took a green ribbon from her hair and tied it through a buttonhole on Billy's vest. Claudine whispered in her French accent, "You know, Billy, long time ago, when a lady favored a knight she give to him a scarf in her favorite color, and he would wear her colors for the good luck."

Billy nodded, listening intently, almost forgetting about the race all together.

"So," she said, "I am tying this ribbon on you to show the others I favor you."

Billy watched her hands as Claudine inserted the ribbon through one of his buttonholes. Her fingers touched his chest and she looked into his eyes and smiled. She kissed his cheek and left. Speechless, he watched her walk away.

"Billy Armstrong, you ridin' or not?" Quinn hollered as he rode by on his black stallion.

Billy and the others rode their horses up behind a line drawn in the dirt. At both sides of the starting line, sticks were placed in the ground with white rags hanging from the branches.

The last rider to arrive was Andrew. When he rode up to the line on Noah, he was riding bareback, a surprise to Quinn and the others who had all saddled their horses as usual. Andrew figured Noah would be even faster without the 30 pounds of tack and there were no rules about it.

Noah pawed at the dust until Andrew laid a hand on the animal's neck. Quinn's stallion, Jit, shook its mane. The silky-black animal's eyes were wide open and his nostrils flared at the scent of the other horses.

Frenchie raised his pistol and fired a shot into the air to begin the race.

Andrew's and Quinn's horses bolted out together, and the three soldiers immediately cut in front of Billy, blocking him. Billy forced his way through and raced on to the cheers of the crowd.

People lined both sides of the path marked for the race, wide enough for six horses to race together at first then narrowing to a width for only two horses between a tree-lined creek and a boulder, before opening wide again. There were a few obstacles along the way—a fallen log and a dry rocky creek bed.

At the far end of the run, a stake held a red bandana. A rider had to grab the flag and race back across the finish line with it to win.

The prizes were a dinner cooked by Rachel and Claudine, as well as a purse of six dollars for the challenge race. Out of sight of the preacher, several men placed bets, hoping to win enough to pay for their next river crossing toll. Quinn bet heavily on his own chances. He planned to win and, if needed, get a little help from his friends.

The dust was flying as the horses neared the narrow path between the boulder and the creek. Noah and Jit were running neck and neck. Billy was trailing with the others close behind. They still had to jump the first obstacle, the fallen tree. All but one rider jumped it successfully, but the cloud of dust behind the other horses was blinding and the last horse stopped short of the log, tossing Shaughnessy into the air and out of the race.

As Quinn and Andrew rode through the narrow break, Quinn tried to kick Andrew off of Noah but missed. The errant move dropped Jit back half a length and Noah galloped on. The next obstacle was the rocky dry creek bed. Andrew leaned forward on Noah and the horse jumped the whole width of the creek, leaving Quinn and Jit behind. Jit slowed and stepped carefully through the rocks, ignoring Quinn's whip. Andrew galloped toward the flag, slowed enough to round the stick, and grabbed the red bandana.

He could tell the next challenge would be getting back past Quinn, the remaining ex-soldiers and maybe Billy.

Quinn stopped short of the turn. He tried to cut Andrew off but Andrew dodged the cheater and jumped the dry creek again, leaving Quinn behind. Jit was limping slightly, but Quinn was still determined to steal the bandana.

Billy and the others made it through the narrow pass but turned around when Andrew raced by them holding the red bandana.

Shaughnessy was standing atop the boulder at the narrow break. As Andrew galloped by, Shaughnessy pulled a rope taut across the path, knocking Andrew off of Noah. The horse stopped as the two men fought in the dust.

Angry and shaken, Andrew punched Shaughnessy in the face with his left then his right fist. Shaughnessy swung wildly as he stumbled backwards. Andrew followed up with two punches into Shaughnessy's stomach.

Quinn rode a limping Jit up to the site and abandoned his horse. After he dismounted, Quinn grabbed the dropped bandana, and climbed onto Noah, just as Andrew knocked out Shaughnessy.

Quinn galloped 50 feet on Noah until Andrew let out a shrill whistle. Noah immediately slid to a stop, and Quinn sailed into the air over the horse's head and landed on his back, breathless in the dirt. Noah ran back to Andrew who mounted the horse and rode toward Quinn. Andrew bent down and grabbed the bandana as Noah ran past a staggering Quinn.

Back at the camp, a cheering crowd greeted Andrew and Noah as they came across the finish line. Billy rode in second, trailed by the two remaining former soldiers. After the crowd turned to celebrate, Shaughnessy ambled in, walking his horse along with Quinn who was leading a limping Jit. The horse was struggling with a stone from the dry creek still stuck in his hoof.

Andrew looked over his shoulder at Shaughnessy and Quinn, then saw the expression on Preacher Crawford's face. The minister was shaking his head. Andrew figured it would be the only horse race on the trip. He started thinking about getting a drink but would wait until after dinner.

Sixteen

It was nine o'clock Sunday morning when Andrew looked at his gold watch and sat down on a tree stump smoking a pipe, not far from Rachel, Claudine, and Daniel who were resting on a blanket. It was time for what had become regular Sunday sermons. Reverend Crawford stood before his congregation.

"Idle hands, idle hands, idle hands are the devil's tools. Maybe you've heard it before. Idle minds, idle minds are the devil's workshop. Maybe you've heard that before too."

Preacher Crawford was just beginning. He knew the wagon train of eighty people would travel together for almost half a year, and he was concerned there would be too much time for mischief among the children as well as the adults. He wanted to reach everyone with his message.

"There are many who have gone before us who recognized the value of keeping our minds and bodies active. There are references in the Bible to idleness. And the founding fathers of this great country understood the importance of using our minds for doing good things."

A gentle breeze flowed through the campground. It was a good morning. Children had been washed by their mothers and fathers. One mother sat on a blanket in the back of the group breastfeeding her young baby. The reverend looked out over the gathering.

"I see a lot of fine folks here in the congregation. Back in Tennessee, I got to know each of you by visiting in your homes. I know you are good, kind people who love your families. As we go forward to establish our church in Oregon, we cannot help but think about the parents or grandparents we left behind. But it is with their encouragement and good wishes that we take this trip. One of my goals is to help all of us find a better life together as a community once we build our church.

"When we reach our destination a few months from now, just imagine what we will have to look back on. We would have crossed a vast portion of this young nation together as it expands from the Atlantic Ocean to the Pacific. Each of us will be a little older and a little wiser. And we will appreciate those who have gone before us even more."

He paused for a moment and took a breath.

"I don't know about you, but I'm feeling good today. I just took a breath of fresh air. I think God and Mother Nature are working hand-in-hand to bring us this good weather, and we should enjoy it. And we can enjoy today and the days ahead even more if we are prepared by having a plan and keeping our minds and bodies busy.

"I want to talk to you about idleness and what I call the three P's of planning, playing, and praying. It's good to keep your mind busy by making a plan. So, plan your day. Decide on the tasks which need to be done. For you mamas and papas, be sure to include your children who are old enough as you make those plans. They learn by the examples you put before them. If you want a fulfilling life, plan your day and share the plan with your family members. And call upon the Lord in prayer to help guide you.

"There are plenty of chores to give your young ones. Doing so will help them learn how to take care of themselves and you. It will help you make this a better trip as your family shares the tasks. So, share your plans and how your family can help you carry them out.

"When it comes to the second of the three Ps, the one about playing, keep in mind having fun with your spouse, children, and friends is part of life too. Through playing, we also grow closer to our children and other loved ones. Through our social gatherings, we can enjoy music, games, and fellowship. We just need to make the playtime a time of goodness. I have seen some folks in our community need to find better ways to use their idle time. Instead of playing cards for money, I hope you will play checkers for fun. Gambling can lead to anger and the loss of money you will need later to feed your families or take care of yourself. Instead of drinking alcohol, I hope you will teach your children or friends a skill. Water is the best thing for our bodies, so drink plenty. Drinking alcohol makes our minds forget how to act right and causes accidents and fights. Some folks find work can be like play if you do it right.

"Share your knowledge of working with livestock, fixing a meal, or exploring the natural wonders around us with your children and friends. We work hard. We walk several miles each day. We water, feed, and care for our livestock, and we need to also water, feed, and care for our families. Part of caring is keeping idle minds and idle hands busy and productive, so make playtime a time of learning too.

"If we turn to the Bible, we read in Ecclesiastes 10:18 the following: *Through sloth the roof sinks in and through indolence the house leaks.'* We see idleness should be avoided and we must be diligent and keep busy with the right things. On this trip we don't have a roof, none of us does. We do hope our canvas wagon covers keep out the rain and wind. We may wish we had a roof, even a leaky roof when bad weather sets in, but the point is we must use our time well. We know it's going to rain sometime, so make sure you're ready for it.

"We all know about leaky roofs already, so let's talk about the other big word I used, 'indolence.' Through 'indolence' the house leaks. The word 'indolence' means someone is avoiding doing something. In the case of the roof, a man ignores the need for repairs. He knows the roof has been leaking, but on the first sunny day, instead of repairing the roof, he becomes idle. He decides to sit in the sunshine and do nothing to fix the roof. The indolence, the idleness will come back to haunt the man because the next time it rains, the roof will leak again and again. Until he decides to repair it, the floor will get wet and furnishings will get ruined.

"Now, I know we all remember what floors and furnishings are. Right now, the only floor we have is in our wagons and our furnishings are piled up in those wagons. But let's think about what the Bible is trying to tell us. Maybe what the Bible is trying to tell us is not something about a leaky roof and a slothful man who doesn't repair it.

"I say the Bible is talking about how there may be something else in our lives that needs repairing or needs tending to. Maybe when God wants us to mind our houses and roofs, He's talking about minding and nurturing our lives.

"So, have you got bad habits making your life less than it could be? Is there a weakness limiting how well you get along with other people—important people like your wife or husband or children or your mother or father or your neighbors? Are you jealous? Are you gossiping? Have you been telling lies, hiding the truth? If so, maybe those sins are your leaking roof which needs repair. And, yes, I said lying is a sin.

"So, don't be lazy. Overcome your idleness. Make the necessary repairs. Change your ways.

"And now to the third letter P, which stands for the word prayer. We should all turn to prayer every day. Turn your thoughts inward and evaluate yourself and your behavior. Try to recognize if you said something hurtful to someone you love and ask God to forgive you and guide you. And while you're at it, it's a good idea to admit to yourself you're not perfect and you make mistakes, just like the rest of mankind. And then apologize to those people you have belittled or you have otherwise harmed with your words or deeds. Pray to find a way to make it right. And then take the steps to overcome any indolence and make things right again. It will lift a burden off your shoulders. The weight of your life will be easier to bear when you plan and play and pray."

The reverend stepped away and Mrs. Crawford stepped forward. She said, "Now let us all raise our voices to the Lord and sing praises unto him by singing the hymn "Come Thou Almighty King." She waved her arms and began... "Come Thou Almighty King, help us thy name to sing..."

During the trip so far, Reverend Crawford had seen the four soldiers drinking whiskey, gambling, and fighting. He had received complaints about those four men from several families.

He pulled Andrew aside to talk about it. As the hymn was finished, and the congregation began to disperse, the reverend stepped over and shook hands with Andrew.

"My sermon today was partly aimed at the men you added to the train to protect us. I'm sorry they didn't attend."

"It was a fine sermon, Reverend," Andrew said. "Those four men probably won't be attending any of our Sunday services. It's the way they are. All of them spent the last three years fighting in the war with Mexico and staying alive by their wits. They're good fighters but are gonna' be short on following the good book and attending church services."

"My concern is, in part, whether they will be sober enough to provide the protection we'll need if we ever come under attack," said the reverend.

"I know what you mean. I'm keeping an eye on them."

"I think also, they could use their idle time differently, such as hunting instead of gambling or by helping other folks instead of drinking or fighting."

Andrew knew he had to address the problem sooner rather than later.

"And," the preacher continued, "I need you to stay sober as well."

Most of the pioneers had returned to their campsites when young James Kincaid and Ella Anderson came up to the reverend and Mrs. Crawford. The preacher had heard about Ella's condition and wanted to provide counsel when she and her parents were ready to listen.

James began, "Reverend, Ella and I would like to get married and wondered if you would do the ceremony."

"I see," said Reverend Crawford. He noticed Ella's pregnancy was starting to show. Her abdomen had started to expand to make room for the baby growing inside her. He was concerned about their sins and their souls.

"Yes, Preacher Crawford," Ella said shyly. "James and I love each other going on a year now, and I think my folks will understand soon enough our getting hitched is the best thing, the right thing. Can you help us? We are both planning and playing and praying about it."

The reverend was touched to know the girl had taken in the points of his sermon. Even though their sin was great, he wanted to help them do the right thing.

"Ella, I will talk to your parents and, James, what about your kinfolk?"

"Reverend, I've been on my own for two years now. My folks drowned when I was ten. My mother fell off a bridge into a river.

She was leaning on a rail and it broke. My father jumped in to save her but they was both washed away. My uncle is a farmer, and he took me in, but he beat me bad once, and I left, taking my mule with me. I been on my own since then, doing small jobs to earn a little money. But I'm a fast learner and will work mighty hard to take care of Ella."

"And our baby," Ella said.

"Come here, children," Mrs. Crawford said and hugged them.

All four joined hands and the reverend led them in a prayer. Then he put his arms around the couple.

Seventeen

Every day Andrew and Billy Armstrong rode around the camp perimeter. In the mornings, they made sure draft teams were getting hitched to wagon tongues in preparation for the day's journey. At the end of the day, they wanted the livestock settled inside the circle of wagons, and the two men asked if anyone needed help with wagon repairs.

For the most part, the settlers knew what had to be done during the day—keep up with their children, look out for wild animals, collect vegetation good enough to eat, and keep putting one foot in front of the other. When the wagons stopped before sundown, the women washed clothes, fixed meals, and schooled their children. The men built campfires, re-shod their animals, repaired equipment, and hunted for game.

There were over thirty children on the trek, from babes in arms to sixteen-year-olds. When possible, different groups of children gathered for story time and their parents would tell tall tales, read from a few scarce books, or play an instrument for a singalong.

One of those children, nine-year old Jackie Vonschoff, usually wore a friendly smile and had a bright spirit about her. Always ready to have fun, she turned a chore into a game, especially when watching over her two younger siblings. Her parents were farmers and dedicated members of the church and its teachings. Thinking of Jackie's future, her father had built a cedar hope chest. Jackie and her mother filled it with colorful ribbons and fabrics for dresses. They also made a beautiful patchwork quilt to put in the chest.

In the early weeks of the trip, Jackie became a friend to Daniel. They liked being almost the same age and enjoyed playing tag, Cat's Cradle, and Blind Man's Bluff. Jackie put up with Daniel's interest in throwing rocks or using his slingshot to hit just about everything. He put up with her occasional tea party, pretended to eat mud pies, and sipped make-believe tea.

There were two other children in their age group, Jeremy and Claudette King, and Jackie loved having all of them gather for tea parties. Only after Jackie had played games like tag or hide-and-seek did Daniel consent to attend one of her teas. Most days there was nothing in the little tea kettle when Jackie poured invisible tea into tin cups. Daniel and the King children pretended to drink imaginary tea and to eat imaginary cakes or cookies, depending on what Jackie had conjured up. Some days they made imaginary fruit pies.

This day, when Jackie poured from the kettle, real water splashed into the cups. Earlier, she had filled her teapot at one of the ponds along the trail. Thirsty, she drank her full cup quickly but held her little pinky finger out like she had seen some ladies do. Jeremy took a sip of the brown tea but didn't like the way it smelled or tasted. It was a little muddy. When Jackie wasn't looking, Daniel and Claudette poured out their tea-water on the ground. Then, Daniel suggested a game of tag, touched Jackie, and said 'You're it,' and off they all ran.

The morning after the tea party, when Andrew rode around the camp, the Vonschoffs apologized for being slow to get ready. They explained Jackie had been up and down all night. Her gut was unsettled and she looked pale, but they would be ready to go as soon as possible.

Jackie's health deteriorated during the morning. Her parents stopped their wagon frequently to help Jackie find some privacy away from the trail. She vomited and had bouts of diarrhea. Her mother dipped a cloth in their water barrel and placed it on Jackie's forehead and neck.

Andrew rode Noah toward their stopped wagon. Even at a slow pace of two miles per hour, he wanted all the wagons to stay close.

"How's the little miss?" Andrew asked.

"I'm afraid she's not well," Mrs. Vonschoff said. "I'm concerned. She should be better by now."

"I'll ask Mrs. Crawford to take a look at her."

Upon seeing Jackie, Mrs. Crawford said, "It's cholera. This child has cholera." The woman turned to Jackie's mother. "Do you know what she's been eating or drinking? Probably yesterday."

"I'm not sure. We all ate the same food." Jackie's mother began to cry. "What can we do?"

"Let's give her fresh water and lots of it."

Mrs. Crawford told Andrew the news about Jackie. It wasn't good, and Andrew remembered Daniel and the King children often played with Jackie. Speaking as kindly as he could, Andrew told the Vonschoffs to position their wagon at the end of the wagon train and to quarantine from the other travelers for the time being.

They had to talk to the other families and when Andrew and Mrs. Crawford checked in at the King family wagon, they too were slow-moving.

"Jeremy is feeling poorly," Mrs. King said as the pair rode up.

Usually, Jeremy was eager to hitch up their mules, but today, it was such slow going for the boy, the parents hitched up the animals.

"It's diarrhea," Mrs. King said, a little embarrassed.

"How is Claudette doing?" Andrew asked.

"She's fine."

"Where's Jeremy?" Andrew said.

"He's in the wagon. The poor boy has been in the bushes this morning, having trouble with his gut. I gave him some dandelion tea."

"May we see him?" Mrs. Crawford said.

"Whatever for?" Mrs. King said as she wiped a wisp of hair from her face.

"He was playing with Jackie yesterday, wasn't he?" said Andrew.

"Captain, you're scaring me," she said.

Mrs. Crawford moved toward the wagon. "Jackie has come down with cholera, and we need to check on Jeremy."

"My boy!" Mrs. King screamed. "You think it's cholera?" The mother was crying, and Mrs. Crawford fought back her own tears as she put her arms around Mrs. King. Then Mrs. Crawford climbed into the wagon to get to Jeremy, as Andrew stepped to the back of the wagon.

"How's the boy look?" Andrew said.

"A slight fever," Mrs. Crawford said, touching Jeremy's forehead with the back of her hand. "Same treatment as for Jackie, I expect."

"So, Jeremy, I'm sorry to hear you don't feel well," Andrew said.

"My tummy hurts, Captain, and I been sick, and I'm sure tired," the boy said.

"Were you playing with Jackie yesterday?" asked Mrs. Crawford.

"Yeah. You know, hide-and-seek," Jeremy said.

"Anything else?" Andrew asked.

"Well, you know, another one of her tea parties."

"And ..."

"She poured us all a big cup of water this time. It wasn't the pretend kind of tea."

"Did you drink the water?" Mrs. Crawford said.

"Jackie drank a whole cup full, but I took a sip and it tasted so bad I poured it out. And so did the others."

"Who else was there?"

"Claudette and Daniel. They didn't drink any of the tea."

Mrs. Crawford and Andrew prescribed plenty of water for Jeremy. They hoped cups of fresh water or dandelion tea every hour would help clear the boy's system. Two hours later he was doing much better. Mrs. King helped him change clothes and bundled his soiled clothes for boiling.

Andrew spoke to Jeremy's worried parents about a quarantine. They would need to move their wagon just ahead of the Vonschoffs' at the end of the train but keep a safe distance away.

As the wagon train kept moving, Jackie was not able to get comfortable. By noon, the Vonschoff family had stopped again and given Jackie more fresh water. Andrew rode up with Mrs. Crawford once more. Jackie's eyes were sunken and her skin was dry and shriveled. Mrs. Crawford put her ear to Jackie's chest and listened. The girl's heartbeat was irregular.

Mrs. Crawford turned to Andrew and the Vonschoffs.

"Let's try some more fresh water. Her body needs more water, and your whole family needs to wash their hands with warm water and soap. Cholera can spread easily. You need to put her bedclothes and anything she's touched like plates or cups into boiling water now."

Andrew stopped the wagon train early while the Vonschoffs built a fire. They burned the girl's gown and put the last clean one on her.

When Mrs. Crawford came by again, Jackie's skin had turned bluish-gray. The family was reading Bible verses and praying along with Preacher Crawford, who was out front of the wagon.

The child died before sundown from the "Blue Death" and many hearts were broken.

Mama Vonschoff wrapped Jackie's body in the patchwork quilt from the girl's hope chest. Though Billy also brought a shovel, Papa Vonschoff insisted on digging the grave for his daughter by himself.

Because of the danger of cholera spreading, the congregation gathered on one side of the open grave away from the Vonschoff family who huddled on the other side, holding hands and crying. The Kings did not attend. The grave was big enough for the child's body and for the hope chest Papa Vonschoff had made.

Holding a Bible, Preacher Crawford said, "There are few words of comfort I can offer. We know Jackie is no longer suffering, and for that we are thankful. Jackie was already an angel here on earth, and I know she is now an angel in God's arms. If we turn to the Bible for solace at this time, we read in Romans: 'For if we live, we live to the Lord, and if we die, we die to the Lord. So then, whether we live or whether we die, we are the Lord's.'" A gentle breeze passed through the camp, bringing a cooling relief to the temperature. The preacher knelt and picked up a handful of soil and sprinkled it into the open grave.

"In search of understanding our loss," he said rising, "we read in Matthew in the New Testament: 'Blessed are those who mourn, for they shall be comforted.'"

As the congregation concluded the Lord's Prayer, Mrs. Crawford and Andrew stepped up to the grave and sprinkled hands full of soil into the site. Then the grave was filled in and rocks were piled on top. A wooden cross was tapped into the ground, bearing hand carved dates of Jackie's birth and death.

Eighteen

By the morning, under the cook wagon in his bedroll, somewhere inside his head, Andrew knew he was dreaming—a familiar dream but one of his most disturbing—a nightmare of blood and death. He saw a blurred image of a tomahawk flying toward him. He heard his horse scratching at the ground. In the gauzy mist of the dream, he could feel the ground shaking and hear footsteps running toward him. A blast from his weapon fired into an Indian's chest. A wail. The fallen man. A knife swinging up. A curse. A flailing gun butt. An eye on the ground. Pool of blood. He woke, gasping for air and touching the scar on his cheek. Glad to be awake again, he could hear Frenchie grinding coffee beans.

The blare of Billy's trumpet playing reveille restored reality.

"Cap'n," Frenchie said, "coffee's ready when you are."

Andrew knew it would be a long journey. He had done what he could to plan the route. He had brought on board the best people he knew to help lead the train, and a few he didn't know but had faith in. He hoped for a peaceful six months but planned to deal with the dangers.

His earlier lectures to the pioneers explained the conditions the travelers could face—not to scare them as much as to prepare their minds for the possibilities. Andrew described the terrain and weather they would encounter. Ray talked about the Indians and hunting for food. They described the daily grind of fixing a quick breakfast and putting a biscuit in your pocket or eating dandelion greens to settle your gut.

Along with Preacher Crawford, who had opened each meeting with a prayer, Andrew and Ray talked more about life on the trail, forts along the way, hitching up draft animals, and looking out for snakes.

Children in the group ignored most of it. Women shook their heads in anticipation of the worst. Men nodded, acknowledging the warnings and accepting responsibility to be aware and careful.

Preacher Crawford closed each meeting with words of inspiration, urging the congregation to help each other, be thoughtful, read the Bible, and pray for guidance from the Almighty, to help establish a new church at the end of their trek.

By the end of another dusty day on the trail, Andrew washed his hair and face in the creek with a little lye soap, and gave extra attention to his handlebar moustache, before walking to the sisters' wagon for a shave and a haircut. Rachel Richards had just finished trimming McFarland's beard when the captain arrived. Animosity had been building between the two men ever since Andrew hog-tied McFarland to the man's own wagon and they noticed a shared interest in Rachel.

"Captain," McFarland said, rising from a wooden chair, "reckon' you're next."

"Yep," Andrew responded curtly.

McFarland handed Rachel a coin. "Next time, maybe I can get a slice of pie too. Ya think?"

"I'll see what I can do. Thank you," she said shaking out a sheet used to catch her customers' hair trimmings.

Andrew took a seat on a well-worn chair. "Well, ma'am, it's been a few weeks. How are you and yours faring?"

"Oh, you know. We're getting used to it now. Walking all day is tiring, but we're doing all right. Daniel's got energy to burn even after putting up the stock."

"Good."

She ran her fingers through Andrew's hair and started working with her scissors. "He does a good job of hitching and unhitching the oxen. Those are big animals, and they're slow."

"Yep, and strong, and they'll do you well on the trip. They can eat sparse grass when a horse won't and still stay healthy."

Rachel had noticed the scar on Andrew's left cheek previously, and she was curious about how it got there. Had he been cut by an enemy, she wondered? Or was it there from a childhood accident. Or maybe the result of a spat with his late wife or some other woman who threw things or lashed out in the heat of anger or passion?

Rachel stopped herself from thinking about it or asking. She held her tongue—a new discipline she was trying out, especially around Andrew.

She dragged a comb through his wet hair again, pulled out a leaf and a twig and started to cut off an inch or two. He's a bit of a shaggy man, she thought, but he was cleaning up nicely. When she finished cutting his hair, Rachel dipped a clean towel into a basin of hot water, rang it out and wrapped it around Andrew's face.

"I'm going to leave the towel on for a couple of minutes to soften your beard while I sharpen the razor." She stropped the razor along a leather belt. Even with Andrew's face beneath the towel, she could understand his words.

"This is two weeks' worth of beard," he said.

"I'll get that off. This razor works well."

"So, you been doing shaving long?"

"Oh, yes," she said. "I shaved my father since I was twelve. The first few times he needed to show me how. And I practiced on a dog we had back then too. Nobody has bled to death, yet, if that's what you're wondering."

"Then I reckon' I'm in good hands."

"You are," she whispered in his ear, as she removed the towel and brushed on a soapy lather from a mug. "Just relax and don't move, or you could be like the fella who lost an ear."

Andrew took a breath, holding still and closing his eyes. "Sometimes your humor passes me by."

"Captain," she said as she pulled the razor down his right cheek.

"Mmm," he mumbled, relaxed.

"I'm going to stop for just a minute."

"Okay."

"And, Captain..."

"Yes."

"Can you take a look? I think it's a rattlesnake coming this way."

Andrew opened his eyes wide and looked down. Ten feet away, a long, fat snake headed toward the chair. Andrew stood up, pulled a knife from a scabbard on his belt and threw it at the snake, pinning it to the ground. As the snake writhed in the dirt, Andrew stomped its head while Rachel screamed.

With the snake dead, Andrew started back to the chair. As he turned around, he discovered Rachel standing on the chair and shaking.

"Yeah, a timber rattler," he said.

Rachel swooned and he caught her in his arms. After Andrew held her for a minute, Rachel's face lost its pallor, her cheeks turned a little pink and she opened her eyes. Andrew still held her. "Ma'am, are you gonna' be okay?"

She put a hand on his chest and pushed herself to her feet. "Yes, Captain," she said. "I don't know what came over me. I've seen snakes before. Maybe I'm lightheaded from being tired."

Andrew brought her a cup of water from the sisters' water barrel. "Why don't you sit a spell and drink some water."

"I'm so sorry," she said. "I need to finish shaving you or you'll look a sight with half a beard."

"There's no rush. Just get your bearings first. I planned on asking you to the dance tonight, but it looks like you'd be better off resting this evening."

Rachel finished the cup of water and shook her head. "No, no. I'm fine. This will pass. It's passing now. I'm feeling better. Really." She rose and pointed for him to take a seat. She whipped up the mug of lather again and re-applied the foam over the dried soap left on his face.

"Be sure and leave the moustache," he said.

"Thank you for taking care of the snake ... and me. I have to say I'm embarrassed."

"Think nothin' of it. I think I'll take the snake to Frenchie. See if he can make a meal out of it."

Rachel took a deep breath and sighed a little. "As far as the dance is concerned, I think I'll be strong enough for a few dances. Claudine and I are giving a pan of biscuits to the event. So, we are going anyway."

She finished the shave and wiped Andrew's face with another warm wet cloth. "There now. You look nice."

"Good to hear. I'll drop by prior to the dance and we'll see how you're feeling. If you like, I'll help you carry that pan."

~ * ~

Meanwhile, Billy Armstrong was walking across the campsite and Claudine intercepted him.

"Billy, is there a dance tonight?" she asked.

"Yes, miss. That's why I'm here."

"Yes."

"I was gonna' ask you to be my partner and go to the dance."

"Yes."

"So, you're saying yes?"

"*Oui*. Yes." She laughed, touching his arm.

Billy had known a few women, learned to drink and gamble, and enjoyed racing horses. Talking sweetly to a socially acceptable young woman was the larger challenge for him. By the age of twenty-two, he had spent two years in the Army, reporting to Captain Greene. After receiving his pension of 160 acres in Missouri, Billy had tried his hand at farming, gave up after a year, and sold his land.

Back at the lead wagon, Andrew shook out his clothes from the day's travel and little clouds of dust drifted into the air. After he changed, Andrew and Billy walked over to the sisters together. The ladies held the men's arms and they were escorted to the dance, with Andrew carrying the pan of biscuits.

A passing rain shower lasted a few minutes. The disappointment the dance would be rained out was replaced by relief when the rain stopped. It had dampened the ground enough to reduce the amount of dust the crowd would stir up.

As the two couples walked toward the group of musicians, some folks began singing "Buffalo Gals."

Though all the travelers had hiked twelve dusty miles, people were energized by the music, food, and conversation during the dance. Men played a fiddle, a banjo, and harmonica providing enough music for dancing. After the first few dances, some of the people started singing their favorite songs. At one point, one of the men announced he would be glad to call a square dance and asked people to break into groups of four.

Andrew and Rachel, and Billy and Claudine, joined together. The caller explained the do-si-do and promenade formations and started the square dance with the help of the musicians. There was plenty of laughter as couples ran into each other trying to follow the instructions. At the end of the dance and the laughter, the whole event started to wind down.

Another Irishman stood up next to the musicians and began to sing in a clear tenor voice. Everyone joined in on the chorus.

Ella Anderson and her beau James Kincaid held hands. He took her back to the Andersons' wagon. Around the rest of the camp, parents started getting their kids ready for bed, campfires were allowed to burn down, and women put away food and washed dishes. The next morning would be another day on the trail. It would come too soon for some if not for all, but tonight they would sleep well, having shared something good.

The night before, Frenchie had said it was going to rain, and sure enough the camp woke up to a downpour as dawn approached. It would be too muddy and miserable to move the train, so Andrew and Billy toured the camp, telling folks to hunker down and stay dry as much as possible.

"There will be days ahead when you'll wish it would rain like this but not today," Andrew shouted to one family above the roar of nature. "Dry days are ahead but today keep your family close and your kids out of mischief. Feed yourselves well and rest or make any repairs you can."

At the cook wagon, Frenchie set up two waterproof tarpaulins of canvas, using poles and ropes. The tarps were staggered in height and overlapped to allow smoke to escape from the campfire. He decided to cook bacon and pancakes which would take too much time on a typical day.

The livestock left inside the corral, formed by the circled wagons, stood in mud. Men and boys tossed in armloads of grass so the animals could feed.

Some other wagons suspended tarps to give the family members somewhere to stand or sit. Mothers held babies and told their children to stay close by or in the wagons.

Andrew knew the creeks to cross would be swollen for a day or so, and the trail would be such a slog it was better to lose a day's travel than spend it digging wagons and draft teams out of mud holes.

Andrew, Billy and Walt, a teamster, were beginning to circle the fire after smelling the bacon, tin plates in hand.

"Pour yourselves some coffee," Frenchie told the group. "I ain't your maid."

Andrew wrapped a cloth around the handle of the steaming coffee pot and lifted it off the fire. "Frenchie, seems I've been pouring my own coffee ever since I met you."

"You ain't the only one," Frenchie said.

"I would have died of thirst otherwise."

"You bring a checkerboard?" Billy asked Frenchie.

"It's in the back of the wagon, next to a sack of coffee beans and the grinder."

"Care to play?"

"Not now. I'm busy burnin' pancakes for you hungry wolves."

"Who's this coming?" Billy said.

It was Daniel.

"Boy, you're up to your ankles in mud already," Andrew said.

"Mornin', ya'll," the boy said. "Our wood's all wet. Can't get the fire going."

Andrew looked across the faces of the other men for volunteers, but they all fell silent and looked at their own fire. He scooped up some hot coals in a bucket. "Little soldier, grab some of those cow chips, and let's get your mama's fire started."

Frenchie handed Andrew three day-old biscuits in a cloth. Daniel grabbed a handful of dry buffalo chips and walked back to his wagon alongside the captain.

"Sorry, Captain. We must look as drowned rats," Claudine said from under a parasol.

"It's always good to see you ladies, no matter what."

"Mama, I got us some fire stuff," Daniel said.

"Over here, Andrew. I laid a fire but it's too wet," Rachel said, "and our tarp doesn't want to stay up." Andrew tied the tarp to their wagon and propped up one corner with a stripped tree branch to divert water runoff. He found three flat rocks and placed them on the ground under the tarp."

"Okay, Daniel, show me how to make the fire," the man said.

As she stepped back under the tarp, Rachel said, "I hope this rain stops soon. We haven't eaten yet. Thank you for your help and these biscuits."

"You're welcome, Mrs. Richards," said Andrew.

"Please call me Rachel. We've a long journey ahead of us, and I think formalities can drop by the wayside."

"Most folks will set aside some day-old biscuits and beef jerky, just in case."

"Look," Daniel chirped. "I got it going."

"Good job," Andrew said. "Blow on it a little and add some sticks or crumbled buffalo chips. That's a good start." He touched the brim of his hat and nodded toward the three wet travelers. "I'll leave you to it."

"*Merci*, Captain," Claudine said to his back as Andrew headed toward the cook wagon. He turned and waved.

Returning to claim his pancakes from Frenchie, Andrew said, "I reckon Cooper is holed up in a cave somewhere."

"He'd head for high ground and shelter for sure," Frenchie said.

"He'll know we've lost a day."

"When it clears enough, he'll keep coming back until he finds us."

Billy and Walt were ending a game of checkers, sitting on two barrels.

While Billy set up the board for another game, Walt turned to Andrew. "Captain, tell me 'bout the land in Oregon. Frenchie said something about big acreage being available."

"Yes, there's lots of land. You know, Ray and I made the trip by horseback last August to mark good campsites on our map."

"It's a good thing you did."

"Yes, and Ray has no interest in farming or ranching, of course, but I looked into the Willamette Valley."

"Is it good for farming?" Walt asked.

"And logging. Lots of fine hardwoods," Andrew said. "When we get there, I'll introduce everybody to the leaders who drafted the constitution for the area, opening up the land for settlers."

"A real boon ..." Walt said.

"Hey, Walt, it's your move," Billy said. And the new game began.

"You will be able to claim 320 acres at no cost," Andrew said.

Everyone stopped what they were doing.

"Good golly! Did you get some?" Walt said.

"It's sitting there, and the view of the trees and hills rolls on for miles, just waiting for me. In fact, I met two families who've already settled next to my land, twin brothers. They agreed to build a small cabin and a corral for me on a hillside near a creek running across my land. I figured I'd need a roof over my head when I get there. And I'll be able to fish in some streams. The cabin is pretty far from those other folks, which is the way we both wanted it."

"Mighty fine," Frenchie said.

"There's land for you too, Frenchie, and if you have a wife you can get 640 acres. So, you better start looking." Everyone laughed.

"Amazing," said Billy.

"Well, I'm no farmer," said Frenchie. "And ain't no husband material."

Andrew said, "You could claim the land, sell off some timber and open yourself a restaurant, if you still want to keep on cooking."

Frenchie rubbed his beard and nodded. "That's something to think about."

Billy beat Walt at checkers and challenged Andrew to a game.

"Okay, Billy. But whoever loses has to walk the whole camp and check on each wagon."

"Sure thing, Captain, and seein' as how you're already wet, you won't mind at all."

"We'll see," Andrew said. "By the way, Claudine says hello. Not that it should distract you.

"Aww, Captain. That ain't fair."

Nineteen

The next day the sky had turned dark again by noon, and the spring rains came in faster and harder. The first few drops were refreshing and cooling, as they landed on the sweating bodies of travelers and livestock. With heavier rain, two inches of fine trail dust turned into slippery mud. It seemed to get worse every step of the way. Before they could reach Fort Childs, the wagons would have to maneuver around a slippery hillside which led to more level ground.

Then it happened.

Jeremiah Anderson was trudging through the shifting mud on the down-hill side of their wagon. His wife, Ada, and daughter, Ella, managed their team of oxen on the uphill side. When the wagon rolled around the muddy hill, the oxen slipped and so did the wagon. Ada screamed. The load of supplies shifted, and the wagon turned over toward Jeremiah, who saw it coming but couldn't get his feet to move fast enough in the sludge. He almost made it out of the way but the frame of the wagon landed on his left arm, pinning him face down in the mud.

As they picked themselves up out of muddy puddles, screams from Ada and Ella brought help running. James Kincaid was a few steps behind the wagon. He had been pushing it up the incline. He got to Jeremiah's side first. The strong boy used his hands to scoop the watery mud away from Jeremiah's face, so the moaning man could catch a breath. Ada crawled on her hands and knees to Jeremiah's side. Ella screamed for more help. They had to get the wagon off of Jeremiah before he lost his arm or suffocated.

Responding to the commotion, Andrew and Billy rode up. They tied ropes to the frame and used their horses to pull the wagon upright, freeing Jeremiah and his broken arm. Four other men unhitched the oxen from the tongue of the wagon, lassoed the animals and pulled them away while Ada and James continued to clear the choking mud from around Jeremiah's face.

Jeremiah cried out as he rolled over and grabbed his injured arm. "It's broke, Ada. It's broke."

With help from Billy and Andrew, Mrs. Crawford fashioned a splint out of pieces of wood and some rope. Jeremiah cried out in pain. Andrew pulled steadily on the man's wrist to straighten out his arm and align any broken bones. Mrs. Crawford tightened the splint ropes. In pain, Jeremiah took his first drink of whiskey in a year. And then his second.

Andrew said, "This will have to do until we get to a doc at Fort Childs. We'll get there late today."

He sent Billy ahead to find a doctor and claim a place for the wagon train to camp near the fort. With the help of James and others, the Andersons' wagon was re-loaded except for some broken glassware and china which was tossed to the side. Jeremiah held his arm in a sling, riding uncomfortably on the seat of the wagon. The re-organized group trudged on as the rain continued to fall.

As the day wound down, Andrew rode up to Fort Childs on his Appaloosa, dismounted, and flipped the loose reins across a hitching post in front of the commander's large HQ tent. The fort commander, Lt. Colonel Ludwell Powell, stepped from behind his carved wooden desk and greeted Andrew with a slap on the shoulder. They shook hands, remembering their times serving together in the Army.

Commander Powell said, "What a sight for sore eyes. I almost didn't recognize you with that moustache. What has it been now?"

"Four years," Andrew said, "and look at you, a lieutenant colonel with your own fort."

"Ha. Right, it's a fort in the making. I've got almost two hundred men building a fort with no outer walls. We'll have several buildings but have an open plan. We'll be more of a trading post but with protection duties as well. We're trying to work with the Indians too."

Powell showed Andrew a schematic layout for the new fort. "One wooden building is completed and the rest will be adobe. Plus lots of tents. We expect thousands of travelers coming through here in the months ahead."

They sat and talked briefly about the plans and shared drinks from a bottle of rye whiskey.

"Your man Billy took our doctor to your camp already. Did the rest of your train get settled in?" asked Powell.

"They're doing it now, and I'm sure they'll want some fresh livestock and supplies," Andrew said. He poured himself and the commander another glass of whiskey.

"Of course, anything we can do to help. I've got a patrol ready to visit your settlers and get an inventory of what they want. We'll assemble what's available," Powell said, putting away the whiskey. "Your greater concern will be crossing the Platte River. The current is fast with all this rain and the crossing areas are deep." Powell looked toward the opening of the tent. "Here comes the new lieutenant who's leading the patrol."

Andrew turned around to greet the young officer and hesitated.

The lieutenant said, "Is that you, Father?"

Captain Greene laughed and hugged Lieutenant Greene. "What a surprise," Andrew said. "I thought you were still at the Academy."

"You must not have received the letter about my graduation. I invited you to come."

Andrew shook his head. "I've been traveling since last fall. Haven't gone home."

"I didn't know you'd be here," Thomas said. "Then Commander Powell said you were coming this way. Figured I'd wait. No need to write further."

Andrew took a step back. "Let me look at you. You look mighty nice in the uniform."

"I finished second in my class. The ceremony was in January."

"I am sorry I missed it, son. I truly am, but I was in Oregon over the winter. Then, rode fast to St. Joseph in order to meet this wagon train. We had a deadline."

Twenty

The sisters, Rachel Richards and Claudine Lafayette, had become popular with everyone on the wagon train. With the other women, such as Mrs. Crawford, Mrs. Anderson, and her pregnant daughter Ella, the sisters exchanged recipes, traded newly churned butter for spices or starter for making bread, and added a little gossip and advice.

The sisters were popular with the men for being easy to talk to and tease, for a dinner for ten cents, or for an occasional free piece of pie. The sisters also sold eggs their hens laid until the birds stopped laying and wound up in a frying pan. The two women traded milk from their cow with the blacksmith to keep their oxen shod.

Rachel and Claudine followed a reliable routine. Because on Sunday mornings most of the camp attended church service, the sisters did their wash the night before, giving their clothes more time to dry before the wagons rolled again on Mondays.

On Fridays before dusk, when there was still good light in the sky, the sisters set out a chair where men sat for a shave or a haircut, or both, for fifteen cents. The sisters had grown up serving and cooking in their late father's restaurant. There they had learned how to talk to customers of every stripe and found joy in taking care of others.

Monday through Thursday, after a dusty day on the trail, the sisters would dispense wisdom or sympathy or a bit of dinner to visitors who wandered by their campfire.

Each night before they tucked Rachel's son Daniel into his bedroll, they washed his sweet face and behind his ears, had him read to them from the Bible, and said a prayer with him.

The party of three travelers continued to adapt to life on the trail and after the first month, a day of respite at Fort Childs was very welcome. The break was helpful to the sisters and the rest of the travelers. An Army patrol arrived in the morning to check on supply needs. The folks were impressed because, no matter their rank, the soldiers were polite and eager to assist the company.

A surprise for most everyone was discovering Andrew's son, Thomas, was present among the soldiers stationed at the fort. Already a lieutenant due to his Academy training, Thomas Greene was leading the patrol. He and his now-civilian father rode into the camp together.

The patrol stopped at the lead wagon first and Andrew introduced his son to Billy, Ray, and Frenchie.

"It's good to meet you all," Thomas said. Then he explained the re-supply protocol.

"And how do you find army life, Lieutenant?" asked Frenchie while offering a fresh biscuit.

"Thank you. Army life is agreeable," Thomas said. "Father tells me the two of you served together for some time."

"I was a cook, a younger cook when your father joined the ranks. He had a lot to learn. But how to eat was not one of them."

With an easy laugh and a smile, the lieutenant nodded toward his group of soldiers. "Nice to meet you all, but I better get this patrol working. We are to get a list of needed supplies and livestock from each wagon and see if we can help with any repairs."

Later, as Thomas was meeting with Rachel and Claudine, a gunshot rang out behind their wagon. The women screamed. Thomas stepped between the women and the direction of the report. He drew his pistol and ran to the back of the wagon. He looked around the back wheel of the wagon and saw a corporal talking to Daniel. The sisters appeared at the lieutenant's side. Then Rachel ran past the officer.

"Daniel, are you all right?"

"Yes, Mama."

She pulled Daniel close. Corporal Ames holstered his pistol. "I'm sorry, ma'am. The boy wanted to take a look at my gun. He's all right."

Calling for his sergeant, the lieutenant stepped up to Corporal Ames and confiscated the man's pistol just as the sergeant rode up.

"Sergeant, I'm placing the corporal here under arrest for endangering these people with the careless handling of his firearm. Escort him back to the fort and to the jail."

"Yes, sir," said the sergeant.

"The corporal let this boy play with his gun and it discharged. Ask the commander for a replacement at once and return here within the hour. Is that clear?"

"Yes, sir," the sergeant said as he led the corporal from the camp.

"My deepest apologies, ladies. Sonny, are you sure you're okay?"

"Yes, sir," Daniel said. "I'm fine."

"Officer, thank you for your actions. I hope the rest of your men know what they're doing?" Rachel said.

"I have to take full responsibility for the man's blunder, ma'am. Again, my apologies. I'm glad no one was hurt."

Andrew had been on the other side of the camp when he heard the shot. He rode up and Rachel recounted the event. He turned to Thomas and thanked him for protecting the women and Daniel, then took Daniel by the shoulders.

"Tell me what happened, boy. You are not in trouble. We just want to be sure what happened."

Daniel looked up at Andrew. "He had a Dragoon Colt, Captain. I heard about 'em, but I never saw one before. And when I asked could I look at it, the soldier laughed a little and then started to pull the gun out. But it went off."

"Do you know what direction the bullet went?"

"Right between his feet in the ground."

"Show us where?" Andrew said.

Daniel pointed to some boot prints in the wet ground. There was a small round hole between them. Thomas stooped down and pried a bullet out of the ground with a knife.

"Sure enough," Thomas said. "It could have gone anywhere. I reckon I'll be able to use this as evidence." He put the spent bullet in his pocket.

Andrew and Thomas went on to the next wagon together. With growing interest, Rachel and Claudine watched as the men, of similar builds and gaits, walked away. Then Rachel glanced at Claudine, who was staring longer than proper.

"And, sister, what are you doing?" Rachel asked in a tone of chastisement.

"*Pas de quoi*, (nothing)" said Claudine, "and you, sister?"

"Perhaps we should read a few Bible verses," Rachel said, "and besides, I thought you and Billy were of mutual interest."

"I still have eyes, sister," said Claudine.

Twenty-one

After riding back to the fort with Thomas, Andrew returned to the sisters' wagon with a dappled gray horse and gave it to a surprised Daniel who immediately climbed into the saddle and rode around the camp. Rachel was carrying a bucket of water back to her wagon and saw her son whooping as he rode past her.

"I don't think it's your place, Andrew, but it's too late now." Rachel stood with her arms folded across her chest, staring into Andrew's eyes from three feet away.

"I'm glad to give it to him. The commander said they had too many anyway, and the used saddle was free too."

"The boy doesn't need a horse. He's got Bessie to ride or even the oxen. What do I owe you?"

"Nothing. And he shouldn't ride a milk cow anyway."

"It's not up to you to give my son anything."

"It was a good thing. Did you see his smile? He's happy."

Daniel returned from his first ride around the camp showing off his new horse. The animal pawed at the ground. Daniel tied the reins to a wagon wheel.

"Did you see me, Mama?"

"Yes, my son."

"Everybody likes my horse and he's friendly. Frenchie gave me an apple. I ate half and fed my horse the other half. He ate it right out of my hand. I held my hand flat like you said, Captain."

Andrew smiled. "Very good, Daniel. Now, what name will you give your horse?"

"I don't know."

"You can't just call him 'horse,' can you?" said Rachel.

"No. I guess not. Is he a paint or a pinto, Captain?" Daniel said.

"Pretty much the same thing," said Andrew.

"Can I call him Paint?"

Rachel patted Daniel's head. "You can name him whatever you want. Have you thanked the captain?"

"I think so." Daniel turned to the captain. "Did I say thank you?"

"You did, and you're welcome."

"I'm gonna feed Paint some grass now," and the boy skipped off, leading his new treasure.

Frenchie banged two pots together—his poor excuse for a bell—and Andrew headed back toward the lead wagon and lunch.

"You did a good thing," Frenchie said, as he handed a tin plate of stew to Andrew. "You'll be a hero to Daniel for the rest of the trip."

"He's a good boy, but his mama's hard to figure. She didn't like me giving him a horse or anything."

"She sure has her own way of doing things. I reckon you'll be glad when her husband shows up," Frenchie said.

"I reckon. You know I asked the commander if he knew of a Carl Richards. There's no Carl Richards at the fort. A couple of men named Richard but no Carl."

"What'd the letter say?" Frenchie said.

"Said he'd meet her at Fort Childs."

"Maybe he's hiding."

"She's not that bad. Just doesn't want to feel obligated to me or anyone. An independent sort." Andrew drank some coffee and swallowed hard. "By the way, what kind of meat is in this stew?"

"It's a mix."

"Of what?"

"Does it taste good?"

"Yeah. It's good."

"Then that's all you need to know, ain't it?"

Andrew scooped himself another half plate of stew. "Where's Billy and Ray?"

"Billy's out wandering around with Miss Claudine."

"Un-huh."

"Ray's gone over to Grand Island for a little entertainment. May not be back until mornin'."

"So, they're both out hunting?"

"Something like that."

"I know Billy can find his way back, but Ray's got a big day tomorrow helping with crossing the Platte. I'll have to go to the island to round him up. While I'm there I'll see if this Carl Richards is around. Rachel hasn't mentioned him lately, and he's becoming a mystery man."

"You got dinner at the fort tonight with the commander, you know," Frenchie called after him.

"Right. I'll be back in time."

A half hour later, Andrew pushed through the doors of The Cleopatra, the first saloon he came to on La Grande Isle. On his quest to find Cooper and Carl Richards, he figured bars and brothels were a good bet. He had Carl's name and a brief description, gleaned from Rachel over the last month, as she made small talk with other folks around the camp.

The bar was full of fur traders, mountain men, vendors, and Army personnel. Men were gambling at tables in half the room. A piano player was busy pounding out a tune which could barely be heard above the noise from the crowd. A gray haze of tobacco smoke filled the bar and floated up to rooms on the second floor. At the top of the stairs, a dark-haired woman was hanging over the railing waving to a man at one of the tables.

Andrew stepped up to the end of the sticky bar and motioned to the barkeep.

"What'll it be mister? Beer? Rye whiskey? How about a redhead?"

"A beer," Andrew said above the din. He settled in next to a man who made a little room for him as the bartender put a mug of beer on the counter. The barkeep picked up a coin Andrew slid onto the bar.

"Anything else?" the barkeep said.

"Yes, I'm looking for a man name of Carl Richards. I'm in charge of a wagon train, and he's supposed to meet up with his wife and son."

"Carl Richardson?"

"Richards. He's a surveyor."

"Don't know the name. He could be anywhere. This island's about forty miles long. Lots of bars, hotels, and other places. Hotels would have a register with names. In this bar, we don't ask for names. Just show us the coins or cash."

"All right. Thanks for the idea. I'll try the hotels."

As the barkeep turned away, Andrew pulled out his gold pocket watch and checked the time. It was going on three o'clock. He needed to get back for dinner with the fort commander soon.

The man next to him said, "Hey there, mister. I'm Oliver. You say you're heading up a wagon train?"

"Yep. Headed to Oregon. I'm the wagon master, Andrew Greene."

"Couldn't help but overhear. Good to meet you," said Oliver. "What does this man look like you're looking for?"

"I understand he has a dark beard, usually wears a gold vest, and stands about six feet."

"Seems like I saw a man like him the other day. Tall man, beard and a vest. Up near the hotel, just up the street,"

"Well, that's quite a coincidence," said Andrew.

"Sure enough. I tell you I'm fixin' to leave anyway. I can walk you up there, if you like."

Andrew finished his beer. "No, I can find it."

"The McHenry's the name of the hotel. Good luck to you," said Oliver as he turned to leave.

Andrew watched the man go as the barkeep came over shaking his head.

"Nothin' agin' that man, but you're right to let him go."

"I still got to look till I find Richards," Andrew said.

"I'll keep an ear out for the man."

"Thanks. I'm running the Crawford wagon train. So, if you see him tell him we're headed west tomorrow."

"Will do. Crawford Company."

"I've also got to find my scout too. You know of Ray Cooper?"

"Cooper? Big man?"

"Yeah. He's been around these parts for years," Andrew said.

"Yeah, Cooper was in here this afternoon. Was upstairs for about an hour. Then he went on. Not sure where. He had one of those new Sharps rifles with him."

Andrew left the bar and walked Noah toward the McHenry Hotel.

~ * ~

Back at the camp, Billy Armstrong tied his horse to a shrub near the sisters' wagon and then walked arm-in-arm with Claudine. The sun kept peeking out from behind passing clouds as the two wandered along the river's edge. They stopped to kiss before returning to Claudine's wagon.

Rachel was hanging newly washed clothes on a rope line when the couple arrived. Daniel was sitting by their small campfire, whittling.

"I'm glad you got away for a walk, sister," Rachel said. "Billy, how are you?"

"I'm fine. It's a welcome break in the weather for a walk," he said.

"We stopped by to listen to a fiddler too," said Claudine.

"By the way, Rachel," Billy said, "did the captain tell you he was headed over to Grand Island looking for your husband?"

Claudine suddenly turned to Billy, as Rachel froze and placed her hand over her open mouth.

"Sister?" Rachel gasped. "I must talk to Claudine, Billy. Please visit with Daniel for a minute."

"Well, sure."

He watched the women step behind the wagon then he sat down next to Daniel. Billy could hear the sisters talking in hushed tones but couldn't make out the conversation. Daniel put a few sticks on the fire and the sisters returned.

"Billy," Rachel said. "Claudine has given me permission to ask you for a walk about the camp. Will you be so kind?"

Billy stood up, "Certainly."

Claudine stayed with Daniel and watched Rachel lead Billy away from the wagons. She saw Billy suddenly stop and put his hand on Rachel's arm as she turned to him. Claudine saw Rachel take a handkerchief from her cuff and wipe her eyes. Billy let go of Rachel's arm and pushed away, leaving Rachel on her own.

"Claudine," Billy said, mounting his horse, "I got to go find the captain. Please tell Frenchie." And he was gone at a gallop.

Back at the McHenry, the desk clerk explained to Andrew no one named Carl Richards had been there, and Andrew walked on.

When he entered the Saratoga Saloon, Andrew saw all four of the men spread around the room gambling. Before he could take another step, a large woman in a revealing red dress brushed up against him.

"Hey, mister. I'm just what you're looking for," she said, leaning into him. "Won't take much of your time, and then you can get to gambling or drinking or both. I got a room upstairs where we can rub on each other."

"Please step back," Andrew said. "Not here for the entertainment."

"Well, you keep me in mind. I'll be glad to entertain you before you leave, 'ya hear?"

McFarland was busy folding a losing poker hand when he looked up and waved his hat in the air. "Hey, Captain," he said, "come on and play a hand or two."

Andrew shook his head on the way to McFarland's table. "I didn't know you boys would be over here till I saw Quinn's black horse out front."

"Oh, yeah," McFarland said, "he gave some boy two bits to guard that animal. I was hoping I could get Quinn to put up Jit in a poker game, but he's still too sober."

The dealer said, "You all playing or not?"

Andrew said to McFarland, "You four had better be sober and back at the camp tonight." Then, Andrew noticed Quinn two tables away. The man was complaining in a loud drunken voice about losing at blackjack.

"Oh, you know us, Captain. We'll be there," McFarland said. "So, you sittin' in for a game or not?"

"Not," said Andrew. "You seen Ray?"

"Nah," McFarland said, returning to his poker game, "deal 'em, men. I feel a lucky streak comin' on."

Andrew asked the bartender about Ray Cooper and Carl Richards, had no luck, and walked out the door.

"Hey, Captain. There you are again," Oliver said outside the Saratoga.

"Oliver, we meet once more." Andrew nodded.

"I've been thinking about that feller you're looking for."

"I see."

"Yeah, and I just seen a man a lot like him. He was going down the alley with a woman. They both seemed a little drunk, but the man had a beard and was wearing a gold vest. Come on, I'll show you the way. There's a little cabin down there past some stables and a store or two."

As they walked down the alley, Andrew could see a small log cabin with drawn window curtains and he could begin to smell the stables. Oliver stepped up to the door and knocked three times.

They heard a woman's voice. "Go away. Come back later."

Oliver knocked three times again.

"She's busy," an angry man shouted as he opened the door.

Oliver pushed Andrew inside, and the angry man tried to slug him, but Andrew ducked, recovered, and knocked the man to the floor, then turned on Oliver.

Oliver yelled, "We don't want no trouble, Captain. Just your gold watch and your money, and you can go peaceful like."

Andrew heard footsteps behind him. He turned. The woman was lifting a hunting knife, intent on stabbing him in the back. He swung around, slapped her across the face, and took the knife away, throwing her into Oliver.

"Back up," Andrew said, "or I'll gut you both."

Oliver backed up against a wall, making a clear path to the door and Andrew took it. He looked back over his shoulder, threw the knife to the side of the alley, and walked back to the main street. There, standing next to Noah, were both Billy and Ray.

"I came for you and saw Noah," Billy said.

"You all right?" said Ray.

"Yes. I came here to round you up and to find Rachel's husband," Andrew said.

"I saw you," Ray said, "from a window upstairs. I was headin' back anyways."

"Captain, it looks like you been in a fight," Billy said. "Your hand is bleeding."

Andrew looked down and saw blood on his left hand. He figured he got cut when he grabbed the knife from the harlot. He wrapped his bandana around his hand.

"Aww, it's nothin', and it ain't easy finding Carl Richards."

"That's what I came to tell you," Billy said, "he ain't here. Rachel said she needs to talk to you."

"What do you mean?" said Andrew as he mounted Noah.

"That's all I know. Rachel wants to tell you something."

"Well, let's get the hell out of here."

And the three men rode out toward the camp.

Twenty-two

Rachel saw Andrew's bandaged hand as he dismounted Noah.

"I'm so sorry, Andrew. I'm sorry," Rachel said. "I have to talk to you, and I'll understand if you want us to leave. I expect there'll be another wagon train coming along sometime," Rachel said.

"What are you talking about?" Andrew said.

"Why you shouldn't look for my husband."

"I just needed a better description," he said, "I should have asked you straight out for one. I know how some men are, and I didn't know what he might be up to on the island. I thought it would be a nice surprise to round him up for you."

"No, no," she said with tears falling from her eyes. Andrew fell silent. "I have to confess something to you." Sobbing, Rachel was having trouble breathing. Andrew started to take her hand. She pulled away and turned her back but continued to cry.

"I already told Billy, so he would go get you," she said as her sobs subsided.

"Told him what?" Andrew said.

"You wouldn't be able to find my husband." She wiped her eyes.

Andrew was growing frustrated after a fruitless search, a fight, and now with time running out to get to a dinner at the fort.

"So, what is it? Has he moved on somewhere else?"

Rachel turned toward him. "No, no." She closed her eyes, not wanting to see the man's face when she told him. "I don't think I have a husband."

Andrew shook his head slowly and his lips tightened. "And that's what you told Billy?"

"Yes. But I didn't tell him why." Rachel lowered her voice. "Daniel knows nothing of this. Just the love Claudine and I can give him. And he misses his grandfather."

Rachel sat down by the campfire and continued. "So, I lied to you to get on this trip. I wrote the letter myself. Claudine and I were so eager to leave New Orleans after our father died. We were headed to Saint Louis, but I heard about the cholera outbreak there. Then, the first wagon master had turned us away. I was desperate."

Andrew couldn't decide whether to slap her or hold her, but he couldn't do either. Sometimes all two people can do is breathe and stay alive. He stood there. He couldn't touch her. Not yet. He couldn't comfort her. He didn't know where to start.

He saw the determined woman he had met earlier break down and reveal her innermost secrets. In his mind he thought of her lies, what she had put him through with her deception, what position she had put him in. And then he thought about what the woman had been through herself. He started to understand her life in a new way.

"I married Carl when I was eighteen. He was older," Rachel began. "A handsome man and he dined often at our family's restaurant. We met when I was seventeen and waited on him each time."

Andrew knew she could experience joy and happiness—he had seen it so many times already. Now he knew how strong she was and some of what she had to overcome in life. He wondered if this was meant to be—their paths should cross so she would come into his life. Could he cast her out for her deception? Would his heart and mind allow it? He remembered when they first met how she had asked him if *he* could be trusted, was *he* a man of honor. And now this. He sat down on a log near her, waiting for her explanation. His jaw was clenched.

"I did love him, and he said he loved me," Rachel said. "He got my father's permission to court me because I was so young at the time. Seventeen. Carl was a surveyor and did some traveling to map out roads and towns across the South," she said, twisting a white handkerchief in her hands.

"Anyway, we began seeing each other when he was in town; off and on at first, but then all the time. His work would take him away for weeks, but he always came back. I kept cooking and serving at the restaurant and waiting for Carl to return. We got married when I turned eighteen. While I was pregnant with Daniel, Carl changed. His trips took longer, and when Daniel was a baby, crying a lot for the first six months, Carl left on another surveying trip, and I never saw him again ..." Rachel said, holding back tears.

"...I never saw him again, I never heard if he was living or dead, but I had to go on living and hoping he was all right. So, I don't know if I'm a widow or divorced. I reckon he abandoned me and Daniel. Being quiet about it with you has almost driven me crazy.

"Maybe he wasn't ready to be a father. I don't know. Claudine has always been by my side. She helped raise Daniel and he loves her. So, when our father died we sold the restaurant and decided to leave New Orleans. It was out of fear and desperation I made up the letter. I am ashamed for it, and I understand if we must leave the train. Perhaps it's for the best, because we are so near the fort. We can probably get on with another wagon train. It's up to you, so let me know, and I'll tell Claudine and Daniel."

Andrew was feeling a mix of anger, disappointment, and sympathy, and he held his tongue for a minute. A piece of wood on the campfire popped and crackled and then hissed. He wasn't sure what to do or what to feel.

"I hear what you're saying. I need to think on it, and I've got to get to the fort for something else," he said. He left Rachel there and rode on.

In her heart she wanted redemption, understanding, and sympathy. She didn't want to be abandoned in the dust. But all she could do right then was watch him shake his head and ride away.

Lt. Colonel Powell had invited Andrew to Fort Childs for dinner and to stay the night in more comfortable quarters. He accepted, partly to spend more time with Thomas and to take a well-deserved break from trail food, get out of the weather, and get a good night's sleep.

Andrew knew the wagon train would be in good hands with Billy, Ray, and Frenchie watching over it. With Rachel's sad story preying on his mind, he rode Noah up to the fort and tied the Appaloosa to a hitching post. A soldier stepped up to put the horse away for the night.

Thomas greeted his father at the barracks door, and they hugged each other again.

Andrew's guilt about not keeping up with the whereabouts of his only child surfaced. "You know, I didn't reckon when I would see you again," Andrew said.

"You must have missed it, the letter I sent you upon my graduation from the Academy. I sent it to our home. I thought you'd be there," Thomas said.

"I think my home is in a saddle these days. Didn't even know you were finishing the Academy. I should have been at your graduation."

"I know you're pretty much of a nomad, Father. Mother always told me. She understood."

Andrew's throat closed up with emotion, and he couldn't speak. His heart still ached for his beautiful Elizabeth. During the day, he pushed thoughts of her away to keep his sanity, but he still dreamed about her every night—holding her, looking into her eyes, smelling her hair. Seeing her smile. Feeling her love. She knew him so well. He lost all those connections to her and all the years he should have had. He knew if he had been there he could have saved her.

Now he realized his son, their son, knew him through the eyes of Elizabeth. Her love was always constant and supportive, and she had instilled a goodness and understanding in Thomas.

The two men talked about the future as only a reunited father and son could. Andrew talked about *Manifest Destiny* and his mission to expand the boundaries of the U.S. to the Pacific. He explained he had land in Oregon and would build a new home, get a new start. But there would always be room in his life for Thomas. He wanted Thomas to join him in Oregon whenever he could. He wanted to make up for lost time together.

All Thomas could do was hug his father again.

For dinner, Andrew expected to be in a dining tent with at least 100 of the soldiers. Instead, Lt. Colonel Powell ushered him into a newly constructed hall. As they entered, ten officers stood and saluted and then broke into cheers and applause.

Andrew looked around the room. "What the hell are you all doing here?" Everyone laughed.

The commander stood next to Andrew and his son. "When Thomas found out from your man, Billy, you were stopping here, we wanted to give you a proper welcome and a surprise. Who knows, one day you may want to return to the Army. There's still time, and we'll always have a need for a man with your experience."

Looking down the tables, Andrew realized he had served with each of the men during his career. He walked around the room, shaking hands, getting a slap on the back or a hug from each officer. As Andrew looked at the corner table, he was surprised to see Frenchie sitting there.

Loud enough for the group to hear, Andrew said, "Frenchie, what are you doing here?"

"I used to feed most of these men. It's about time they fed me."

There was laughter around the room.

"I thought this would be one night I wouldn't have to look at you," Andrew said.

"I was thinking the same," Frenchie said.

There was more laughter.

When some men gather there is good-natured ribbing. It can go too far, but Frenchie and Andrew had such a long history and friendship they knew each other well—one ornery man and another ornery man, relieved to be off the trail and among friends.

Andrew shook the hand of one of the officers. "The last time I saw you, you were covered in mud from a battle in Illinois."

"It was a terrible time, and I remember you had blood on your face."

"None of it mine, I'm glad to say."

"It was worth it. We routed Black Hawk."

"Commander Atkinson really liked it."

And so it went. Each officer recalled their time with Andrew. The last officer said, "I remember getting to spend some time at your farm with you and Thomas. He was twelve then. Elizabeth was generous with such hospitality. You both were. I could tell why you loved each other. I was sorry to hear of her passing. The war with Mexico was just starting when I heard."

The commander eventually got everyone's attention. "Gentlemen, there'll be more time for a visit later, but we've got staff eager to serve a meal."

It was a three-course meal: First, a salad of greens, second a feast of buffalo, wild boar, corn, green beans, potatoes and spoon bread, and the final dessert course was cherry cobbler. Everyone was full and satisfied by the end. Andrew leaned back in his chair and smiled at his son and the commander.

Frenchie shouted, "Speech, speech," and everyone turned to look at Andrew. He waved the idea away, but others joined in, "Speech, speech."

Andrew shook his head and rose to address the group.

"First off, let me give a word of thanks to all of you for this wonderful dinner and for your presence here this evening."

He turned toward the commander. "Thank you for bringing together these fine officers, and, of course, Frenchie." Frenchie nodded his approval as a few officers chuckled and Andrew continued.

"It is an honor to be back among soldiers, especially the ones who I commanded, even though most of you now outrank me. And though there's a letter floating around a post office somewhere in Tennessee which would have told me, it was a wonderful surprise to find my son is stationed here. He and I had not talked in two years and today we shared some fond memories during our reunion. With a career in the Army, all of us learn too well of the challenges, sacrifices, and dangers ahead of us, and behind us. I look around the room and I see friends I need to thank, because if it wasn't for you, I wouldn't be alive. And I see a few faces because I saved your butts." The officers applauded and then quieted down.

"I bet you thought I was through talking." More laughter.

"Tomorrow, as you know, I'm leading our wagon train across the Platte, headed west eventually to Oregon. I know it isn't gonna be easy. Seems like much of what I do isn't. But I'm glad to be a part of expanding our young country all across this continent. It is our country's destiny. America's Manifest Destiny." Andrew sat down to applause.

Smiling, Commander Powell stood. "I thought you were just going to say thank you. I didn't know you were going to run for office." Everyone laughed. The commander then handed Andrew a present wrapped with string. "In recognition of your new responsibilities as a wagon master, our company wanted to give you a memento in honor of your visit with us. So, please accept this gift from all of us here at the fort and think of us when you use it somewhere in the mountains."

Andrew unwrapped the package on the table, not sure what he would find inside. To everyone's amusement, he pulled out a pair of long red underwear.

When the laughter died down he said, "I don't know what to say, gentlemen. except these will come in handy. When I see the first snowflakes fall near the Rockies, I'll put these on and think of you all." Everyone applauded.

"This has been a fine meal and now, gentlemen," the commander said, "unless you have other duties, let's retire to the hall where good whiskey and fine tobacco await."

Finally, with his head full of memories and alcohol, Andrew found a cot to his liking and fell asleep. This time he would welcome his dreams of Elizabeth and battles fought beside his comrades long ago.

~ * ~

The next morning, during the first full day at the fort, the sisters wanted to rest. Life on the trail had not been easy, and they were eager to wash clothes, sort their wagon, and prepare for what was to come. However, the misfiring of the corporal's pistol was a disturbing reminder that danger could come from within the camp as well as without.

Like all the other pioneers, Rachel and Claudine needed to prepare to continue the journey. They took an inventory of their supplies to determine what was needed for the months ahead or until they could reach another fort or trading post. Though the wagon train was at a standstill, it had been a long day.

An Army patrol had visited everyone, inspecting wagons to make sure the schooners were readied for crossing the Platte River. Soldiers re-applied hot tar underneath a few of the wagon beds to seal out water which would help the wagons float across, if need be.

Toward the end of the day, after washing, cooking, eating, and cleaning up, the women watched Daniel care for their milk cow inside the corral of wagons. They praised him for doing a good job and for a lifelike horse he had whittled earlier with his folding knife. At a neighbor's campfire, they drank apple cider and joined in a song. Then the sisters and Daniel settled down for the night.

Rachel and Daniel prepared to sleep in their wagon in case it rained. The pair arranged a flat area across bags of flour and meal and folded a blanket across themselves with bags of clothes for pillows.

Claudine preferred to sleep below the wagon, lying inside her blankets on the ground. A waterproof tarp protected her body from dampness, and the oversize bed roll kept her comfortable in her nightclothes as the evening temperatures fell.

Both women missed the beds they had to leave back in New Orleans. Along with the soft mattresses, quilts, duvets, coverlets, and down pillows, they missed the smell of breakfast cooking and warm rolls from their oven. They often dreamed of their future home full of furnishings they would find in Oregon.

As wagon master, Andrew posted a watchman duty roster every day. It listed the names of men who were to walk around the camp in four-hour shifts at night. Armed with rifles and carrying lanterns, two men would guard the camp starting at 10 p.m. The second shift of sentries was on duty from two to six.

The sentries began their meandering rounds while all the campfires burned down to coals. Everyone else settled down for the night. The crescent moon cast an intermittent light across the land as clouds passed before it and shadows chased each other into the night.

At the sisters' wagon, Claudine was dreaming of getting settled in Oregon and could see green pastures spreading before her, but her sleep stopped abruptly when she woke to a man's hand across her mouth.

"You be quiet or I'll choke you dead," he slurred, pressing his body on top of her.

Claudine's arms and legs were trapped, pinned inside her blanket. She didn't have time to take a breath as the man's other hand closed around her neck. All she could do was move her head in silence and try to breathe again.

The man peeled back her blanket and ran one hand down across her body. She could smell the whiskey and tobacco on his breath and the stink of his body but couldn't see his face in the darkness. Claudine moaned "No, no" and struggled out of the blanket. The man slapped her face. Suddenly, with her legs free, she kicked her knees into her attacker's exposed groin and he grunted. She felt his weight fall on her again. His hand pressed her mouth closed once more.

For a moment, Claudine saw the blade of a knife reflected in a sliver of light as a cloud passed by the moon. She saw the blade raised and closed her eyes.

"No! Leave my aunt alone." It was Daniel with his whittling knife, stabbing the man in the back once, twice.

The man cried out and swung an arm at Daniel, knocking him against a wagon wheel, and the boy fell silent, which gave Claudine enough time to reach for her derringer and fire a shot toward the dark figure—no time to aim— just shoot. The man cried out, hit her with his fist, and stumbled away. She could hear him running.

By then, Rachel had screamed and jumped from the wagon. Claudine heard other footsteps running toward her and then a rifle shot. The sentry knelt down, holding a lantern close to her. Rachel reached for Daniel who was conscious and rubbing the back of his head. She touched him and felt warm, wet blood.

The sentry said, "I shot at him, Ms. Lafayette. I heard your scream. I may have hit him as he rode away. Are you all right?"

Within minutes, half the camp came with lanterns and torches, worried for the sisters and desperate for an explanation.

Rachel wrapped a blanket around Claudine who was shaking with emotion and exhaustion. "Someone attacked Claudine, and Daniel is hurt. Where is Mrs. Crawford? Please give us some room and some privacy."

Mrs. Crawford arrived and tended to Daniel. By lamplight, she could see the cut on his head was minor but Daniel was crying.

Rachel held him close.

"I got him, Mama. I got him," Daniel sobbed.

Billy Armstrong shoved his way through the crowd and pushed the sentry aside. "Claudine, what happened?" He turned to the group of people and asked them to leave.

Billy held Claudine in his arms and she held onto him. Sobbing, she told Billy she was all right. She was angry and worn out and wanted to be left alone with Rachel. She needed time alone. Claudine's face had turned pale and her cheek was swollen from the impact of her attacker's fist.

"Who was it?" Billy insisted.

"I don't know. He smelled of whiskey. He was drunk and heavy. He tried to ..."

"Did he?"

"No. No. Daniel saved me. And, Billy, I shot the man."

Billy pulled her close and kissed her face.

"The man tried to choke me," Claudine said. "When my gun fired, in the flash, I could see he only had three fingers on one hand."

The sentry told Billy the man had ridden off west toward the river, and Billy was gone.

Twenty-three

After spending the night in the Fort Childs barracks, Andrew rode back to the Crawford camp. He thought about the wonderful Army meal along with the camaraderie he had so missed from his days in the military. He enjoyed seeing his son and learning about Thomas's hopes for the future.

As Andrew dismounted from Noah he saw Frenchie. "Did I hear gunfire out here last night?"

"*Oui, mon ami*. When I returned I was told Claudine was attacked by a man. He tried to rape her." Andrew's jaw tightened and he looked toward the sisters' wagon. Frenchie could see anger rise into his face.

"But she's all right. She fought him off, and Daniel helped stop the man ..."

Andrew had heard enough and mounted up, ready to ride to the sisters' schooner. Then, he held Noah back.

"Who did it?"

"Not sure," Frenchie said. "A three-fingered man, I heard."

"That bastard Quinn."

"Maybe."

Andrew looked around the camp and back at Frenchie.

"Where's Billy?" He figured he knew the answer.

"Billy left at sunup. He's gone huntin' I expect," Frenchie said.

"I hope he knows what to do."

Claudine and Rachel were washing tin pans they used for breakfast, and Daniel, his head bandaged, was sitting by the campfire.

"How are you, boy?" Andrew asked, kneeling down and gently touching Daniel's head.

"Where were you?" the boy said. Daniel used the same words Thomas had said when Andrew arrived too late on the day Elizabeth died. It would have been easy for guilt to wash across Andrew again, but now he figured he deserved at least one night off and, of course, Daniel was frightened.

"Don't mind him," Claudine said. "We are all okay."

"We missed you yesterday," Rachel said. "I hope your son is well. Did you hear the camp is celebrating two things today—a birthday and a wedding?"

Andrew could tell the subject of the attempted rape would not be discussed in front of Daniel.

"Mademoiselle Ella turns seventeen today," Claudine said, "and she and James are to marry. Mr. Anderson said so at dinner."

It being their last day at the fort, people in the camp were busy getting organized. Led by Thomas, a patrol returned, herding fresh livestock and driving wagons laden with supplies. Men and women at each covered wagon received and paid for the goods they had ordered. Fresh, well-rested oxen and mules were traded for trail-weary animals. The patrol would return the next morning.

As the wedding party gathered, Ella Anderson was a pretty bride, wearing ribbons in her hair and carrying a bouquet of prairie flowers. She was dressed in a borrowed blue hoop skirt and escorted toward Preacher Crawford by her father, his arm still in a sling, as it would be for the next six weeks.

James was well-washed and groomed, hair brushed, and he was dressed in his cleanest clothes, including a new shirt. His budding moustache was still filling in. He could not stop smiling.

Mrs. Anderson was overjoyed, and Mr. Anderson was content. After James had joined the wagon train, Ella's parents found him to be trustworthy and reliable. They realized how much he cared for their daughter and future grandchild.

People brought other food and small gifts for the reception, and the Army gave the couple a mule. All the pioneers attended the ceremony and birthday celebration. There were two cakes: one to celebrate Ella's birthday and one to celebrate the wedding.

Rachel signaled to Andrew to meet her aside. "As you know, Captain, I'm not one to beat around the bush," she said, as she arched her back and stepped toward him. "I have to know if I need to make other plans or if we are crossing the Platte with you today."

Andrew studied her as she stopped in front of him with her arms folded across her chest.

"Mrs. Richards, I have given this some thought," he said. "I am disappointed you lied to me so carefully. You even forged a letter from your husband."

"Yes, out of desperation. I admit it."

"I remember when we first met and you asked me if *I* could be trusted."

"I know it must burn in you and rightly so."

"I see you are somewhat recovered from our last meeting when you were forthcoming with your history."

"We all have a past following us around."

"Whether we like it or not," he said.

"Whether we like it or not."

"I know life is full of troubles."

"It is, more for some than others," Rachel said and then she tried to let the man speak uninterrupted. She found her resolution to hold her tongue to be a challenge.

"It is not lightly I arrived at my decision, Mrs. Richards. I have been impressed with your ability to conduct yourself on this journey by way of running your wagon team and contributing to the success of our train."

He continued, "I am conflicted. I must take the measure of each emigrant and balance what is best for the overall wagon train."

"I see."

"Not having your husband to accompany you and Claudine creates a problem. The wives of the men can get jealous, the advances toward you both by the ex-soldiers and others. I am concerned."

"And I have appreciated your own attention." She smiled and then tried to fall silent.

"And I have done so as a courtesy to escort you in your husband's absence."

"I see."

"Not that it hasn't been pleasant."

"I see."

"So, I hope you understand you have challenged me several ways."

"Yes," she said.

Andrew could smell the scent of lavender drifting toward him. He wanted to say more. More about luring him. Deceiving him. About how she made him feel. The dishonesty. The lack of respect. A moral code.

"I know I have been in the wrong, Captain. I have confessed. I do not know, now, if I can endure the remainder of this trip with the guilt I feel. Will you be holding this against me and mine if we continue? Should I make the decision myself to withdraw? It doesn't sound like there is room for forgiveness and a way forward."

They were interrupted when Thomas rode up with his patrol to help with the crossing. He stopped his horse near the pair.

"Good morning, Father."

"Son."

"Is everyone ready to roll?"

After a pause, Andrew responded, "Yes, Lieutenant. Everyone is ready."

Andrew looked at Rachel and said stiffly, "I'll see you after the crossing. Stay safe, madam."

She turned toward her wagon, relieved, and hoped the matter was resolved.

Ten minutes later, Andrew saw Billy ride into camp, leading Quinn's unmistakable black stallion Jit, but there was no Quinn. Andrew figured Billy would have slung Quinn's dead body over the horse, no matter when Billy would have found it. Maybe the bastard got away.

"He couldn't have gone far," Billy said, as he tied Jit to a wagon wheel. "There's dried blood on the saddle. I waited all night along the river. I had to wait till daylight to see under piles of driftwood and amongst the cottonwoods. In the dark, I set the lantern down to try and draw him out to shoot at me. But nothin'."

"You think he tried to cross?" Frenchie said.

"Only if he can walk on water," Billy said, pouring himself a cup of coffee.

Andrew said, "Frenchie told me about it. The women folk aren't talking, at least in front of Daniel."

"You know, Captain, I'd of killed Quinn if I found him," Billy said.

"Wouldn't be surprised."

"All of us would want to shoot him," Frenchie said. "Why don't you get cleaned up and go see your girl?"

Andrew said, "You know galloping off into the night is a good way to get yourself killed, or worse yet, get your horse a broken leg."

"Yeah. I know," said Billy.

"You can't see where you're going," Andrew continued. "There's plenty of holes and rocks spread around and a cliff or two."

"Tell Quinn," Billy said, as he walked away, still fuming at not finding the man who had harmed his girlfriend.

"You sure he ain't dead?" Andrew called after him.

"Not by my hand ...not yet anyways."

"Get cleaned up before you go," Frenchie said.

"Thank you, Mama," Billy replied.

"I can still kick your arse," Frenchie said.

Andrew said, "Get on with it. We got to cross today."

He walked Jit over to Quinn and McFarland's wagon and found McFarland hitching up their team of oxen. McFarland saw him coming and stopped to roll a cigarette. He licked the edge of the paper to close it and lit it with a match.

"You gonna use up all your matches," Andrew said.

"I got plenty," McFarland said, taking a puff. "Looks like you're missing a rider."

"You seen Quinn?"

"Naw," said McFarland.

"He ain't in the wagon?"

"What the hell?"

"A man with three fingers tried to rape Claudine last night."

"So I heard. Bad business. I was passed out."

"Billy found the black along the river. There's blood on the saddle."

"You can leave him," McFarland said, pointing to a wagon wheel. "Hitch him over there."

"In case the owner returns?"

"I was sleeping when it happened. Woke up to the ruckus."

"He's a dead man, you know."

"Wouldn't surprise me. If'n so, I get the horse."

Andrew looked in the wagon and walked away. He left Jit behind.

Fighting fatigue and trying to stay awake, Billy poured water over his head and washed his face. He chewed a string of licorice and took some to give to Daniel and the women. Claudine walked up to him as he got to their camp. She kissed his cheek.

"No sign of him," he said and pulled her close.

"Thank you anyway."

"It ain't over. Found his horse."

"We're crossing today," Claudine said, touching Billy's cheek. "Can I help?"

"No. We're all ready. Daniel's been quiet, off and on. He really doesn't understand. It's just as well."

Daniel saw Billy, ran over and hugged him around the waist.

Billy knelt down. "Hey, Daniel. You were awfully brave last night. You did the right thing."

Daniel's eyes filled with tears and the boy quietly buried his head in Billy's shoulder.

Twenty-four

Last night at the fort, Andrew had discussed ways to cross the churning Platte River with the commander. Because of heavy spring rains, the currents were swifter, the water deeper, and the Platte wider where it had overflowed its banks, making the necessary crossing more treacherous.

It was clear the best way to cross the river was by Indian ferry. The Cheyenne had constructed a crude dugout raft of boards and cottonwood logs, bound by ropes, and driven by poles, and paddles maneuvering the currents. The large ferry could hold two full wagons at a time. The unhitched teams of draft animals had to swim alongside during the crossing.

At normal river levels, the time to cross to the west bank was half an hour. The swollen river would require an hour to cross as the raft crews had to deal with floating debris. Commander Powell had warned it was not unusual for some animals to lose their footing in the deep water and drown, or be swept away, possibly reappearing on the same side where they began but half a mile downstream.

The Cheyenne charged nine dollars per wagon and two dollars per animal. It would take most of a day for all to cross, assuming there were no other wagons waiting to use the ferry. Some days there were many wagons lined up and waiting on both banks.

The only other option was to ford the two-hundred-yard-wide river. The Army had found a channel with fewer hidden tree stumps where wagons could cross but it was still dangerous and deep. If there were no incidents, it could take an hour or more for a team to take a wagon across by a combination of pulling part way, swimming in the ten-foot deep water and pulling once the draft animal's hooves reached the river bed again. If the draft animals panicked or lost their footing trying to pull a wagon, all could be lost.

The herdsmen decided to drive their frightened cattle across the channel, losing one calf under the churning waters.

During the first month, the travelers had driven their wagons across creeks and shallow rivers, but today they faced the swollen and treacherous North Platte River. It had to be crossed. Staying on schedule was vital to avoid the worst snows in the Rocky Mountains still months away. The heavy spring rains in Nebraska had overflowed the river's banks, making it wider, deeper and more dangerous—over 200 yards across, and up to 10 feet deep.

Andrew stood on the seat of the lead wagon. "The Army is going to help us today to get to the river and stay organized. As you've been told, the ferry is the safest way to cross. I know some of you want to avoid the cost. But once you see the river, you'll understand it's worth the money, considering the possibility of losing your belongings or your people in the river.

"After your wagon gets loaded onto the ferry, the trip across will take about an hour, if all goes well. The ferry can take two wagons at a time, so this is gonna take all day. We got twenty wagons." Andrew looked at the sky. "I hope we can have a little sunshine.

"Now listen," he said to the restless crowd. "First, I'm takin' this lead wagon and Frenchie is taking the cook wagon across to set up a new campground. Ray and Billy will stay on this side to be on the last ferry, along with the Andersons and Crawfords. So, we'll have someone on both sides to help you in and out."

At the river's edge, the travelers could see a fallen tree floating down the Platte. Across the river they could see what was left of a wrecked wagon, turned on its side and trapped under a fallen log, the torn white canvas flapped in the wind as if the wagon had surrendered to the waters.

The Indians spoke little English, but they knew what to do. Andrew put Noah's saddle and tack in the lead wagon then stripped to the waist in case he needed to jump in the river. He wasn't about to lose his horse.

Andrew looked across the river, then scanned the sky and saw buzzards circling overhead. Probably a dead animal washed up on the shore.

While waiting to cross, Ray and Billy checked the next pair of wagons and helped tie down any loose supplies. Any travelers who couldn't swim were to stay seated on their wagon or stand beside it and hold onto a wheel.

Halfway across, in the deepest channel, one of the Indians clapped his hands and pointed to a large jagged log floating rapidly toward the ferry. It would do little damage to the ferry but was big enough to injure the animals in the water. Andrew joined two of the crew in a canoe to intercept the oncoming obstacle. They tossed a rope around it and pulled the log past Noah and the other animals.

Seeing Noah's eyes were wide and the horse starting to tire, Andrew jumped from the canoe and finished the crossing swimming next to his horse until its hooves touched the riverbed. Then Andrew rode the horse he loved bareback to the shore to start setting up a camp where everyone could gather.

Vultures were ever present on the journey west. Catching thermals and circling overhead, the dark brown-feathered fowls were constantly looking for carrion, the dead and the dying. Andrew was used to seeing the ugly birds. He knew what it meant after an animal died on his family farm back near Memphis. He also knew what it meant when he saw the birds above a newly silent battlefield.

Before crossing the North Platte, Andrew saw the feathered creatures swirling up in the air on the other side of the river, a tenth of a mile downstream. Out of his concern for the safety of the people and livestock in the Crawford Company, he needed to investigate the source of the vultures' interest. If a mountain lion had left part of a carcass behind, it would mean an animal of prey was nearby.

Such an animal was known to attack vulnerable humans. With children and babies in camp, Andrew wanted to determine what kind of death or dying the birds were tracking. He didn't expect to eliminate the birds, didn't really want to. He did expect to protect the camp from some of the dangers awaiting them.

After he and Frenchie crossed, they found a good wide area to set up camp off the trail. Andrew left Frenchie behind, saddled Noah, and rode along the shoreline looking for turkey vultures on the ground. He had seen them close up in the past. He knew their ugly, bald red heads, beady eyes and hooked yellow beaks made their bodies perfect for picking out the meat of a carcass, getting into all the crevasses clear down to the bone.

He remembered seeing roosts for some of the birds in the trees on La Grande Isle, the site for saloons full of men pursuing their hobbies or addictions of drinking, gambling and whoring.

As he rode down the shoreline, Andrew wondered which animals were less desirable, the debauched humans or the disgusting-looking buzzards.

Emerging from a stand of cottonwood trees onto a clearing, he found twenty vultures surrounding carrion. Most of the birds were waiting to feed and flew up into trees, leaving one picking at the flesh of a dead animal. It was a young bear cub. It must have died from disease or drowned and then washed ashore by the high waters. The carcass was no more than two days old.

Andrew dismounted, letting the reins fall to the ground. Noah would stand and wait but didn't care for the smell of a rotting carcass and the horse pawed at the ground.

"Just hold on, Noah," Andrew said over his shoulder. "I want to see what killed this cub."

Noah shook his head and mane, then whinnied his disapproval.

The last vulture took flight toward the trees as Andrew approached on foot. The cub had been attacked, probably by a cougar, based on the tracks in the wet ground and because the body had been dragged to the site and partially covered with leaves, a habit of the big cats.

Andrew heard a muffled huff and a whinny behind him and turned, expecting to address another complaint from Noah. Instead, a large grizzly bear was staring at him from fifteen feet away. It had to be the cub's mother.

The only weapon Andrew had on him was a hunting knife. His pistol, still wrapped in oil cloth for the crossing, was in the saddlebags on Noah. His rifle was in a scabbard attached to the saddle, fifteen feet in the other direction.

To try to scare the bear away, Andrew stood and spread his arms, attempting to look bigger. The bear rose up on her back legs, standing six feet tall. It looked to weigh about 300 pounds. Four-inch claws were extended and the animal opened its maw, revealing its sharp white teeth. Then it roared.

Andrew knew he had to save himself and Noah. He bent down slowly, picked up a piece of driftwood and drew his knife. He stood back up; the grizzly raised its paws in the air, preparing to charge.

It was only after the bear fell down dead at his feet that Andrew heard the sound of the gunshot. He looked back across the Platte and there stood Ray Cooper, holding his Sharps rifle above his head—at two-hundred yards away. Andrew knew Cooper was a hell of a shot. He also knew he'd hear about this shooting for the rest of the trip, probably every night around the campfire. And he'd be glad to hear it.

Andrew took a final look at the body of the mother grizzly. He figured he would send Frenchie back to carve out some bear steaks for the camp, but first things first. Andrew strapped on his pistol and mounted Noah.

He was about to ride back to camp when he saw another mound of leaves, possibly another cub, and had to check it too. The mound was larger than the first one. As he pushed away the leaves, Andrew realized it was the body of what was left of a man, facedown. Could it be Quinn? He checked the swollen arms and hands and rolled the body over. The man had a full beard, wore the remains of a leather-fringed coat and had all his fingers.

It wasn't Quinn. Andrew couldn't believe the three-fingered bastard could survive a bullet in his stomach, a musket ball in his back, and a 200-yard swim. Maybe the sentry missed.

Twenty-five

There was a new baby on the journey. Only a few months old when the wagon train left St. Joseph, little Jane Pike was not too fussy, but if hungry or wet she would cry and her mother Martha would quickly see what was needed.

Much of little Jane's life, so far, was spent being rocked in a wooden cradle her proud papa Henry had built. It was made of cedar and lined with pretty cotton blankets. The rocker legs of the cradle were shaped to allow it to rock from side to side and one end had a wooden canopy to provide shade. The other end was plain except for a heart-shaped cutout. It was all nailed together with wooden pegs and very sturdy—a good thing, especially when the family crossed the Platte River.

The construction of the Indians' dugout ferry had been put to the test all day, transporting two wagons at a time, with the crew pushing aside floating debris, as the craft crossed the expanse of rough waters. The current was swifter than usual and downed trees or branches flowed across the path of the ferry, requiring the crew to be vigilant, lest a jagged log strike the ferry or the livestock swimming alongside.

With the Pikes' wagon and McFarland's onboard, the ferry was heavily loaded. McFarland had claimed ownership of Jit and along with eight oxen, two other horses, and a milk cow, the livestock was swimming the best they could in the deep water. Mama Martha Pike had placed baby Jane in the cradle which was rocking on the seat of their wagon. Baby Jane's parents were holding hands, as a caring couple, and standing on the deck of the ferry, watching the river roll by and the Indians' crew work.

Upriver three trees had fallen together into the Platte and were now headed in tandem toward the ferry as it crossed the deepest part of the channel.

All the Indians saw the thatch of broken trees coming and yelled to each other. The crew, along with the Pikes and McFarland, hurried to the same side of the ferry. Half the Indians jumped into the water at the same time to pull ropes that tethered the animals together. The oxen were mooing in fright as their heads bobbed in and out of the water. The animals strained to keep their heads out of the water to breathe.

Desperate, the Indians pulled the oxen away from the path of the oncoming trees. McFarland yelled and pointed toward Jit to get the Indians to pull the horse to safety. The Pikes were pointing toward their milk cow and horses and yelling to get the Indians to protect their animals.

One of the floating trees rammed the side of the ferry, missing all the animals but jarring the big raft. Upon impact, the Pikes and McFarland fell onto the deck. It was a close call. The ferry held together but it rolled with the impact and the waves.

It was then that Martha Pike heard the cries of little Jane and turned toward their wagon only to see the cradle was gone. In horror, she saw it floating downstream with the crying baby still inside. Without a word, Henry Pike ran past his wife and dove headfirst into the river. He was not a good swimmer, especially in the rough waters. Everyone was yelling and screaming for help.

Still onshore and waiting to cross, Billy Armstrong saw the collision and heard the screams. He saw the cradle splash into the river. He and Ray pulled a canoe from the dock and paddled furiously toward the cradle, hoping to reach it before it sank or tipped over, spilling the now quiet baby into the rushing waters.

Well below the cradle's path, a lone Indian heard the commotion and rode his pinto fifty yards into the water. Up to his waist in the river, the Indian pulled an arrow from its quiver and attached a long thin leather strip he used for fishing. He pulled the string of his bow back, aimed carefully, and shot the arrow at the cradle. It stuck in the top wooden canopy and the man was able to slow the cradle long enough for Billy and Ray to get to it. Baby Jane was saved.

Henry Pike had disappeared beneath the waters.

The long and dangerous day turned into an unsettled evening. The loss of Henry beneath the waters of the Platte preyed on Andrew's mind, and now there was the question of what to do for the distraught widow Martha, and the baby. Andrew felt one of his most important responsibilities was keeping his people safe from harm, but he knew he couldn't control everyone's decisions or the impact of Mother Nature. He couldn't be in charge of everyone's destiny. He had enough trouble determining his own.

What if Henry had not jumped in the river? What if he could swim better? What if the couple had not placed the cradle on the seat of the wagon? What if the Indians could have kept the log from hitting the ferry in the first place?

Once all the wagons got across, Emily Crawford spent the rest of the day at the side of Martha and baby Jane. Emily, too, felt the loss of Henry, whom she had watched grow into a caring husband, and her heart ached. She had known Martha all her life as well. Emily gently encouraged Martha to take care of herself and eat so she could nurse the baby.

Martha was in shock. Was she to turn back now? How could she go forward? Martha held the baby close and rocked her body back and forth, sitting on a log near a campfire.

"Here, Martha, drink some water and eat some dinner," Emily said at sunset, offering Martha a cup of water and a tin plate of stew. "Jane needs you, and you need to stay healthy."

"I can't believe he's gone. It happened so fast," Martha cried.

"I know."

"He didn't say anything. He saw the cradle go in and followed right after it," Martha said.

"The men have looked up and down the river."

Baby Jane began to fuss and then cry.

"I think Jane is hungry," Emily said.

Martha brought the baby to her breast. "We've got to find him, Mrs. Crawford."

"The Army looked on the east side, and our men looked on this side until dark. They'll look again when morning comes."

"I'm not leaving here until we know for sure."

"Maybe we can get the Army to help again tomorrow."

"I can't do anything until I have Henry back or until..."

Martha couldn't say the words: 'they find his body.' It was too much to think. It would be bad luck. She had to have hope.

Andrew believed in sharing the wagon train duties with the other travelers. As the group's leader, he wanted to set an example. It was why he served as one of the sentries some nights.

After the challenge of crossing the river, the pioneers were glad to set up their tents and cook dinner as darkness fell. While campfires burned brightly, the parents let their children run wild for a while—best to get them worn out a little to have even a chance at a peaceful night of sleep.

The tale of how sharpshooter Ray Cooper had felled the grizzly from 200 yards spread through the camp quickly. People learned the story from Frenchie and Ray, and added their own versions as part of the gossip. The women were surprised to receive fresh bear steaks from Frenchie. He said to fry them or chop them up and make chili.

Later in the night the weather cooled, and a hazy mist of rain created a fog which wandered through the camp, rising up from the river's edge and surrounding the tents and animals like a shroud. Vision was so impaired people walking around looked like ghosts in the night. Once the camp settled down to sleep, though, the ghosts stopped appearing.

Andrew's turn as one of the two sentries would expire at two o'clock in the morning. Duff was the other sentry. Fortunately, he was awake and sober. Carrying a lantern and weapons, the two men walked the perimeter in opposite directions with the purpose of guarding the tents and corral.

Protecting the camp from wild animals hunting for easy prey was one mission for the sentries. The mountain lion or another bear could be on the prowl. Andrew also thought with over a hundred horses, oxen, and mules confined in the circled wagons, the wrong sound or wrong scent could spook the animals and lead to a stampede. He knew a stampede would endanger lives and property, and it could take days to round up scattered animals.

As Andrew dutifully walked between the churning river's edge and the east end of the camp, he could hear the continuous roar of the water. He paused, and with light from the lantern, he looked at his pocket watch to see it was almost two o'clock. He figured the fog would lift by morning with the sun's rays warming the atmosphere. He wanted to explore farther down river for Henry Pike with what little time they had. He knew the train had to stay on schedule or risk running into trouble with the fall snows near the South Pass. As he closed the face of the watch, he looked up and saw a figure moving toward him.

"Who's there?" Andrew said, but the roiling river drowned out his voice. He spoke again, louder this time. "I say who's coming? State your name."

There was no response, but the figure kept coming, silently. Then, he recognized it was Martha Pike, carrying baby Jane in her arms. He stepped beside her.

"Martha. Martha. Look at me. What are you doing?"

Still no sound from Martha. She was walking, trance-like, toward the bank of the river. The baby was asleep in her arms, wrapped in a blanket. Martha's night clothes dragged across the underbrush. She didn't stop.

Andrew stepped in front of her, "Martha, it's me, Andrew." She came to a halt. "Martha, say something." She stared into the distance. Her body was in front of him but her mind was somewhere else.

Rounding the sentry route, Duff approached them.

"What's going on, Captain?" Duff said.

"Duff, I'm holding Martha here. She was headed for the river with the baby. Go find Mrs. Crawford and bring her. I'll wait. Be sure you can find your way back in this fog."

"Will do," Duff said, and he hurried toward the wagons.

Emily came along quickly and said, "I'm sorry, Andrew, I was supposed to be watching them, but I fell asleep. I thought Martha was doing all right."

"I found her a few steps from the river. I think she was headed in, wanting to be with her husband."

"Oh, goodness." Emily draped a shawl around Martha's shoulders. Martha was crying, but at least she was awake.

"Where's Henry?" Martha said. "I can't go anywhere until I find him."

"Let's go back up to the tent, Martha," Andrew said.

He and Emily escorted the mother and baby through the fog. They found the tent. Andrew stirred their campfire and added wood.

"I'll stay up and watch her," Emily said. "Maybe you can ask one of the other women to come help."

"No need," Rachel said, walking over in her boots and night clothes. "I heard the commotion. I'm surprised Martha lasted this long." She sat next to Martha and offered to hold the baby, but Martha shook her head.

Soon, two other sentries took over and began their routes around the camp. The cloaking fog stayed until the sun broke through at sunrise. Martha, exhausted, fell asleep until Jane began to cry again.

As the air cleared and the sentries returned to their tents, a disoriented man stumbled out of the woods below the camp. He cried for help, once, twice, and fell to his knees. It was Henry Pike, bruised and battered but alive.

Twenty-six

The eighty souls on the trip to Oregon—different ages, different dreams—were adjusting to life on the trail. The six-month trek would be a test of everyone's maturity and patience. Dealing with the physical stress of the daily routine, wrangling draft animals, and enduring the elements would be exhausting.

The travelers would miss the relatives and the lives they left behind. The longing would cause tears and trauma for many. Yet it would be a time of growth and awakening. People would reach a new awareness of self and their place in the world. Growing children would shed some toys and learn to ease the burden of everyday work their parents faced. At times tempers would flair and self-control would face new challenges.

Through all the growth and strife, life would go on. Personalities and relationships would evolve. One day a scared and weary young boy might cry baby tears from frustration while standing in the middle of a fast-flowing stream. The next day the same boy would accept more responsibility with a new determination. He and others would refuse to be defeated by the trail.

The day had been long and hard on everyone. Heat radiated from sunup to sundown. Rocky creek beds along the Oregon Trail strained wagon wheels, axles, and ankles. Andrew pressed for two more miles out of the travelers, trying to make up for a lost day earlier due to a rainstorm that wouldn't stop.

Finally, reaching safe and plentiful water by a river, the train halted. To ease their lives, folks had started preparing dinner in groups of two or three families near their wagons. Women and girls made fires and shared the cooking chores while tending to younger children. The men and older boys put draft animals in the corral of circled wagons, pitched tents, did a little hunting, and started to pester the women for the evening meal and maybe dessert.

While folks were settling in after sunset, Billy rode up from the back of the train. "Cap'n, looks like a fist fight's comin'."

Shirtless to cool off, Andrew was lying on a blanket with his stocking feet propped up on a log. "Why are you telling me?" he said, rising and quickly stepping into a pair of leather moccasins.

"I figured you should know."

Andrew clicked his tongue three times and Noah appeared. He mounted the horse bareback to ride next to Billy. "I mean, why didn't you stop it instead of coming up here?"

"I was just passing by a couple of wagons and seen two men talking close, next to a campfire—you know, face-to-face. From what I've seen, it was headin' toward a fight."

"Who is it?"

"Elder Reese and Lester Allen."

By the time Andrew and Billy arrived at the wagons, the two neighbors were wrestling in the dirt. Reese grabbed Lester by the hair and swung a fist up into the man's face.

Andrew dismounted. "Stop it, you two."

He and Billy pulled the men apart.

Reese was the first to speak. "He got what's comin', Captain. He's been staring at my wife all day. Carolyn said he's been winkin' at her like somethin's up."

Lester wiped his bloody nose on the back of his hand, "It ain't true. I had somethin' in my eye is all. I wasn't winkin'. This dust got in my eyes all day."

"Both of you sit down and shut up," Andrew said. "You know the regulations. No fighting. Everybody agreed and signed the papers."

Both of the fighters fell silent and looked down at the ground in front of them, expecting some type of punishment.

"I can penalize both of you," Andrew started. "Reese, I've not known you to fight in the past..."

"It ain't right," Reese said. "I know my Carolyn is a pretty woman and younger, but it ain't right to stare at a man's wife, no matter what. I'll not have it."

Andrew turned to Lester. "Should I ask Mrs. Reese about this?"

"I don't know; I ain't done nothin'," Lester said.

Andrew didn't stop. "But you *were* looking at her?"

"Well, Captain, she's a lot better to look at than the back end of a wagon all day."

"All right. Here's your orders," Andrew said. "Tomorrow, Lester, move your wagon to the rear of the train. You hear me?"

Lester looked at Andrew, irritated. "Yes, I hear you."

"Any more fighting from either of you and I'm charging you ten dollars each."

"He started it," Reese said, pointing at Lester.

Andrew crossed his arms and looked from one man to the other. "Let's make that twenty dollars each, then. Would anyone like to say anything else?"

Both men shook their heads. Lester got up and stumbled to his wagon where his wife Teresa was staring at him with her arms crossed over her chest.

Billy and Andrew headed back toward the front of the train. By then the only light was coming from campfires and a partial moon.

Holding a lantern, Daniel was running into the path of their horses.

"Pull up, Billy," Andrew said. Both horses stopped quickly. "Hold on there, little soldier."

Daniel stopped and looked up.

"What are you doing out this late?" Billy said.

"I had to pee."

"Well, that's a good reason, but you almost got run over," Andrew said. "You doing all right?"

"Yes, sir. I watched those men fight too. But not too close."

"I was wondering..."

"So, Captain, are you like the sheriff? I saw you stop it."

"On this trip I am."

"So, you can tell people what to do?" Daniel said.

"Yes, I'm in charge."

"Of everybody?"

"Yes," Andrew said.

"Of everything?"

"Yes. Everything."

"Includin' me?"

"I expect your mother is in charge of you first," Andrew said.

"Then your Aunt Claudine," Billy added.

"Then me," Andrew said.

Rachel stuck her head out of her tent. "Daniel, what are you doing?"

"I'm just coming back, Mama."

"Evening, Rachel, I hope we didn't disturb you," said Andrew.

The woman stepped out of her tent, still dressed from the day. "We are eager to get ready for a good night's sleep, as soon as things quiet down. Did Daniel get in your way?"

"No, we're just passing on up to the lead wagon. Sorry to disturb you."

"You ride around much at night, Captain, after we're all asleep?"

"Sometimes. Tonight, Billy and I had to take care of something."

Before Daniel entered the tent, he looked over his shoulder at his mother and said, "There was a fight. He's the sheriff, and he's in charge of everybody."

Rachel folded her arms and looked up at Andrew. "I see, and perhaps you can wear a shirt next time, Sheriff."

"My apologies. I was in a hurry."

As the men rode on, Rachel watched them. She thought she saw a scar on Andrew's back, but it could have been a shadow. Hard to see.

"Thank you for stopping the fight, Cap'n," Billy said, "I s'pect Lester may also get an earful from his wife."

"Yep. There'll be some more suffering then. But we all need to save our strength for the trail. Fights can get worse with knives and guns about. Next time you see a fight coming, don't look for me. Stop it yourself before it spreads. I know you can do it. Of course, if you're outnumbered, give me a holler."

Billy nodded. "Reese may have found it easier to punch some person 'cause you can't punch the dust or the sun."

Andrew shook his head. "You may have the beginnings of a good tall tale there."

"You mean sort of like 'the day Elder Reese punched the sun'?"

"Something like that," Andrew said. "Hey, who's on sentry duty tonight?"

"At ten o'clock it's McFarland, then Shaughnessy at two."

"By the way, Billy, where were you when you saw Reese and Lester squaring off?"

"Well, I was within seeing distance."

"Something tells me you were jawing with Claudine a few wagons away."

"I was just making my rounds."

"How is Claudine?"

Billy smiled. "As pretty as ever."

"I knew you were there."

"Ahh, Captain."

"If you had your thinking-cap on, you would have done something different about a brewing fight."

"I was already a couple of wagons toward you when I realized what was going on. I figured I might need you anyway."

"Don't let a woman distract you from what you should be doing."

"It ain't easy. I sure like to listen to her talk and she smells good too."

Andrew saw a match flare up near the ex-soldiers' wagons. "Let's remind McFarland he's on duty tonight."

McFarland exhaled a puff of smoke as Billy and Andrew reined in their horses. "You remember you're on sentry duty tonight, don't you, McFarland?"

McFarland took another drag on his fag. "Yeah, Captain, me and Shaughnessy at ten o'clock. I got at least an hour to go. After ten years in the Army, I know what I'm doing."

"And remind Shaughnessy. He's on too."

"Will do, Captain. We'll keep your camp safe. Not much going on anyways," McFarland said, spitting into his campfire. "I'll have a lantern lit by ten and my shotgun loaded. By the way, when's the next payday around here?"

"As I told you when you signed up, first payday was when we reached Fort Childs. Last payday is in Oregon."

"Assuming we make it," McFarland said.

"You're here to see we do," Andrew said.

"If I have anything to say about it," said McFarland, as he leaned back against the wagon.

And the pair rode on.

~ * ~

The next morning the routine began again. There was a daily rhythm to the wagon train as it moved along, created by the sounds of wood and metal rubbing and banging as the prairie schooners stumbled along dusty ruts in the Oregon Trail. The creak of leather harnesses and saddles and the pop of whips blended with the voices of kids, adults, and animals, along with the sound of a harmonica.

Once it left Fort Childs and crossed the swollen Platte River, the wagon train left behind most living green things—no more island of trees, no more verdant grasses. With the dryness of the plains, whether there was a wind or not, there was always a billowing cloud of dust rising to the sky, stirred up by hundreds of hooves and the feet of humans. The dust could not be avoided and settled on the livestock, the pioneers, and their possessions.

A sea of bandanas, wide-brimmed hats, and flapping bonnets tried to stem the tide of penetrating dust, but to no avail. A little relief would come when the train stopped, briefly, near noon. The pioneers watered their livestock and themselves, chewed on biscuits and jerky, and applied bear grease to overworked wheel hubs.

It would be the end of the travelers' hot 10-to-12-mile journey most days before it made sense to go to the trouble of pouring a bucket of water over their heads. Some would bury their faces in the running waters of a creek or river to clear their eyes, ears, and noses of the dust. Some used the water to rinse their hair and face while others bathed their whole bodies with lye soap and water. Though not every day, women would throw their family's soiled clothes into wash tubs for soaking or against washboards for scrubbing, then hang them out to dry on ropes strung between the stilled wagons.

And the next day it would begin again. The creaking, squeaking cacophony, the swirling dust, the effort to cover up or wash bodies and clothes.

Twenty-seven

Ray Cooper had recommended a friend of his, Walt Toler, as the man for the job of teamster to manage the lead wagon. Walt was added to the train because Andrew needed to be free to ride up and down the line of wagons, for people who needed help and to round up any stray animals. He needed to be free to respond rapidly to any dangers.

Walt was a big mountain of a man who knew how to drive teams of mules, horses, or oxen. He walked beside the six oxen every day, goading the team along. He was handy with a bullwhip, deadly with a range of firearms, and an ardent student of the Bible. Walt was ready to go farther west and found he liked talking with Preacher Crawford of an evening about the scriptures.

Like the preacher, Walt had read the King James version of the Bible from cover to cover. Unlike the preacher, he had the freedom to interpret the meaning of the verses as he chose, without regard to the teachings of a seminary or the doctrine of a particular religious sect.

He had favorite verses, including John 3:16 – *"For God so loved the world that He gave His only Son, that whosoever believeth in Him should not perish, but have everlasting life."*

Walt looked forward to discussing the gospels of the New Testament with Preacher Crawford when their paths crossed, including the talk Nicodemus had with Jesus.

The teamster was a quiet man. He once had a wife and young daughter but four years earlier they had succumbed to influenza while Walt was away on a buffalo hunt with Ray. It had broken his heart.

On this day, after three hours in the growing heat of the day, with the train kicking up a cloud of dust, there developed an occasional light breeze at Walt Toler's back, blowing from east to west, providing minor relief from the temperature. Ray Cooper was out a day ahead, scouting the trail for the next campsite which would have a good supply of water and grasses. Andrew was riding Noah halfway back in the train handing out slices of jerky to children and encouraging them to keep up with their parents.

Walt looked to the north and saw a figure moving toward the trail in the distance. He squinted and realized it was someone toting a bedroll and a sack. As the train and figure got closer, he could see it was a girl. She raised her hand and waved weakly to him and Walt waved back. She dropped her possessions, fell on her face, and stopped moving.

Walt shut down the team of oxen, and all the wagons behind started creaking to a halt. The man grabbed a goat bladder bag of water from below the driver's seat and ran as fast as he could toward the fallen girl. She wasn't moving when he knelt beside her body.

"Hey, girl. Hey. Can you hear me, child?" He turned her over and poured some water on her sunburned head to cool her. Her skin was dry and blistered. Her lips were cracked and scabbed. She opened her eyes and stared blankly at Walt. He began to cry at the sight of her, propped her up against his knee, and poured water into her cupped hands. She sucked at the pool of water and he filled her hands again.

He heard footsteps running toward him and the hoofbeats of Andrew's horse.

Frenchie ran up with some hardtack and a canteen. Andrew dismounted.

"Walt," Andrew said. "What have we got here?"

"I don't know where she came from, Andrew. She's like a little lost fawn and in bad shape. I don't think she can talk, she's so dried out."

Frenchie broke off a piece of hardtack and said, "Give her a bite of this and some more water. Looks like she's been traipsing around for days in this heat."

Mrs. Crawford pulled up in the buckboard. "What is that child doing out here?"

"Let's get her in the wagon," Andrew said, putting the girl's sack and bedroll on the bed of the buckboard.

Billy rode up and dropped the reins of his horse next to the buckboard. The rest of the folks on the wagon train watched and waited to get underway again.

Walt stood, lifted the exhausted girl in his arms, and laid her against the bedroll.

Mrs. Crawford pointed to a pink gingham bonnet blown against some scrub brush. "Billy, that must be her bonnet. Put it on her head for some shade. Give her a bit more water but not too much. Let's see if she can keep it down."

Andrew said, "We need to find out where she came from. She may have a family out somewhere looking for her as we speak."

Walt said, "She came down from the north, best I could tell."

"We've got to get this train moving again," Andrew said. "I've got plenty of daylight left. I'll backtrack her. Billy, get the wagons rolling."

"Yes, sir. She's left a pretty clear trail from here," Billy said. "Of course, she could have been walking in circles."

Andrew said, "Well, I'll see what I can find north of here. It's where the tracks lead. I'll catch up with you before sundown either way."

"Yes, sir. Take extra water in case people are out there dying of thirst. I can't imagine the girl could have traveled very far."

Walt tossed Andrew a bladder of water and the wagon master trotted off, tracking to the north.

"I'm gonna get her a little shade and more water, if she can tolerate it," Mrs. Crawford said. The preacher's wife turned the buckboard back toward the wagon train.

"All right, let's get moving again," Billy said. "Walt, you know you saved this girl's life."

"I'm glad I saw her. I'm sure she understands our kindness. I just hope she can talk soon."

"Her tongue is all swelled up from lack of water," Billy said. "It could be a while before she can talk much. Could be days."

Billy and Walt got the train moving again. Everyone wanted to know about the girl, so Billy explained it to a few people and let the rumor mill roll. He figured the news would take folks' minds off the heat for a spell.

Andrew followed the girl's footprints northward for an hour, and he saw buzzards circling in the distance. He figured in one hour on horseback he had covered the path she walked in a whole day, maybe two. Who knew how long it took her to decide to look for help. In one more hour, he crossed a dried-up creek bed, passed a masa, and then stopped at the start of a playa. He looked across the flat, dried-up land and saw buzzards gathered on the ground near the remains of a burned-out wagon.

The canvas cover had turned to ash and blown away except for a tattered strip hanging onto one of the hooped bows. Before approaching the crippled wagon, Andrew kept his hand on the butt of his pistol while he scanned the horizon, looking for signs of life or silhouettes of riders who could be a threat. Then he dismounted.

He walked his horse toward the burned prairie schooner. Everything was charred and ruined. When he walked to the far side of the wagon, he found the dead bodies of a man and a young boy. The buzzards gathered there took flight. A pistol and a broken shotgun lay nearby. A dusty rag doll lay next to the wagon. A woman's gingham bonnet was caught in a stand of grass nearby, the same pink fabric used for the girl's bonnet.

There was nothing left of the food or possessions on the wagon except a broken chest of drawers. The wagon's front axle was split and an unburned wheel lay on the ground. Andrew could see the impressions of several sets of horseshoes. Maybe some raiders or other desperate travelers who had already moved on.

He piled the decaying, swollen bodies together, laid dried grass and the wagon wheel on top, and set the pyre on fire. He knelt on one knee and said a prayer, asking God to save their souls and to protect the girl.

Andrew put the rag doll and the bonnet in his saddlebags and headed back south. The mother was missing. No telling how long the young girl sat there by her father, waiting for him to get up and take care of her, waiting for her brother to get up and play a game. The desperation of starvation and thirst finally convinced her to seek help or die.

~ * ~

A few days later, Rachel and Claudine were dishing out a dinner of fried fish, rice, and canned peaches for themselves and Daniel as Andrew walked by.

"There's some extra for you, Andrew, if you like," Rachel said.

"Oh, I think Frenchie is cooking dinner as we speak. Not sure what. Where'd you get the fish?"

"I caught 'em in my net," Daniel chirped. "Five fat bream."

"Well, good for you, little soldier. It smells good. And are those peaches," Andrew said. "I may be planning to eat at the wrong table, if we had a table."

Rachel spooned a bite of each item onto a tin plate and handed it to Andrew.

"Thank you," he said.

"Claudine and I put up the fruit last summer," she said.

Claudine said, "We can use the empty jars for drinking glasses."

"Or I can use 'em to hold fireflies or frogs," Daniel said.

"So," Andrew said, "Daniel, have you ever been frog gigging?"

"No. What is it?" Daniel said.

Rachel said, "Andrew, I'm not sure ..."

Andrew said, "We can go frog hunting sometime, Daniel."

Rachel said, "We used to buy them from some men in New Orleans, for the restaurant."

"Oh, good. Then it would be okay to take him out some night?" Andrew said.

"It's very different from buying frog legs already in a bag," Rachel said, "It isn't the thing for Daniel to do, Andrew."

Andrew stopped talking and looked at Rachel as if waiting for her permission to continue. She was getting used to saying his first name, instead of saying Captain Greene or captain. Since her revelation about her missing husband, she felt more at ease in addressing him as Andrew, partly because he had been her escort for most occasions from the beginning of the journey, but mostly because she poured out her heart about being abandoned. Revealing one of her deepest secrets to him had brought them closer together, eventually, with the passage of the last few days.

Daniel said, "Momma, can I do it?"

"Let's wait, sweetheart. That type of thing is done late at night, and it would be way past your time to be in bed."

"But I'll be with the captain."

"Let me think about it. In a little while you need to wash up the dishes and get ready for bedtime."

"Yes, ma'am," Daniel said. Later when he gathered the plates, he looked at Andrew and nodded his continued interest in frog gigging.

~ * ~

By the time Andrew got back to the cook wagon, Frenchie was doling out ladles of stew onto plates for the three ex-soldiers, plus Billy, Walt, and Ray.

"Good thing you're back," Frenchie said. "I saved a few servings."

"What are we having tonight?" Andrew said.

"It's a mix of potatoes, carrots and meat."

"And the meat is...?"

"You're getting awful picky in your old age," Frenchie said.

Ray said, "It's prairie dog and rabbit. All fresh."

Billy said, "Tastes good. Where were you, Cap'n?"

"Walking around camp."

Frenchie said, "What was Rachel serving tonight?"

"I got a bite of fish and peaches, thank you, Frenchie. But this tastes good too. Even if it is made of varmints."

McFarland said to the other ex-soldiers, "It's our turn to wash up tonight. Make sure the kettle of water is boiling good when you put things in."

Andrew said, "McFarland, how's Jit working out for you since Quinn disappeared?"

"The horse told me he wants to race your Appaloosa again when you get permission from Preacher Crawford," McFarland said.

All the men chuckled and looked at Andrew expectantly.

"That could be a while," Andrew said to a few moans from the men. "Maybe when we get to Fort Laramie. Just keep any bets quiet and make it a clean race. Not like last time."

Andrew finished his dinner and looked back down the trail. In the distance, for the second night in a row, he could see the flicker of a small campfire.

Even before Frenchie started breakfast the next morning, Andrew rode Noah eastward, back down the trail. He had to satisfy his curiosity about the mysterious campfire.

Stirred up by the hooves of his ambling horse, dust followed a lone rider along the Oregon Trail, his back to the rising sun. A shadow cast ahead of him. A hawk circled overhead hunting for movements of small prey as its next meal—nature's way, survival of the fittest.

Gripping his pistol, Andrew rode Noah out from behind a mesa. "Hold on there," he said to the rider whom he recognized.

Quinn halted the nag and moved his hand toward his gun.

"Hold on, I said, or I'll drop you where you are," Andrew said.

Quinn rested his hand on the cantle of his saddle. "Might of knowed it was you."

"I've seen your fire the last two nights."

"Mmmm."

"I'm surprised you made it across the Platte," Andrew said.

"Floated on a log, washed up not far from that bear cub."

"So, you saw."

"From a distance. Kept low."

"Thanks for the help."

"I lost my guns."

"Looks like you found some."

"Some fool broke his neck falling off this old horse. Figured I could use his possessions."

"Remember what you did?"

"Not real sure. I was probly drunk as a skunk." Quinn coughed and spit on the ground.

"Bad business." Andrew kept his pistol aimed at Quinn.

"That explains the lead in my gut and knife wounds in my back," Quinn said.

"Well, I have to say you are tough to be so stupid."

"We gonna' have a problem?"

"You hurt that young woman."

"Which one?"

"The one you tried to rape."

"Oh...was that the little French thing."

"You're a pretty sorry fella."

"If it makes you happy, I don't feel so good," Quinn said. "Gut shot. Fever and all. Hungry. Ain't et nothin' but snake. Could use a shot of whiskey."

"Reckon I need to take you in." Noah took a step forward and Andrew pulled on the reins.

"Ain't no jail around here, Captain. Or is it sheriff?"

"There's a jail back at the fort."

"I don't think so."

Quinn drew his pistol fast and fired a bullet toward Andrew.

Andrew already had the drop on Quinn and fired a shot into his chest.

Quinn fired a second errant shot. A bullet to nowhere.

A second bullet from Andrew's pistol found Quinn's chest again, and the rider fell to the ground dead. Echoes from the shots faded away and clouds of gun smoke floated on the wind. The hawk screeched from above.

By the time Billy rode up, Andrew had slung Quinn's body across the saddle on the nag. "I thought I heard shots," Billy said.

"He resisted arrest."

"Wish I'd been here."

"Not up to you," Andrew said.

"So you say."

"Better this way."

"You're the sheriff."

"His wounds were infected. I don't think he had long to live anyway and he knew it. We ought to take him up to the train, so folks will see justice has been done."

"That's fair. Claudine will rest easier knowing he's gone."

"Doubt she'll like it, but it's the thing to do. We'll bury him alongside the trail."

Twenty-eight

Late-afternoon temperatures were tolerable. Brief rain showers dampened the trail dust, and later white clouds drifted overhead. Walt goaded two pairs of oxen pulling the lead wagon. A spare pair of yoked oxen walked right behind the wagon. Walt was the first to spot the outline of two men on horseback when they crested a hill at least a quarter of a mile in the distance. They rode easily toward the train with the sun at their back. Walt grabbed a long pole with a red flag attached to one end, waved it to the left of the wagon and left it hanging from the seat until Billy rode up.

"What is it, Walt?" Billy said, matching the gait of his horse to the speed of the wagon.

"Some riders comin' up ahead."

Billy glanced up the trail. "I'll let the captain know. Keep looking and keep your weapon handy." He reined his horse back to find Andrew.

It was rare to run into folks headed east on the Oregon Trail, especially this time of year. Well before the two riders could reach the wagons, Andrew made sure the three ex-soldiers were on alert. Billy cautioned the rest of the travelers to have their weapons at hand. The leaders would assume the two riders were friendly until proven otherwise, but it paid to be cautious.

Andrew and Billy rode up a ways to intercept the riders. The purpose was to keep the wagon train moving while the riders were met and evaluated. One of the riders had a long black beard. The other one had a thin red moustache. They were both wearing side arms and had rifles tucked into scabbards on their saddles. The men's rough clothes looked like they had been on the trail for some time.

"Howdy, mister," the black-bearded man called, bringing his horse to a halt and looking at Andrew. The mustachioed rider stopped as well and leaned forward, resting his arms on the pommel of his saddle.

"Stranger," Andrew called back, "who am I addressing?"

"I'm Pete Burrows," the bearded man said, "and this here's Otis Jones. We're just a couple of Jayhawks working along the trail as needed, headed to Saint Jo or Independence. Figure we can sign on with one of the wagon trains as scouts. We know the territory pretty well."

"Good to meet you. I'm Captain Greene, and this is my right hand man, Billy Armstrong." The rattling noises of the passing wagons reminded Andrew to keep things moving.

Burrows said, "There's some good water up ahead a few miles over the hills. We passed your scout, the man with the Sharps rifle."

"Ray Cooper," Billy said.

Jones said, "Yeah, he may be up there waitin' for ya—just past the water. Looks like ya got a fine little wagon train of folks. How long you been on the trail?"

"About forty-five days," Billy said.

"Headed to Utah, are you?" Burrows said. looking at Andrew.

"No. On to Oregon," Andrew said.

"Well, we best move on," Burrows said, and the men tapped their boot heels into the sides of their horses to urge them on.

"Nice to meet ya. Have a good trip," Jones said.

Andrew and Billy gave a nod and touched the brims of their hats as the duo rode past the train.

"Seem like decent folks," Billy said.

Andrew said, "Could be. You know the bearded fella looks familiar."

"You met him before?"

"Not sure, I can't figure it out yet."

Billy waved at Claudine as she walked past. She was followed by three chattering children along with Daniel. Her shotgun was strapped across her back.

Andrew dismounted and knelt, looking at the hoof prints left by the visitors' horses. "Look at this, Billy."

"What is it, Cap'n?"

"The dirt is soft enough to get a good imprint of their hooves. Look at this one. It's the front right."

"I see it. There's a little chunk out of the shoe."

"Shaped like a V."

"Yeah."

"When I tracked down the lost girl's family and found their wagon, there were lots of hoof prints. Shod and not shod."

"Un huh."

"And I saw the same V in the ground around the wagon and those dead bodies."

Billy said, "So, it's the same horse?"

"Seems like the same horse."

"There's probably lots of chipped hooves and shoes out there."

"Could be, but it was the front right shoe back there too."

Billy and Andrew stood and looked to the east after the last wagon passed. The riders had disappeared.

Andrew said, "Did you notice while black beard was going on about their work plans the other one was staring at the train?"

"Well, sort of. Now you mention it."

"I think he was counting."

Billy said, "The wagons?"

"And the number of men."

"So, they were sizing us up? What are they up to?"

"That's it, Billy. The bearded man. That's it. His face was on a wanted poster back in St. Joseph. I saw it when I was tacking up bulletins."

Billy frowned. "You think Ray's all right?"

"Damn."

Earlier than the usual stopping time, and before reaching the hill ahead, Andrew said, "Circle 'em up and let's camp here tonight."

Billy blew five short blasts on his bugle—a signal for everyone to start making the circle. Walt responded by guiding the lead wagon off the trail to the right and making a broad arc through the scrub brush. There was a slight rise to the land toward the west, and there would be plenty of room for the pioneers to pitch their tents on the perimeter.

Frenchie steered the cook wagon around to the left and halted the team as it met the lead wagon head on. The remaining wagons split to the right and left, completing the circle. The herdsman moved his thirty head of cattle. He and his drovers would settle the herd downwind from the camp.

The last rays of the sun disappeared below the horizon. On his rounds, Andrew saw Emily Crawford shaking out a blanket as he passed by. Preacher Crawford, reading his Bible, looked up and nodded.

Andrew said, "Has the girl we found talked yet?"

"No," Emily said. "But she's eating and drinking regularly. Good enough for now. She's in the tent lying down. We're calling her Cathy."

It had been three days. The girl, found wandering beside the trail, had endured the loss of her family. Everyone waited for the traumatized waif to find her voice.

"Have you tried a different language?" Andrew said.

"A little French and Spanish. It's all we know. Nothing yet. She may be so overcome she can't speak yet."

"Should we take her back to Fort Childs and let the Army figure things out?" Andrew said.

"I don't know. She's very dear and shy. Should she go through another change?" Emily said.

"You and the preacher want to keep her?"

"Don't know. That's a big conversation. Big decision."

"Let's settle on something by the time we get to the next fort."

"How far?"

"Fort Laramie. About three weeks," he said, walking on, leading Noah.

"We'll see how she's doing. And how the preacher and I are doing."

"That ought to do it," Billy said.

"Okay, and I've got a mission for you," Andrew said. "But let's go talk to Frenchie."

~ * ~

"So, what's your plan, Andrew?" Frenchie said, as he turned a team of oxen into the corral.

Andrew said, "I figure Billy and I will walk ahead after dark and see if there's a gang up there."

Billy said, "Campfires and such. We don't know where Ray is. They may have him."

Frenchie said, "So, let me understand this. Based on a passing conversation with the bearded guy, who says he's headed to Missouri, you recollect he's really a wanted outlaw based on a sheriff's poster you sort of remember seeing back in St. Joseph?"

Billy said, "Well, if you say it like that..."

"... Yes, Frenchie," Andrew said, "his partner was counting our wagons and guns as we rode by."

"Andrew's right, Frenchie. I saw it too," Billy said.

"Wait while I catch up to your thinking, Andrew," Frenchie said. "What are you going to do if there is a gang, and they have twenty or thirty desperados waiting for you to sneak up on 'em?"

"It's reconnaissance," Andrew said.

"And who will you report back to? Yourself?" Frenchie said.

Andrew put his hands on his hips. "Well, we can sit here and wonder if there's a gang coming over the rise tonight, or we can take a walk and count some heads. And we need to find out if they have captured Ray."

"They knew about his rifle," Billy said.

"So, what do you want me to do, Andrew? Wait till I see you two high tailing it back here with twenty riders chasing you?"

"That's why we are here to talk to you. We want to figure out the best defense for the camp. If they've got Ray, we have to get him out to safety first, or they'll use him as a hostage and make demands."

Frenchie stroked his beard. "You think the two men who came by returned up ahead someway?"

"Probably."

"We need to figure out which direction to place our lookouts and to aim our weapons," Frenchie said.

"You're in agreement then?" Andrew said.

"Yes, if you think we're going to be attacked, we need to make sure what we're dealing with. If you find out there's a small army, say, thirty gunmen coming at us, it would be better to get a rider to the closest fort and get an army of our own out here."

"I don't think we have time," Andrew said, "because Fort Childs is thirty miles behind us. It would take almost eight hours to get there, organize a troop, and get back here. If we're lucky."

"That's better than not having them at all," Frenchie said. "We can probably hold off a gang for a while. It sort of depends on when we send a rider and when you stir up the hornet's nest which may be over the hill."

"And if there even needs to be a fight," Billy said.

Andrew said, "We need a good rider with the freshest horse." Both men looked at Billy.

"I thought I was going with you up the trail."

"Change of plans," said Andrew.

"Captain, you know I'll do what's needed," Billy said. "I'll ride all night."

Frenchie said, "Before anybody rides anywhere, we need to know what we've got on our hands. If it's a gang. If they've got Ray. How many guns and men ..."

"I know, of course." Andrew nodded. "So, as I said earlier, Billy and I are walking over the hill a couple of miles on reconnaissance."

Frenchie said, "Just in case you do come running back with a gang of outlaws on your tail, I'll get Walt and those ex-soldiers ready."

"Plus the two sentries," Andrew said.

"May as well get everyone ready," Frenchie said, "and hide the women and children. And, by the way, you know Rachel Richards is a good shot."

"And Claudine and the boy," Billy said.

"Keep the boy out of it," Andrew said.

Frenchie said, "I reckon you two should tell those two you're leaving."

"What does that mean?" Andrew asked.

"I got eyes. So does the whole camp," Frenchie said.

"Captain, we were already invited for dinner," Billy said. "I forgot to tell you."

Andrew looked at Billy and then at Frenchie.

"You know, you either do something or don't," Frenchie said. "Hoverin' in the air don't do anybody any good."

Andrew and Billy rode up to the sisters' wagon. Claudine was stirring a pot over a campfire and placing hot coals atop a Dutch oven while Rachel and Daniel were cutting up carrots and potatoes. "Here's our company," she said to her sister and nephew.

"Evenin', Claudine," Billy said, dismounting and removing his hat. He kissed her.

"*Bon soir, ma chere.*" She hugged him. "Good to see you, but dinner will not be until later."

"Evening, ladies, Daniel," Andrew said as he dropped Noah's reins.

"Hey, Captain," Daniel said, "look at all the carrots Ma and I chopped."

Andrew said, "It all looks good, but we need to postpone our dinner plans till another time."

Rachel put down her knife. "Andrew, the camp seems to be stirring. What's that all about?"

"Well, I'm not sure yet. Billy and I are going ahead soon and trying to get an answer for you."

"Is that why Mrs. Crawford is rushing over this way?" Rachel said.

Andrew turned around as Mrs. Crawford passed in front of the fire.

"Andrew, I need to talk to you right now," she said, pulling him away from the others. Rachel followed them to the back of the wagon.

"I must tell you, as those two men rode by our wagon our orphaned little girl almost knocked me over trying to burrow into my arms. She was pale all of a sudden, trembling, and buried her head in my chest."

Andrew said, "I knew it. I bet she recognized them from the attack on her own family."

"That's what I figured. She still can't or won't speak, but I think that's the reason." Mrs. Crawford headed back to her wagon.

"What's this about?" Rachel said, touching Andrew's arm.

"It's why Billy and I have to go up the trail now. We think there's a gang a few miles ahead. Up to no good. May have Ray."

"Oh, no." Rachel said, putting her hand over her mouth. "So, what are you going to do? The two of you? Arrest them?"

"No, nothing like that. We need to find out what we may be up against."

"Andrew, I'm tired of guessing. Tell me."

"We are just asking each wagon to have their weapons handy and to keep their children close."

"Because ..."

"What I just said. There may be a gang over the hill."

"Coming to kill us all?" Rachel said.

"I wouldn't say that," he said.

"You don't seem to be saying any of it."

"My apologies. You three have been through a lot, and I didn't want you to be overly concerned," Andrew said.

With her face close to his, Rachel said, "So, your message is to just have our guns ready in case we're attacked in the next few hours by outlaws who will butcher and burn us all out. Is that the message?"

"You know, sometimes I find it difficult to have a conversation with you."

"Maybe there's a problem with the language you use."

"What?"

"For a man of your rank and experience, I expect more."

"Well, this is all I got for you tonight," Andrew said.

He turned to go to his horse and get Billy when Rachel pulled him back. She put her arms around his neck and spoke into his surprised face.

"I'm sorry," she said. "You can wear me out. It's only been some six weeks, but I feel like I've known you for a long time, and I don't want my new good friend to get hurt trying to take care of everyone but himself. Do you understand me?" A tear ran down her cheek.

"I do," he said and put his arms around her, pulled her into him and kissed her for the first time—for a long time.

Then Andrew and Billy turned and began their walk by the light of a quarter moon and stars. They took their pistols, knives, and carbines but left their canteens and anything else liable to make a clanking noise.

Two miles later they knelt behind a stand of mesquite shrubs.

"Stay low," Andrew said.

"I can see a campfire from here," Billy whispered.

"We're downwind. Their horses won't smell us for a while. Let's take a minute to look. See if you can find any signs of Ray."

"You see the three men near the fire?"

"Yep, let's move a little closer and to the right," Andrew said.

Billy nodded and followed Andrew toward a boulder at the base of a butte leading into the narrow canyon. They froze when they heard footsteps crossing a layer of shale and heard voices.

One of the strangers said, "… and they all looked good to me. But we can give Barney the oldest one. He won't care." Both of the strangers chuckled.

"There's bound to be cash in that lead wagon. Hey, gimme that bottle again. Don't go hoggin' it."

"We got a half case left."

"George is making some kind of spoon bread for dessert. Should be ready 'bout now."

"I don't wanna miss that, and tomorrow's gonna be a good day. I wanna try out that Sharps, once they're in the valley."

"Did you see that redhead?" … and the voices and the footsteps faded away across the shifting shale toward the campfire.

Andrew looked at Billy.

"Did you hear?"

"The Sharps?"

"They got Ray somewhere."

"Or at least his rifle."

"We don't know enough yet. We need a head count and have to find Ray."

"Got to get closer."

"We can't ride into this tomorrow. They know we're coming."

Andrew and Billy worked their way around the boulder, bypassing the shale field.

Andrew whispered, "They want a lot more than our money and horses."

"Some bad business. We gotta find Ray."

"And that Sharps."

"Tonight?"

"Damn right."

For the next half hour, they watched the group of men around the campfire. Counted six, standing or sitting. All drinking from jugs or bottles. A man sat on a barrel next to a two-man tent, holding a shotgun across his lap.

There were three more tents and campfires visible past the main campfire.

Billy said, "Hard to be sure how many we got to deal with."

"My guess is four men per tent, except for the big one—sleeps six—so maybe twenty."

"About even then."

"Except these are all killers," Andrew said. "Where are their horses?"

"Must be way past the tents."

"Let's circle around. See how many horses they got."

"Did you see? Two of the men have passed out on the ground."

"Good time to move."

The pair took three steps and the outlaw on the barrel suddenly looked up in their direction. Billy and Andrew froze then lay on their bellies. It could have been their shadows moving in the dim light caught the guard's attention, or their eyes reflecting flames from the fire.

Sliding off the barrel and walking toward the fire, the guard bent over and talked to his black-bearded leader who handed him a half-empty bottle.

As the guard turned around to walk back to his barrel, Billy and Andrew rose and moved across the trail. They found a rope corral with twenty horses. There was no sentry.

Andrew said, "That's Ray's horse at the end. Once I get Ray and his rifle out of there, cut all these horses loose."

"How's that now?"

"Ray's got to be tied up in the small tent where the guard's posted."

"Wait a minute, Cap'n. That'll stir up the whole camp. There'll be twenty men coming for us."

"Sleepy, drunk, and on foot," Andrew said.

"You know you got to get past that guard."

"Then there'll be nineteen left. Better save some of those horses for us," Andrew said over his shoulder and disappeared back toward the campfire.

Two minutes later, a knife slit the back of the tent and Andrew stuck in his head.

"I been waitin' for you," whispered Ray Cooper, "cut these damn ropes, will ya."

"Where's your rifle?"

"Doesn't matter. Only one bullet anyway. I tossed the rest in the barrel that idiot's sittin' on."

~ * ~

Twenty minutes later, Frenchie heard horses coming, lots of horses in the night. He could barely make out three riders at the front.

"McFarland, you ready?" Frenchie yelled.

"I see 'em. I'll take the one on the right. You shoot the middle one. Walt, take the one on the left.

"Hold your fire!" Frenchie shouted. "Hold your fire. It's the captain."

Billy had tied six horses together and scattered the rest.

"Thanks for not shootin' us," Billy said.

"Who's strapped across the horse?" Frenchie said.

"A bonus. He's been throwing up," Andrew said.

"There still a bunch up there?" Billy said.

"They're not going to like it when they wake up," Andrew said.

Twenty-nine

It was six the next morning. The camp was just starting to stir when Emily Crawford heard someone coming and looked out of the tent.

"Mrs. Crawford, he's missing, I tell you. I don't know where he is. I think he's run away." Ella was in a state. Her face was red from running.

Mrs. Crawford stepped out of the tent. She sat Ella down on a stool. "Stop now, Ella, and tell me what you're talking about. And where are your parents?"

"James is gone and so is his old mule. Momma and Daddy are still sleeping. I think he's left me. Just doesn't want me or the baby anymore. I'm beside myself," Ella said.

Preacher Crawford called from inside the tent, "Emily, is everything all right?"

Emily talked toward the tent. "You best go ahead and get ready for the day, Horatio." Then she turned toward Ella. "Maybe he's out looking for game or something."

"No. It can't be. He would have left me a note. He always tells me or leaves me a note if he goes off anywhere. This morning I reached out for him and he wasn't there. I just tossed off the covers and came to see you, because I don't want my parents to find out. You know how my daddy is."

Most other folks were getting out of their tents, shaking out blankets, or building fires to cook breakfast when Billy blew his bugle.

"Let's go back to your wagon, Ella. It's good to let your parents know what's going on. Nothing's for sure yet. I'm sure James will show up. He loves you so." The two women walked toward the Andersons' wagon.

They walked past Frenchie, who was putting a coffee pot over a fire. "Mornin', ladies," he said.

Emily said, "We may need Andrew."

"He was up late last night with the gang leader he captured, so he's sleepin' in a little I 'spect," Frenchie said.

"I'll let you know." Emily and Ella walked on.

The Andersons were up and worried by the time Ella and Emily arrived at the wagon. After another search of the rumpled covers used for Ella's and James's bedding, Ella found a note on a piece of paper. It read: "Gone for cavalry. Love, James."

A half hour later, the whereabouts of James was clear. He and a platoon of cavalry were seen coming from the east by Billy, who alerted Andrew.

By seven, hungover gang members realized their boss had disappeared, they were mostly horseless, and they were surrounded by cavalry. The discovery didn't stop the outlaw with a thin red moustache from raising his rifle and getting shot by a trooper. Silhouettes of cavalrymen in every direction were enough for the fifteen remaining members to raise their hands in surrender.

The cavalry faced the task of tying up each outlaw and rounding up a mount for each criminal before hauling them to the next fort for prosecution.

"Thanks for your help finding their horses," Lieutenant Ingram said.

"It's the least we could do," Andrew said. He slapped his broad brim hat against his leg, letting loose a puff of dust.

"I need to let you know something," said Ingram.

"What?"

"In one of the tents we found a woman. Says she's about four months pregnant and has been a captive for almost a year after her wagon broke down."

Andrew shook his head. "Those bastards."

"She's been beaten up. Got bruises and a black eye."

Andrew winced. "Can you take her to the next fort? There's not much we can do for her here."

"Best thing, I reckon," the lieutenant said. "The gang's been having their way with her. She's pretty addled. Can't blame her for being a bit crazy. She saw them kill her whole family."

"One of our people is a midwife and nurse. Does the woman need to see her?"

"The doc at the fort can see to her, but she does have a cut. It needs tending. So yes, sir. She could use some patching up before we leave. Probably good to let her talk to another woman anyway. She could use a bath too."

"All our people are thankful for you getting here in time."

"The Kincaid boy rode all night to get us. Seems like a hero to me."

"We thought he ran off until his wife found a note he left behind. If you'll take the woman to the tent near the buckboard, I'll let Mrs. Crawford know you're coming."

"But that ain't all," the lieutenant said. "My sergeant said there's a second woman from the same tent, a little hard to understand. She was hogtied and half naked when he found her.

He cut her loose and gave her some privacy to put on her clothes. He thinks she speaks something like German and some English, maybe Amish. Sounds like she's been held for a week or so. She's got bruises on her arms and legs."

"Can you take her to the fort too?"

"Yes, sir. I reckon she should see your medicine woman too, though. She's been roughed up, you know, by several of those men."

"They should all be hung, if you ask me."

"Yes, sir, but we'll have to see what the commander and courts have to say. We can take both of them to the fort, if they're okay to travel tomorrow."

The two freed women were escorted by troopers to the camp and on toward the Crawfords' tent. The women were something to stare at by the folks on the wagon train and gossip whispers started flying. Emily and Rachel were waiting for them and aware of their problems.

The preacher and the mute girl they had found along the trail and named 'Cathy' were near the buckboard. Cathy was holding a bucket of feed for one of the horses but when she saw the women, she dropped the bucket and ran screaming toward them.

She said something for the first time, "Momma!" Both the woman in a calico dress and the girl cried and fell into each other's arms.

That night, it may have been exhaustion from lack of sleep or stress catching up with him, but after dinner it was happening again. Andrew was missing the taste of whiskey. He knew McFarland would have a bottle handy and went to visit the ornery sentry.

"Cap'n." McFarland said offering a half-empty bottle to Andrew. "You're always welcome. Rest your bones."

"Thanks." Andrew sat down on a barrel. "I figured you'd have a bottle or two going around."

McFarland pointed over his shoulder. "I got a case packed in a bed of straw and boxed up. Better than gold out here."

Andrew tossed a small bag of dried meat to McFarland. "Here's some bison jerky to go with it."

McFarland uncorked another bottle. "Shaughnessy and Duff are on sentry tonight, so I'm glad to have the company. Let's drink to the end of the gang and to the cavalry."

"And to better days ahead." Andrew nodded. The men carefully tapped their bottles together. "Not that I would have *minded* shootin' a few of 'em."

McFarland took another drink and leaned back against a wagon wheel. "Yep. I reckon. You know I been hearin' more 'bout gold in California."

"That so?"

"Reckon me and the boys will head down there after we git you all to Oregon. I think we could use a man like Billy too."

"I don't know about that."

"I talked to him earlier. Seems interested. Good way to make a fortune."

Andrew drank from his bottle of whiskey. The pair could hear coyotes screaming to each other in the darkness.

"I wonder if those coyotes are going to spook all the cattle," Andrew said.

McFarland shook loose tobacco into a white cigarette paper, licked the edge, and rolled it up. He struck a match across his pant leg and lit the fag. "Did you hear 'bout one of the wranglers who fell off his horse the other day?"

"No."

"He was worn out. Fell asleep. Wound up in the dirt."

"I've seen that happen before, including myself, during the Seminole war. Not enough time to rest with all the troop movements and attacks waiting 'round every bend."

"The trail boss let him lie there for a few minutes, gettin' forty winks. Then nudged him awake and off they went."

"Lucky he didn't break his neck or something," Andrew said.

A light breeze rolled through the camp and McFarland tossed a handful of buffalo chips on the campfire and puffed on his cigarette.

"I sort of miss my buddy Quinn," McFarland said.

"A sorry outcome. You know it was him or me."

"Sounded like he was a goner anyway."

Andrew lit his clay pipe. "The wounds were infected. Looked bad."

"Did you ever hear how Quinn lost his fingers?"

Andrew looked from McFarland to the flames in the fire and shook his head. "No."

"It weren't long ago, during the Mexican war, 'bout two years now."

"In a battle?"

"Naw, but it could uh been. I saw it happen from a distance after we won a battle, but before I could do anything. Quinn had a habit of wanderin' off sometimes. After a battle or durin'. That particular day I saw him ride off toward one of them walled-off haciendas. Some kind of fancy estate. Figured he was lookin' to pilfer anything he could carry. 'Bout then I had to round up my other men, get some help for a few wounded, and all. You know."

"Un-huh," Andrew grunted and took another sip of whiskey.

"So, then I go lookin' for Quinn 'cause we needed a head count. He might'a been in some trouble by then, I figured." McFarland inhaled smoke and blew it out. "So, I come up to a little rise and can see over the wall surroundin' the villa and there's Quinn. He's got some woman down on the brick patio outside the house. She's strugglin' and he's on her. I see him slug her, and I start ridin' to stop him, but just then I see this Mexican officer, a general it turned out, ridin' like the wind on a black horse."

Andrew shook his head slowly and pursed his lips. "Quinn had a bad habit."

"So, Quinn's pullin' up his pants and finally sees the general galloping toward him and waving a sword. I can't do anythin' but I'm whippin' my horse to get there. Quinn picks up a pistol and fires it at the Mexican just as the sword swings down on him. Quinn tried to get out of the way, but the general's sword caught those two fingers. By the time I get there, the general's dead, and Quinn's cryin' 'bout his fingers. I wrapped a bandana tight on his wrist to stop the blood. The woman run in the house.

"I figured she's gettin' a gun or somethin', so I help Quinn up on the black and we get out of there. I left him with the camp doc and returned to my regiment. The next day I see Quinn and his hand's bandaged up and he's ridin' the horse. He named it Jit."

McFarland took a drink and set a deck of cards on a barrel between the two. "You want to play Brag or somethin'?"

"All right," Andrew said, taking another drink.

McFarland dealt the cards and won the first two hands. The more they played and drank, the more McFarland won.

"You know," McFarland said. "Seems you and Rachel are gettin' mighty cozy."

Andrew stared at McFarland. "I don't know it's any of your business."

"Just sayin'."

Andrew finished his bottle of whiskey and set it down.

McFarland continued, "I fancy the woman myself. Just don't know where you are with her."

Irked, Andrew said, "Reckon I'm through for the night here." He stood up a little wobbly. "And jus' to be clear, I have my own plans for her and me. So it'd be good for you to try fishing in a different pond."

"That's why I'm askin'."

"And good night to you, sir."

"Come agin'."

Andrew walked back to his own tent and crawled in. He was ready to return to his dreams.

Thirty

After the outlaw gang surrenered to the cavalry, Emily Crawford treated the woman's wounds and tried to soothe her mind. At Fort Laramie, the desperate woman would have to decided her bleak future. Reunited, Cathy and her rescued mother were headed to the fort as well.

It had been two days since Andrew kissed Rachel when he dared to show his affection, on the verge of his foray into the night to uncover the gang. It was when he had to protect the safety of the wagon train and its remaining seventy-eight souls. The train had lost little Jackie Vonschoff to cholera. It lost ex-soldier and rapist Donald Quinn to a bullet from Andrew's gun.

Now Andrew had to continue to lead the train and its precious human cargo safely to Oregon. He knew he could only do it one day at a time, one incident at a time. He rode among the stirring pioneers. He encouraged them to get packed, hitched up, and on their way for another twelve of the 2,000 mile trek.

Those same two days were part of the same routine of walking under a hot sun and dealing with dust. Rachel was packing her wagon and saw Andrew coming. He had just helped the Andersons load their wagon and was making his way toward her. She was waiting her turn after breakfast, stowing a griddle in the back of the wagon.

"You all about ready to get underway?" Andrew said.

Rachel shook dust out of a blanket. "I think you don't listen to me when I talk to you." It wasn't how she meant to start the conversation but, once said, it was out. She had two days of built-up thinking, tossing and turning to set free. Two days of listening to her heart and its desires and fears.

Andrew looked down on Rachel from Noah, stopped, and stepped to the ground. "I'm here," he said. He could tell by her words and tone he had at least one problem.

"Do you know what I'm talking about?" Rachel said, staring into his eyes.

"Probably not. Would you like to walk?" Andrew let the reins fall from his horse and reached for Rachel's hand, but she pulled away.

"I'm talking about the horse, Paint, for my son," Rachel said. She thought, *who is Andrew to give a gift to my boy? What does he expect in return?*

"The horse again?" Andrew said, his voice rising. "Daniel needs it. He can't ride the cow."

Andrew collapsed a cooled iron tripod from over Rachel's doused campfire and stored it in the back of the wagon.

"The idea of a night frog hunt," Rachel said. *Didn't he have enough to do without taking my son on some misadventure? Was it even safe at night to go anywhere?*

"It would be fun. It was just a suggestion anyway. Something he might find entertaining."

From in front of the wagon, Claudine waved at Andrew. She and Daniel were pushing their yoked ox teams into place. Andrew waved back.

"He's eight," Rachel said.

Andrew returned his gaze to Rachel. "He's a pioneer." They dodged a neighbor's draft team being goaded toward one of the wagons.

"And I want you to tell Billy to be careful with Claudine," Rachel said quietly.

"I thought we were talking about Daniel," Andrew said.

"Not now."

"Careful about what?"

A few other travelers seemed to be listening but turned away when Andrew looked around.

"Her feelings," Rachel said.

"She seems fine."

They started walking past other families who were packing wagons.

"Tell him anyway."

"I did already, at the beginning. I told Billy we've got five or six months together and don't break any hearts."

Rachel stopped, put her hands on her hips. "So, you knew what he's like to start with?"

"I told myself the same thing."

"About Claudine?"

"About no one in particular. And do you know what your sister's like?" *He thought of Claudine's French accent, her outgoing spirit, and of Billy's fascination.*

"She's friendly," Rachel said.

Andrew's eyebrows arched. "All the men like her, but of course nothing wrong with being friendly. They like how she walks and talks."

"Sometimes to a fault," Rachel said.

"Unguarded," he said.

"Don't blame her." Like a mother hen, Rachel wanted to protect not only her son but her younger sister.

"I'm not blaming anyone for anything, and Billy is just a young man."

"Like all young men?" Rachel said. She knew Claudine was headstrong, enjoyed using her feminine wiles, and was infatuated with the attention Billy showed her.

"Better than most," he said.

"She's got big ideas."

"I don't know about that ... so, what do you want me to do? Tell him to stop now before it goes further?"

"For the best."

"That's what Claudine wants?" Andrew said. He pushed back his hat.

"It's what's best."

He wasn't going to let that stand and was still trying to figure out what was happening. "So, has she complained?"

"No. I see it in her."

"A complaint?" he said.

"She's too friendly," she said.

"Maybe you should talk to *her*." Andrew was getting frustrated trying to keep up with the conversation and get the train moving. He felt like he was watching a town of prairie dogs popping out of their holes. He didn't know which animal would jump up next.

"I know what's best," she said.

"I don't like to get between people."

"I'm not happy." She blew away a fly and kept her lips set in a frown.

"Who's supposed to be happy?" His wrinkled brow betrayed his concern.

"What?" she said.

"You, Billy, Claudine, Daniel?" He knew it wasn't him.

They circled back to the side of Rachel's wagon, away from Claudine and Daniel.

"Where have you been?" Rachel asked, shaking her head. She finally got to the point. What her heart wanted her head to say, to ask, no matter the answer.

Noah whinnied from a distance, still waiting. Andrew looked toward the horse and made a double clicking sound with his tongue and cheek. The animal trotted up to stand behind the pair.

"I've been here, of course," Andrew said. He picked up the reins.

"Why haven't I seen you?"

"You see me ride around all day." He looked into her hazel eyes. He saw a flash of passion there. *What could I do now? What would she want?*

"I expected you to come."

"Come?" he said.

"To me. Don't mix me up." She stopped.

He stopped, let the reins fall, and faced her again. He took both her hands and held them to his chest. She let him do it and felt the beating of his heart and the vibration of his voice.

"I haven't forgotten you or the kiss. Our kiss."

"It meant a lot to me," she said.

Andrew looked into her eyes. She smelled good. He noticed her sigh. "I should have come." It finally dawned on him.

"I was stirred." Embarrassed at her own openness, Rachel's eyes began to glisten with tears and her cheeks were turning red.

"It was my fault for not coming," he said. *He cared for her. Didn't want to do any harm. He saw her tears ready to fall on her soft pink cheeks.*

"Did it mean anything?" she said. *Afraid to know and afraid to not know but had to.*

"Does this?" He pulled her close, kissed both her cheeks, and then her lips. They stood there with their foreheads touching. She stepped toward him pressing her body into his. He knew the rumor mill would rumble about their display of affection for the rest of the trip.

"That's much better," she whispered. "I didn't know what to think."

"I had some thinking to do myself." He could feel her ample bosom against his chest and felt her breath on his face.

"You can include me, you know," she said.

They stood there. She held his hands. He wasn't ready for this. Not now.

"There's a past. I'm still living there part of the time," Andrew said.

"So am I."

"I still see Elizabeth in my dreams," he said.

"I've been sad year after year and been alone for too long."

"She and I grew up together, woven together—then ripped apart. I lost her forever."

"And so you went to war?"

"And more." Things he wouldn't talk about. "But the war gave me purpose."

"Like this wagon train?" she said.

"I need a purpose. A direction. Some North Star. A destiny to pursue."

"I hadn't heard from Carl for eight years. I was living in a haze, a fog."

Rachel watched as Andrew straightened, stepped back, and reached into the pocket of his vest.

"Lieutenant Ingram gave me this message. It's from Colonel Powell back at Fort Childs. I asked him to find out what he could about your husband."

"And you've had it for two days?" she said.

"It's nothing definite."

Rachel opened the note: *Have contacted Department of Treasury and General Land Office, requesting whereabouts of Carl Richards. More to come.*

"So this is why you've been avoiding me."

"I don't know. I hadn't thought of it that way. Maybe that's so," he said.

"You don't know if I'm free," Rachel said. She couldn't blame him if he didn't trust her.

"I don't know. Neither do you."

"And if I am free?" Could she trust him with her heart, her son, her sister, her life? Could she trust her own feelings? What could she count on?

"That brings us back to what started this conversation, I reckon. We've got maybe four months to go, and I don't want any broken hearts."

They heard Billy sound his bugle to alert the train to saddle up and head out.

"Your heart or mine?" she said.

"Yes. Neither yours nor mine."

She kissed him again.

"What's that for?" he asked.

"I'm glad you came by."

"I think I may go crazy waiting to hear something definite, waiting, holding back," Andrew said.

Even though she already knew more, Rachel said, "Then we'll go crazy together."

~ * ~

Mid-morning of the 60th day, the prairie schooners creaked and moaned their way west again along the dusty Oregon Trail. Andrew rode Noah to the back of the train. He stopped beside Billy, who pointed down the trail.

"See the dust cloud," Billy said. "Someone is coming at a pretty good pace. Probably twenty or thirty horses."

Andrew pulled out his telescope. "I can see them. Cavalry. Flags and about that many. My guess is they are on maneuvers. I'll keep the train going. The soldiers will be here soon enough."

The column of soldiers came to a halt. Billy greeted the lieutenant as he rode up. "Hello. What say you?"

"We're headed to Fort Laramie and patrolling for hostiles. By the way, we met up with another wagon train coming this way about two days back."

"We're making pretty good time. I doubt they'll catch up," Billy said.

"Our troop is passing through, but I have a message for your wagon master, Captain Greene."

The officer and Billy trotted along the trail and found Andrew coming toward them.

"Lieutenant," Andrew said.

Billy said, "They're on their way to Fort Laramie."

"Sir, I have a message for you from Colonel Powell." The young officer handed a pouch to Andrew who pulled out a letter and read it. His jaw tightened, and he slowly shook his head.

"Thank you for bringing this such a long way," Andrew said. "Your troop is welcome to rest and visit us at the next river crossing. We could use some help, I expect, if you have time. Billy, see what Frenchie has we can feed this man and fill his canteen. I've got to see someone."

Andrew rode up to Rachel who was goading her team of oxen.

"I must talk to you," he said.

She handed her goad stick to Daniel and stepped with Andrew to the side of the trail. The wagons kept rolling by.

"What is it?" she said.

"It appears you and the truth are still strangers."

"Whatever do you mean?" Rachel sighed.

"A rider from the fort just gave me this." Andrew handed her the letter.

She took the piece of paper. "I don't like your tone. What are you talking about?" Her lips moved while she read the message.

Andrew said, "This here is what I've been waiting for, some confirmation regarding the whereabouts of your Carl Richards. It says your husband died almost two months ago in St. Louis from cholera."

"I can read it." When Rachel looked up again her eyes were filled with tears.

"You said you hadn't seen him in eight years," he said. "You didn't know where he was."

"I *didn't* know where he was."

"Colonel Powell found out easily enough. He wrote to Washington to the Department of the Interior."

"Well, the Army has more resources than I."

"Remember the first day, when you brought your donkey wagon to St. Joseph, had you indeed come from New Orleans?"

"Of course. My father just died. We sold the restaurant. We had to leave. Everything Claudine and I have is in that wagon."

"Why don't I believe you?"

Rachel folded her arms across her chest. "I suppose you are a suspicious man. I don't know what else you want to hear."

"The truth would be nice."

"I am tired and fed up with this suspicion."

"Solve this mystery for me then."

~ * ~

Before the next break on the journey, Billy rode up to Andrew. "Cap'n, Preacher asked you come see him."

"Anything in particular?" Andrew asked.

"Didn't say." Billy rode on.

The cavalry was preparing to move out. The troops were mounted on their horses and pulled along the gang members' horses at the rear of the platoon. After getting medical care and a night of safe rest, the pregnant woman had recovered enough to ride a horse. She rode at the front near the lieutenant. The reunited mother and daughter known as 'Cathy' rode next to the sergeant.

A few hours later, the wagon train stopped near a stream so folks could water themselves and their animals, Andrew walked to the Crawfords' buckboard. "How are your horses doing, Preacher?"

Preacher Crawford tied off the reins on the side of the seat. "Afternoon, Andrew. They're holding up fine. Emily has some biscuits left from this morning. Would you break bread with me?"

The preacher motioned for Andrew to take a seat on the buckboard. "I have to tell you some of our parishioners talked to me this morning."

"A concern?" Andrew said.

"Yes. I hear you and Mrs. Richards were kissing and hugging out in front of everybody."

Andrew took a bite of biscuit and looked straight ahead at a stream cutting across the trail. "I'm not surprised, Preacher, many people want to get in other folks' business."

Preacher Crawford rested his hand on Andrew's shoulder. "You must remember something. We are both leaders of this wagon train, and as one of the leaders I need you to set the right example, the right kind of behavior, above question."

Andrew shifted in the seat and took out his gold watch to check the time: 12:30.

Preacher Crawford continued. "My point is it's not proper for you to carry on with a married woman."

Andrew thought this might come up. "I see."

"Or for a married woman to interfere with you."

"Preacher, I just received a message this monring from Commander Powell. Rachel is no longer married. She's a widow."

"Well, from what she said this morning, I've been *avoiding* her for a few days. You know she said she was abandoned by her husband, something like eight years ago, after the birth of her son. So, frankly, I've been escorting her to keep some of the other men away."

Preacher turned his hat in his hands. "You think you can stop pursuing her?"

"I do find myself drawn to her."

"It's been a challenge for me to keep quiet, Andrew, what with the amount of drinking going on with those ex-soldiers and the betting on the horse race ya'll ran. There are fistfights and drunken men. I need you to straighten out a few things, to set an example of how to behave. The folks are watching me and you. We need to set an example."

Andrew ran his fingers through his hair and twisted the ends of his mustache.

"But I need you to set a moral example for this rolling community," Crawford said.

"I hear you, Preacher," Andrew said. A mixed wave of remorse, guilt, anger, and disappointment churned in his mind. "I'll talk to Rachel as soon as I can."

An hour later, the last wagon in the train creaked by Andrew and Rachel, who were lost in conversation.

"Like I just said, what Preacher Crawford says is we have to stop being affectionate and close to each other in front of the people on this trip. They're all talking and some have complained about how we're acting in front of their families, their children and all. The preacher wants to know the truth about your husband and your marriage, and he wants to hear it direct from you."

"All right," Rachel said, waving away the dust in the air. "But I'm just going to tell this once, so you and I have to meet with the preacher. The sooner, the better. Right now is good for me. How about you?"

He knew Rachel had a temper, but he hadn't seen her so mad. Andrew was torn; torn between finally hearing the truth, if he could believe the next explanation, and trying to keep his heart intact. All he knew was what Rachel told him, and what Colonel Powell had reported.

Rachel and Andrew rode double on Noah past the entire wagon train and up to the Crawfords' buckboard. The Crawfords pulled over and stopped. Rachel asked the preacher to hear her explanation, and asked Emily to stay too. The four stood next to the buckboard near a dry riverbed. The rest of the train of schooners kept rolling by, led by Billy.

"I know everybody on this train wants to know more about me, Preacher, as well as you," Rachel began somewhat calmly.

"It's unfortunate it's come to this, Mrs. Richards, but it will be helpful to know more, if you can share it," Preacher Crawford said. Emily put her arm around Rachel's shoulders.

"In January of this year," Rachel began, "I myself had just learned my missing husband's survey team was in St. Louis. So, I figured he *had* to be there. It had truly been eight years since I had seen or heard from him, and I was determined to confront him and end the uncertainty of my life." She paused to breathe. Andrew tossed Noah's reins across a wheel of the buckboard.

"In New Orleans, with my father dead, and being a woman on my own, I was having trouble with bankers and finances." Rachel put her hand to her forehead. "Andrew, my knees are giving out. I feel faint."

She took two steps and knelt. Andrew handed her his canteen. Emily lifted a blanket from the back of the buckboard. They all four sat in what little shade the wagon provided.

"Drink this," Andrew said. "Do you want to wait?" Rachel took two swallows and shook her head.

"It was a long journey by steamboat," she continued. "By the time we got to St. Louis, a cholera outbreak had begun. I told Claudine to stay with Daniel at a café, and I would look for Carl."

Andrew saw Billy looking toward them from farther up the trail and waved for him to keep going. Rachel took another drink from the canteen.

"So, you found him?" the preacher asked.

"I was so angry with Carl. What he put me through. How he had abandoned Daniel. My father hated Carl for it. So did Claudine. The survey crew told me Carl was in the hospital. I wasn't allowed in at first. Finally, a nurse let me in but warned me he had cholera and not to touch him."

"Did he even know you?" Emily said.

"Yes. He cried as soon as I walked in," Rachel said. "He was exhausted and his skin was a pale blue color. He could barely speak. He apologized and asked forgiveness with tears running down his face. He was a broken man. The nurse told me he had less than a day to live. You know, I didn't wish such a thing on him. I wouldn't. I only wanted peace in my life and to get a resolution, but not in such a way." She took a breath.

"He knew he was dying. Carl told me where his money was. I could have all of it. He wanted me to have it. He was able to write a note to the bank and told the nurse to give me his wallet. I left him. There was a lot of chaos in the town. It took some doing but the bank complied. By the time I got back to the hospital he had died."

"So, you lied to me from the beginning," Andrew said.

"Andrew, is that all you understand from what I told you? Why don't you arrest me, Sheriff? Go ahead and shoot me like you shot Quinn. I'm a criminal."

"I didn't say that."

"Do you understand what it's been like for me? *I was abandoned.* My father and Claudine kept me going. If I hadn't sought Carl out, I would still not know. He never asked about his own child. He had a small fortune by the end. It's only right that I use it as much as possible for Daniel, for his future."

"Yes, of course," the preacher said.

She bowed her head again and then rose. She faced them.

"Andrew, I'm so sorry I had to lie to you. I don't know if you and I can have any kind of future. I think it might be best we stop at the next fort and I'll wait for the next wagon train."

"I don't want that," Andrew said.

"I'm sorry I lied to you. I thought it wouldn't matter once we made it to Oregon. You understand I was trying to protect my son and my sister as well as myself. I didn't know I would care so much about you."

Andrew nodded. "I hope we can find a way to put this behind us."

"I'm not perfect, Andrew. I think you want perfection, and if you do, you'll never find someone who is. Maybe the next woman will wonder if you are perfect with a perfect past of your own." She was sorry as soon as the words escaped her lips. "I'm sorry to sound so bitter. It's been so long since I could rely on anyone besides myself. Yes, I lied and I am sorry."

Andrew's mind flashed on his time under a table at the Bluff Bar, Molly, and drunken nights. He helped Rachel keep standing, "I'm not perfect. I'm angry," he said. "I asked Colonel Powell to find out about your husband. Knowing more now makes me feel like a fool. You knew his whereabouts and fate all along. How do you think that makes me feel?"

"I was desperate. I still am. I don't know what awaits us at the end of this miserable trip. This is all I can do now. It's best to let me be." She began walking toward the train.

"Do you want to ride?"

She ignored him, the preacher, and Emily. And kept walking.

Thirty-one

"Mama said to bring this to you," Daniel said as he appeared next to Andrew, who looked up from the overturned bucket where he was seated. "Hello, Daniel. What have you got there?"

"Dessert. It's good. Anyways, I like it. Strawberry pie."

Andrew opened a linen tea towel to discover a slice of fresh baked pie on a china dish along with a sterling silver fork.

Frenchie looked up from the campfire where he was scraping the remains of burnt biscuits out of a Dutch oven.

Andrew said, "You want a bite, Frenchie?"

"No, not me," he said. "Hello, Daniel."

"Hey, Mister Frenchie."

Frenchie said, "Andrew, did I ever tell you how to catch a duck?"

Daniel and Andrew looked at each other and then at Frenchie.

"I don't think so," Andrew said.

"How do you catch a duck?" Daniel said.

"First, you dig a little v-shaped ditch, wider at the front, deeper at the back point," Frenchie said.

"Is this for any duck?" Daniel said.

"Pretty much," Frenchie said. "They gotta be walking around on the ground—not flying. So, you dig the V and take some kernels of tasty corn and lay about five in a row leading up to the opening of the little ditch. And then you put some more in the V going down all the way to the deep end where it's narrower."

"So, a mallard," Daniel said.

"Yes, a mallard will do."

Andrew said, "Then what?"

"Once the duck eats the corn all the way to the narrow, deep end, you run up and capture it."

"Why don't it fly away?" Daniel said.

"Because the ditch is so narrow at the deep end, the bird can't spread its wings."

Andrew ate a second bite of strawberry pie. "This sure is good pie, Frenchie. Sure you don't want some."

Frenchie shook his head. "No, but thanks."

Daniel looked at Andrew, who winked and finished the last of the pie.

Andrew said, "Let's take this beautiful plate and special fork back to your mama, so I can thank her."

They left the campfire behind and Daniel said, "Captain, why did Frenchie tell us the duck story?"

"Don't worry about it. Frenchie has lots of tales to tell."

As the pair walked away, Frenchie called out, "Andrew, let me know if you see a trail of corn kernels."

"Just keep on cleaning that pot, Frenchie."

~ * ~

On the 81st day, the Crawford Company reached the Continental Divide. The 20 wagons in the train stopped early at 4:00 o'clock to celebrate. Low grasses covered the plains, relieving the pioneers of constant dust clouds. They could all see the Rocky Mountains rising before them. Preacher Crawford and Andrew called everyone together.

"This is one of the special days we've been talking about," the preacher said. "You won't see a fence along here or any signs, but we are standing along the Continental Divide of this great country, which means the next time it rains the water will run off toward the Pacific Ocean instead of toward the Atlantic Ocean. The rivers we cross will now run toward the Pacific Coast."

"And," said Andrew, "you will want to know this is about the halfway point of our long journey."

Everyone cheered. Men yelled and threw their hats in the air. Women and children screamed and laughed. Babies cried.

"Tonight," said Emily Crawford, "our families will celebrate with cakes and pies. There will be a baking contest, music, and dancing. Of course, everyone is invited." There was more cheering. The women smiled at each other, all eager to show off their baking skills and have fun.

"For those of you who are just learning about this great divide," Andrew said, "it runs along the mountains from way up North almost to the North Pole and way down South, past Mexico, all the way to the tip of South America. Tomorrow we will head through the South Pass to get past the Rockies. If our good luck continues, we have beaten the snow and bad cold weather."

After dinner, a square dance for all who wanted to join in, games with small prizes for children, and a few stolen sips of whiskey out of sight of Preacher Crawford made for a fun evening. After tastings by a group of five judges, Emily Crawford's mincemeat pie of venison, raisins, and spices won the baking contest. Frenchie's Dutch oven peach cobbler received great praise as did Rachel's apple crumb cake. Both Frenchie and Rachel were pleased their canned fruit had held up so well.

~ * ~

The weather began to change. Threatening clouds filled the sky, blocking out flickering stars. A new moon was dark. Children were rounded up and families gathered in wagons or tents in anticipation of a coming storm. Campfires died down and everyone turned in. Except for the sounds of shuffling hooves of oxen and horses, a quiet darkness fell across the camp. The temperature dropped, and a chilling wind began to blow.

When the rains came, so did flashes of lightning and claps of thunder. Restless animals were getting close to panic. In the dark, unseen rivulets turned into flowing waters. Weary wranglers mounted up and rode their horses around the herd of cattle. No one wanted a stampede of the skittish beasts. Sentries calmed the draft animals in the corral of wagons. A herd breaking out of the corral could destroy equipment, trample tents, and end lives.

Rain beat on the canvas covers of the prairie schooners and tents. It was a real test of the layers of linseed oil designed to keep water out.

By morning, the storm had gone, leaving in its wake muddy puddles, wet animals, and shaken pioneers. Andrew and Billy made their rounds to see who was soaking wet and who needed help building fires for breakfast. Bags of dried buffalo dung would be the fuel of choice, because hard-to-find wood or brush was saturated.

Rachel walked up to the lead wagon where Frenchie and Andrew were starting to pack for the day's journey. "I'm looking for Daniel. Did he come to you with another question and a stomach ready for breakfast?"

The men looked at each other and back at Rachel.

"No," Andrew said, "haven't seen him."

"Well, do you know where he is?" she said.

"We haven't seen the boy today," Frenchie said.

Andrew asked, "When did you see him last?"

"He got up before sunrise. Put on his boots and walked out to find a place to pee. I fell back to sleep. This morning I guessed he'd be up here visiting you."

Andrew told Frenchie to finish packing. He took Rachel by the arm. "Let's go back to your tent for a minute."

"Claudine and I have already packed it in the wagon."

Andrew turned to Frenchie. "Please find Billy and Ray and send them to Rachel's campsite."

Rachel said, "Andrew, you're scaring me. What is it?"

"I don't know. That's why we're going to your campsite."

"Oh, Andrew."

"Could be he found something of interest or just wandered off. I expect he'll be along soon. Let's go see."

Billy and Ray met up at Rachel's wagon. "We've got a missing boy," Andrew began. "Daniel left the tent before sunup and needs to be found. Ray, please do some tracking as best you can in this wet ground. The boy's wearing his boots. Billy, ride from wagon to wagon. He may be visiting or asleep somewhere."

After a few minutes Ray came back. "Let me show you what I found, Andrew."

Rachel said, "Not without me."

Ray led the two to the edge of camp on the north side. "I followed Daniel's boot prints this far. Then, you see them other prints? Those are moccasins."

Rachel grabbed Andrew's arm. "My boy!"

"One set of moccasins," Ray said, "there are some drag marks here. Must have been a little struggle. Then just the moccasins by themselves but deeper, like an Indian carrying something heavy."

"Oh, God," Rachel started crying.

"It's the Shoshone, I bet," Andrew said.

"I can't believe they'd come out during the storm and at night, but, yeah, this is Shoshone territory," Ray said.

Billy rode up. "Nobody's seen Daniel this morning ...what's going on?"

"Indians took Daniel," Rachel cried.

"All right, Rachel," Andrew said, "we'll get him back. Don't worry."

"I'm coming with you," she said.

"No. I need you here when we bring him back. You and Claudine need to stay with the wagons."

"He's all I've got. I have to go find him."

"I can't let you go. It'll be hard enough rescuing him without protecting you at the same time."

"He's all I've got, Andrew. You have to bring him back safe and sound. You hear me?"

"Of course," Andrew said. "Ray and I will go."

Ray and Billy walked a few steps away, following the tracks.

Andrew said, "Billy, get this train moving. We'll catch up as soon as we can."

Rachel said, "Shouldn't Claudine and I wait here, Andrew?"

"No. It won't be safe. I'm sure the Indian lives somewhere around here with his tribe. I think the Shoshone are trying to warn us to keep moving on through their territory. Daniel was just in the wrong place at the wrong time."

Rachel fell into Andrew's arms. He held her close and whispered to her. "I'll get him. I'll get him."

She looked at him with tears running down her face. "Dear God, please save him. Be careful and get him back to me."

"Billy, help Rachel get to her wagon, and tell McFarland and the rest of the men to keep their weapons handy. The Shoshone may come back. Ray, mount up. We're leaving now."

A few minutes later, Ray dismounted near some sage. "By these footprints, they're going toward the hills."

The land fell away into a swell of cottonwoods. Ray took a few steps. "Here's where they mounted up. The droppings are cold. It's been three or four hours, my guess."

"They could be watching us now," Andrew said. They mounted up and pressed onward next to each other while Ray kept an eye on the hoofprints left by the Indian's horse.

"At least there's no blood," Ray said. "I'm thinkin' an Injun wanted a slave or some bargaining chip."

"For food maybe. Why not steal the cattle?"

"Wranglers were guarding the herd all night."

"What were our sentries doing?" Andrew said.

"Good question to ask when we get back."

"The Shoshone should know we're passing through, not homesteading here."

"Maybe they want to parlay. They'll probably see us coming."

"They wanted a hostage because they don't trust us."

"Understandable."

"Daniel's got to be scared and mad."

"Should we try and grab a few of their tribe?"

"I'd go for the horses when it comes to trading."

"Hard to do with just us."

Two hours later, Ray and Andrew began to smell smoke. There were signs of more horses and worn paths cutting through the grasses. They dismounted and hid their horses before ascending a grassy hill, staying low. When they got to the crest of the wooded knoll, it ended in a cliff and a valley appeared below them.

A wide, tree-lined stream ran through the valley in front of a village of twenty Shoshone teepees. The village was active with women washing at the edge of the stream and children chasing each other through the camp. Horses were in two corrals at either end of the village. Some braves were standing or sitting around campfires. Buffalo hides were being cleaned and stretched by another group of women. Animal bones lay nearby at the base of wooden drying racks.

"These trees offer pretty good cover," Andrew said. "Isn't it about two-hundred yards to the teepees?"

"I reckon," Ray said.

"What can you do with your rifle?"

Ray looked at him. "Ask the dead bear back at Fort Childs."

Andrew pulled out his telescope and aimed it at the camp. "I need to see signs of Daniel. I don't want to get the wrong tribe."

"What can you see?"

The men heard the beat of horse hooves, fell silent, and lay flat in the grass. A party of five braves galloped down a trail toward the camp. A deer carcass was slung across the last horse.

"A hunting party," Ray said.

"I expect they'll be in camp for a while now. There may be more out somewhere." Andrew passed the spy glass to Ray. "Take a look at the tent near the first corral."

Ray held the glass to his eye. "I see what you mean ...and there's a brave takin' in a bowl of food now. I bet it's for their hostage. Otherwise, I'd expect to see a squaw doing that."

"We need to make a plan. Here's what I'm thinking ..."

All the Indians saw him coming. Andrew and Noah ambled to the edge of the camp. He held up both his arms, a sign of peace. Six braves surrounded him and pushed him to the ground. Noah reared up and the Indians backed away. Andrew hollered, "It's all right. Down. Down," and the horse settled but pawed at the ground.

The Indians pulled off Andrew's buckskin jacket and shirt. He was led toward a campfire and pushed to the ground face down. They held spears pointed at his back. Two braves wrestled off his boots. They whooped loudly at their prize.

Even with his head down, Andrew could see women and children at work fixing food, weaving, and skinning small game. There were other whites in the camp—three women dressed in Indian garb who looked like they had been there a long time. One of the women looked at him and shook her head. She looked back down at her work when a Shoshone woman slapped her.

"Daniel," Andrew shouted, "Daniel, can you hear me?"

A muffled voice came from the first teepee, "Captain, I'm here."

Andrew felt something hard hit his head.

He woke up, still lying on the ground, hearing a new voice in English. "Hey, Mister Captain. Mister Captain." Andrew struggled to sit up. In front of him squatted a thin white boy, a few years older than Daniel. "You wake up now."

"Who are you?" Andrew said.

"Chief knows why you're here. To get boy. We watched your wagons for three days, crossing our land."

Andrew could see the boy more clearly now. His long, light hair was braided and his skin tanned.

"What's your name? How long have you been here with the Shoshone?"

"They call me Chayton. Means falcon. Before Shoshone, my name was Tom Dixon. Now Chayton."

"How long?"

"Maybe three years. Shoshone killed my family. Took me."

"Where's Daniel? The boy. Where is he?"

"Safe in the teepee. The chief will talk to you now. Come. I'll tell you what he says."

Andrew rose and walked shirtless and barefooted behind Chayton toward a large teepee in the middle of the camp. Two braves followed behind, carrying spears.

The chief stood outside the tent, arms crossed. He wore a long headdress made of eagle feathers, beads, and leather. His chest was bare except for a breastplate made of buffalo bones. His hide pants led down to beaded moccasins. Andrew stood with his shoulders back and looked the chief in the eye.

The chief stared back at Andrew, then spoke only to Chayton who translated, "Chief Matho says he sees by scars on you that you are a warrior. He also says you are foolish to ride into our village."

Andrew looked at Chayton. "Tell him I am only here for the boy, whose mother is crying for him."

Chayton translated the words. More braves encircled the trio. Chief Matho talked more.

Chayton said, "I tell you this will not be easy. The chief says *wasi'cu*, white men, cross our land too much. Bring disease and death."

"Then why take one of us captive?" Andrew said.

"To save your head from being cut from your body, I will not tell chief that. The boy will replace our brave's son who died with fever. What else can you say?"

"Tell him I must leave with the boy today, or I will call on the gods to rain down terror on this village."

Chayton looked from Andrew to the chief, swallowed hard, and spoke the words. The chief snorted, put a hand tightly on Chayton's shoulder, and spoke in anger. Chayton translated, "He says you have proved yourself crazy. He does not believe your power."

"Ask him what he wants in exchange for the boy."

"He will not."

"You didn't ask him."

"No need to."

"Ask him what he wants in trade for the boy."

Before Chayton could translate, Chief Matho raised his right hand in a sweeping arc and began chanting. Drummers began a steady beat.

"You are a fool, *wasi'chu*," Chayton said. "The chief will show you how little you are now. He must please tribe. Our people want revenge against the white man."

The steady drum beat acted as a call for all the tribe to gather. The braves and boys formed a circle. Andrew recognized the formation, a fighting ring. Every member of the tribe held a stick or club.

Chayton spoke. "Each of these lost family or friends because of white men, by disease you brought or in battles. The chief's young son died last year by sickness brought by white men. You must pay for their deaths."

Two of the Shoshone hit Andrew with clubs and pushed him to the ground in the middle of the ring of Indians. He felt the points of spears at his back. He knew he had to win whatever fight was coming or die trying.

Chayton poked Andrew's ribs with a club. "Get up now, if you want to live."

Feeling pain throughout his body, Andrew rose to his knees then stood.

Chayton looked in Andrew's eyes. "The chief said, if you live, you will have passed our test of a warrior."

Andrew realized this fight was a game for the chief and the tribe. Entertainment and revenge. Something to prove power over him, and over white men everywhere and over the wagon trains crossing their lands.

An Indian woman stopped in front of Andrew and placed a bucket of water with a gourd in front of him. "*Mni*," she said and walked away.

"She said water," Chayton said. "That's my mother. My Shoshone mother."

Andrew drank water from the gourd and poured water over his head and arms.

"You may die here today, Mister Captain." Chayton looked toward a group of braves and back to Andrew. "Chief asks what is the boy to you. Is the boy your son?"

Andrew said, "He's not my son, but he's the son of a woman I love."

"Where's his father?"

"His father is dead ...Is that you asking, or the chief?"

Chayton went on. "You will fight Wirasuap for the boy, means bear spirit. He took the boy."

"I don't have any weapons," Andrew said.

"No weapons. Look there."

Andrew turned and saw the brave, Wirasuap, waiting for him. The Indian was stripped to his waist and barefoot, wearing a leather loincloth, and holding no weapons. Andrew's ears were still ringing from the noise and blows to his head.

Would this be a fight to the death?

Chayton said, "If you win, you take boy. Wirasuap win, we keep boy."

Before Andrew could protest, two braves slapped his arms with reeds and pushed him to the ground again. He landed on his hands and knees, his arms bleeding from many small cuts from the reeds. Wirasuap was fifteen feet away and shifting from one foot to the other. All the Indians began chanting and the drums continued a deafening rhythm. Andrew could only guess there were no rules.

The din from the shouting crowd and drums merged into a continuous roar. Andrew rose to his feet. Wirasuap took two steps toward him. Andrew ran forward, jumped, and slammed both his feet into Wirasuap's chest, knocking him to the ground. The chanting suddenly stopped. It began again as Wirasuap rolled over then stood with anger in his eyes.

Andrew thought of the combat instructions his father had given him years ago and his own battles. He flashed back to his fights to the death with sworn enemies. His body ached. He saw Wirasuap grab a handful of dirt. He knew what was coming. The Indian charged and threw the dirt toward Andrew's face. Andrew put his hands up and closed his eyes and swung his right fist toward Wirasuap. The blow landed on Wirasuap's face but it didn't stop him from launching his body into Andrew's.

The two men wrestled on the ground, rolling over and over. Each man trying to put a choke hold on the other. Wirasuap grabbed Andrew's hair and pulled his head back, exposing his neck. Andrew flipped over Wirasuap's body, forcing him into the dirt. Andrew pressed his knee into the small of the Indian's back. Wirasuap tried to crawl away, but Andrew held on and pressed the Indian's body into the dust. Wirasuap gasped for breath.

Three braves ran into the circle. One kicked Andrew in the ribs. The other two pulled Wirasuap to safety. The drums stopped. Andrew felt another blow to the back of his head.

When Chayton poured a bucket of water on his face, Andrew jumped up ready to fight again. "You can stop now." Chayton said. "Chief says you were lucky Wirasuap and tribe not kill you."

"I don't want to kill anyone. I just want the boy back," Andrew said.

The two walked to the chief's teepee followed by braves. "I see you are a good warrior, good fighter."

"It's time for the boy and me to leave," Andrew said.

"Maybe, maybe not. The chief is not sure."

"Sure of what. The fight's over."

The chief and Chayton talked. The chief shook his head, crossed his arms and looked from Chayton to Andrew.

"Chief Matho says it's time to talk trade."

"I have nothing to trade. I won the fight. Does the chief not abide by his own rules? Is he a man of his word to be trusted? Ask him."

"No. I will not say that to chief and get us both killed."

Chayton turned to the chief and talked. The chief nodded and a buffalo hide was spread on the ground. They motioned for Andrew to sit down with them. His boots and clothing were returned. Then the chief and two braves sat cross-legged.

"We talk trade now," Chayton said.

Andrew said, "I didn't agree to trade."

"It's a good day to stay alive. Yes?"

"What does the chief want, and I want to see the boy is all right."

Women brought food and drink to the men on the blanket. Chayton talked with the chief and then turned to Andrew. "It is the way of the Shoshone to share good things with the whole tribe. Man should be humble even in victory."

Andrew drank water from a gourd. "Where's the boy?"

Chayton looked toward the first teepee in the village. "Still in the teepee. He is well."

"Before I talk any trading, I want the boy here."

Chayton interpreted for the chief who nodded. A brave brought Daniel to the hide. When the boy saw Andrew he burst into tears and fell into his arms. Andrew hugged Daniel. "Are you all right, son?"

"Are they going to kill us?"

"No. I'm trying to get us free. It's going to take some more time. Sit here with me quietly."

Andrew turned to Chayton. "Tell the chief we must leave today, soon, or I will call upon the gods for help."

Chayton translated for the chief who smirked and shook his head then talked to Chayton.

"Chief says you must trade for the boy. He does not believe in your gods."

"What does he want?" Andrew finally said.

Chief Matho raised one eyebrow and pointed a finger at Andrew. "Horse."

Andrew looked from the chief to Chayton who said, "You keep the saddle. We give you other horse."

It was not a time to negotiate further. Andrew loved his loyal horse, but he let out a low whistle then clicked his tongue three times. Noah trotted up.

"Agreed," Andrew said.

Daniel had stopped crying. He ate some of the food and drank water. "Captain, is there another way?"

"This is for the best," Andrew said. He removed the saddle and tack from Noah and talked quietly to the horse. Then he turned back to the Indian boy.

"Chayton, so he doesn't get upset, explain this to the chief. I want to show him I can talk to one of my gods. I'm going to use my rope and pull this buffalo skull to the top of the totem pole, so the god can reach it."

"That's not good thinking," Chayton said, but he told the chief what was happening. The chief laughed, shook his head, and waved a hand to keep everyone calm.

Andrew threw a rope over the top of the pole and tied a sun-bleached buffalo skull to one end. He quickly pulled it up to the top of the totem. The chief and braves laughed and watched as Andrew started to dance in a circle in front of the pole. The braves pointed and imitated Andrew. Daniel watched, wondering what was going on, then Andrew stopped and held both his arms into the air.

Andrew shouted, "God of thunder, show the chief your power." Chayton interpreted for the chief.

Andrew kept standing, repeating his plea loudly, "God of thunder, show the chief your power."

Suddenly, the skull shattered. The pieces fell to the ground just as the sound of a thunderclap reached the ears of the tribe members. They all fell silent. Andrew turned to the chief whose eyes were wide in disbelief. The chief waved his hand and spoke to Chayton, who interpreted for Andrew and Daniel.

"Chief says take your horse back now. Leave. Never come again."

Though his braves were cowered by the shattered skull, Chief Matho recognized the clap of thunder was the report from a rifle. He quickly realized Andrew was not alone and there was at least one skilled rifleman in the distance who could not only shatter an animal skull but could shatter a chief's skull. It had been a good day of revenge for his tribe, but the chief knew when to stop displaying his own power. He would fight another day.

Thirty-two

To the west, when the wagon train stopped for the day, Rachel saddled Daniel's horse Paint and rode fast back down the trail to look for her son. Claudine followed after her on a borrowed horse. From his position at the lead wagon, Billy saw the sisters ride out.

He wasn't about to let two women head back into Indian territory alone. He yelled to Frenchie, "If we aren't back in half an hour, send McFarland and his men to get us."

Minutes later dusk was approaching when the two women saw Andrew, Daniel, and Ray riding toward them. Everyone stopped. The women jumped from their mounts, and Daniel found sobbing comfort in the arms of his mother and then his aunt.

Rachel pulled Andrew to her, crying. "Thank you for saving him. You know he's what I live for." Then she saw cuts on Andrew's arms and red welts on his face. "What happened? What did they do to you? Are you all right?"

"I'll be fine," Andrew said, wincing. "I need some salve and some rest, though. I think Emily will fix me up."

"Mama, you should have seen it," Daniel said. "The Indians were mean, really mean. They beat him with sticks and kicked and hit him. I had to stay in a teepee. It was sort of dark in there, but I could see through a hole what was happening."

"Oh, Andrew." Rachel reached up to touch some clotted blood on Andrew's head but he stepped back.

"It's tender, Rachel. I got hit in the head a few times," Andrew said.

"Oh, Andrew, I didn't know if I'd ever see any of you again. I was beside myself." She put her arms around Daniel and Andrew.

"Mama, they wanted to keep Noah, and then Captain Greene danced, and Mister Cooper shot a buffalo skull from way off, and the chief told us to get out, and we did."

"You should see the expression on your face," Ray said to Rachel. "And I've never seen Andrew dance like that before."

"It may seem funny to you people, but Claudine and I were worried sick," Rachel said.

Billy said, "Let's get back to the wagons before Frenchie sends a rescue party out for us."

When they all reached the camp, the preacher's wife Emily was waiting for Andrew as he entered the Crawfords' tent. Rachel came right behind. "I figured you might need something," Emily said. "What did they do? What happened?"

"Nothing much. Really." Andrew said. He glanced from Rachel to Emily. "Maybe we should talk in private."

"I'm not going anywhere, Andrew," Rachel said. "I can tell you need some care, and I'm staying. Emily, let me know what I can do, please."

"Get the shirt off him," Emily said, "and wash his wounds. Then swab each cut with this alcohol." She handed a bottle to Rachel who sniffed it.

"Is this whiskey?" she said.

"Yes, it's the best alcohol we got," Emily said. "He'll probably fuss about the sting and then smell like a brewery, but that's all we got."

Andrew grimaced as Rachel helped remove his bloodstained shirt. Some of the dried blood stuck to his arms, and removing the shirt pulled off a few scabs, opening the wounds again. Rachel got her first close look at Andrew's new wounds and old scars.

Emily looked up and down Andrew's arms and back. "What did they do, Andrew? Tell me."

"These are mostly from sticks and clubs," he confessed. "I had to fight the Indian who kidnapped Daniel."

Rachel put her hand to her mouth, not wanting to gasp or cry out.

Emily pressed on. "Did you kill him?"

"No, it wasn't like that."

"I see you've got some head wounds. Some lumps. Dried blood," Emily said.

"Just fix what you can. I got things to do," Andrew said.

"Now, you just hush up, mister," Emily said. "You can be ornery, but if we don't do this as best we can, you may get an infection."

"Rachel," Emily said, "go ahead and dab or pour whiskey on him. It's better than his wounds getting worse. I need to go mix up a salve, and I'll be back in a few minutes."

"Let me have a drink before you bathe me in it," Andrew said, taking the bottle out of Rachel's hand. He swallowed hard and gave the bottle back. "Just start at my shoulders and let the booze run down my arms. Then concentrate on the worst ones a second time."

"Oh, Andrew, I'm so sorry." She began to cry.

~ * ~

Frenchie invited Rachel, Claudine, and Daniel to join the lead wagon for dinner. The campfire was large and warm. Rachel brought a Dutch oven filled with a mix of canned fruit, flour, cinnamon, and sugar to be cooked for dessert. The ex-soldiers, Walt, and the leaders sat around the fire as Frenchie passed out plates of food. Patched up, Andrew leaned against a wagon wheel and Rachel sat beside him.

"This here's a stew of venison, beans, and rice," Frenchie said.

McFarland said, "Cap'n, I paid attention to your directions and my men found signs of a group of mule deer. We came upon some within half an hour this morning."

"They dragged one back here," Frenchie said, "in time for cleanin' and cookin' for tonight."

After dinner, folks returned to their own tents. Andrew pulled the cork from a fifth of whiskey using his teeth. He nodded at Frenchie, his lone companion for the cool evening, who nodded back. After a drink from the bottle, Andrew sat down on a three-legged stool by the campfire and began to pack tobacco into the bowl of his clay pipe. His saddle and blanket were nearby on the dry ground, making it an easy crawl if the liquor did its magic by midnight. He passed the bottle to Frenchie, who took a drink and savored the biting liquid.

"Rachel seems like a good woman, taking care of you and all, *mon ami*," Frenchie said.

Andrew took another sip of whiskey.

"I thought she rubbed you the wrong way. That first day," Andrew said, "bee in her bonnet, I remember you saying."

"Now I'm thinking she was pretty desperate, knowing more of her life."

Andrew poked the fire with a stick. Sparks from the campfire floated into the dark night like orange short-lived stars. "You two been talking?"

"Some," Frenchie said.

"Anything in particular?"

"She was raising her boy by herself and working all the time," Frenchie said.

"Ummm ... she had Claudine, of course, and her papa till last year," Andrew said.

"He was bedridden. Needed caring. She ran the restaurant by herself then. Of course, Claudine was a good help."

"I told you about Rachel's husband dying."

"*Oui*. I think you were hard on her."

"Frustrated. Angry. I felt lied to for a long time."

"You hold her to a high standard, yes?"

"I reckon."

"A perfect woman for a perfect man, eh?"

"You know I'm not perfect."

"It's good to be reminded no one is, yes?"

"So, what brought *this* into your brain?" Andrew passed the bottle to Frenchie.

"I was just thinking ahead, *mon ami*."

"To the end of the trail?"

"*Oui*. Pondering what's next."

"After you get there?"

They could hear muffled conversations in nearby tents.

"After *we* get there," Frenchie said quietly.

"Well, you know I've already got land to build on and farm. I expect to raise horses, sell some timber, grow what I need," Andrew said.

"Build an empire?"

Andrew shrugged. "I don't know ...so, what do you want to do?"

"Seems I've got a few weeks to figure it out."

"Plans can change ... neither of us planned to fight in the Mexican War or lead a wagon train, but here we are."

"We've been in and out of the Army for a long time," Frenchie said.

"I'm glad to be through with it ... you know, running a farm isn't easy. Takes a lot of hands."

"Guess so."

A light breeze changed direction and blew smoke toward Andrew. He moved the stool to a new spot and settled.

"I could use someone to run the house while I'm out in the fields and at markets or auctions. Keep up with things."

"Probably will need a cook," Frenchie said.

Coyotes howled in the distance.

"Or a partner."

"To take care of the household. Run things."

"Or you could work with your new friend Rachel and open a restaurant. Towns always need a place to eat. There'll be a lot of hungry mouths to feed, I expect. Get the right place and you could live upstairs. Maybe run for mayor."

"I think the whiskey is hittin' you," Frenchie said. "Being mayor is the furthest thing from my mind. Don't care for people much and sure don't want their problems. Ain't gonna' sit in meetin's or give speeches."

"So, managing a household or a farm sounds like a possibility?"

"One of the better possibilities."

Andrew stretched and yawned. "I think that's all I can ponder today. I'm turning in."

"I'll let the fire burn down some. See you in the mornin'."

Thirty-three

Daniel ran as fast as his eight-year-old legs could run, looking for help. "Captain, you gotta come quick. Mama's caught in the water."

Andrew reached down from his horse, grabbed Daniel by an arm and pulled him onto the saddle. They galloped toward the river.

Rachel was stuck in quicksand.

She had cried herself hoarse yelling for help and was sunken to her waist by the time they arrived, her white bathing gown soaked through. After Claudine had gone back to camp for soap and towels, Rachel had been left alone and waiting impatiently. She didn't want to wait and chose the wrong part of the riverbank to get a bath.

As Andrew dismounted, Rachel pleaded, "Don't look upon me. I'm almost naked, and I'm going to drown."

Andrew said, "You'll be all right, Rachel."

She pleaded, "You've got to promise me you'll protect Daniel when I'm gone."

Andrew wasn't sure what to say. He was too busy trying to save her. "You're not going anywhere."

He tied a bowline knot in a rope and tossed it to Rachel. She continued flailing in the pool of murky water, still crying, and sunk up to her chest.

"Put the loop over your head and under your arms," he said. "Lie down on your back. Stop struggling. You won't sink. Lie still."

She grabbed for the rope and did as he instructed, sticking her arms out to her sides, thinking she would drown and disappear without ever being truly in love and leaving her son to be an orphan.

After she floated on her back for a minute, the mud at the bottom of the pit finally released her feet. Rachel could feel the strength of Andrew's arms scooping her out of the murky water. She buried her face against his neck. Thanking him and God.

Andrew took her muddy body to the safe part of the eddy and rolled her in. She screamed when she bobbed out of the waist-deep water, wiping her face. She turned her back on him and chastised him for pouring her in. He laughed, relieved, but knew he would pay for it later.

When Andrew turned to leave, he was surprised to see both Claudine and Daniel running toward him, ready to push him in the water. He stepped aside and the charging Claudine fell past him into the water with Rachel. Daniel jumped on Andrew's back and they both fell in. It was the first time the sisters and Daniel had heard Andrew laugh and they liked it.

Billy watched them from atop the hill and could tell it was a good thing.

Thirty-four

The next day, Preacher Crawford was determined to help the rolling community of pioneers keep the faith. In addition to Sunday morning church service with its sermon, every Wednesday evening he conducted a prayer service which consisted of everyone gathering, sharing food, and a shorter sermon about living a Christian life.

Women brought food and their families, no matter how tired they may be. The ladies knew their folk would follow the victuals and then stay for the fellowship, singing, and inspiration. Andrew made it clear all should attend, including the ex-soldiers.

"Welcome, everyone," Preacher Crawford began. "This is a wonderful evening and we have to thank all the families who brought food for our bodies. And thank the Lord for our arrival at this point in our journey. We have come safely through dangerous parts of our trip like the storms, outlaws, and Indians, thanks to Andrew Greene, Billy Armstrong, and Ray Cooper." There was applause and some whooping from the crowd. The children weren't paying much attention. They didn't understand how close they had been to danger.

"This meeting is meant to inspire all of us, and every now and then, some of you have something to say to the group. So, right now, I'm going to turn things over to Mr. Anderson for a few words." Preacher Crawford stepped back and Anderson, hat in hand, took some uneasy steps to stand in front. His left arm was mostly healed but still in a sling.

"Well, thank you, Preacher," Anderson said. "Uh, I ain't much for speechifying, but I know I'm among friends who'll forgive me." He motioned for James Kincaid to stand beside him, and his new son-in-law obliged.

"I ... asked Preacher and Captain Greene to say somethin' bout James, but they said I should be the one to do this, so that's why I'm standin' here." He put his good right arm around the shoulders of James. "Ya'll know James here and my Ella bein' recently wed and all. And I have to admit I ain't been treating him as best I could. But I tell you he's proven himself in a big way a couple of times, and I want to state in front of all o' you, my opinion has been changed by his good actions."

James looked at his father-in-law, not knowing what was coming, but liking it so far. He scratched his head nervously.

"Before Fort Childs, when our wagon turned over on me in that terrible storm, I could'a drowned in the mud, but James was there to help keep me breathin'. And he saved us all when he took it upon hisself to ride his mule through the night and bring back the cavalry." The crowd cheered, clapped, and whooped again. Some said, "Thank you, James" out loud.

"Well, that's all I got," Mr. Anderson said and he and James stepped back into the congregation.

Preacher Crawford stepped up. "Let us bow our heads and pray. Dear Lord, we are gathered here tonight due to Your grace and Your blessing to protect us and keep us safe. We thank You for guiding us and our leaders on this long journey. We know it will bear bountiful fruit upon our arrival in Oregon. Thank You for sending us good men like James to be part of our church family. Thank You for the hands of the wonderful folks who prepared the food we are about to enjoy, and bless us in the days ahead. In Your name we pray. Amen."

Several congregants responded with their own amen. The preacher said, "I see most of you have a plate of food now and that's fine. Go on and get some if you haven't. As you eat I'm going to say a few words and then ask Mrs. Crawford to lead us in a hymn, and then we can all visit."

The preacher started talking about paths of righteousness, the Oregon Trail, and the direction of one's personal journey. Andrew was sitting on a blanket next to Rachel and Daniel. He placed his hand on hers and she wove her fingers into his. They smiled at each other. Daniel noticed and he smiled too.

Billy and Claudine sat at the back of the group on the tailgate of the sisters' wagon. They kissed and started sharing a plate of bacon, beans, and rice.

"I see your Rachel and Cap'n Greene getting close these days," Billy said between bites.

"*Oui, mon cheri*, it is a good thing, no?" She leaned against him and offered him a spoon of food which Billy accepted.

"Yeah, I reckon. You know, little Daniel comes to see the cap'n most mornin's with some kind of question. Just visiting probably."

"I think he misses his *pépé*, his grandfather, you know. Our *pére*, our father, was ze only man in Daniel's life all his years. Now, maybe, he needs a strong man in his life. Of course, Daniel likes you too. You are so good to him, yes?"

"Oh, yes, he's a fine boy."

"Rachel and I take care of him now like he has two mothers. You know I never knew my mother. Rachel has raised me along with our *pére*. She is my sister and my mother, I think."

"Something tells me you two will never part," Billy said.

"Of course not. Why should we? Daniel is like my son too. My family."

Emily Crawford began to lead the congregation in a hymn.

"I want to sing too," Claudine said. She hopped down from the wagon and walked toward the crowd.

Thirty-five

Almost a year later, in September 1849, after her marriage to Andrew, Rachel's water broke and she moaned with each contraction. The baby was coming. Midwife Emily Crawford was with her. They were having tea when it happened. Andrew was out felling trees for a new cabin, tired of living in a one-room cabin. He had taught Daniel how to wield an axe safely. A puppy was nipping at the boy's feet.

The air in Willamette Valley was clear and clean. The pastures were turning brown with the coming of autumn. Andrew wanted to get his life with his new wife right this time for his own wellbeing and for hers. So did she—for his sake, for hers and Daniel's.

The span of twelve months had been a good time for healing. Rachel needed to put the regrets of her life with Carl behind her. His death made it possible to begin. She was sad that Daniel had lost his father all those years ago, but she knew he needed a better example of what it was to be a good man. She knew she needed a loving husband for herself.

Rachel had been drawn to Andrew from the first day when she proved she could shoot straight, but she couldn't say anything. Andrew was a mystery to her. He was in charge and judging, because he had taken on the responsibility to protect all the souls on the wagon train he would lead for the next six months. Though he was an experienced leader, he wasn't perfect. She knew no one was or is.

She had learned more of the hard parts of Andrew's life and then watched him deal with every new challenge. She knew about his scars, and now their intimacy answered many of her questions about his loyalty and heart. She knew he could be trusted.

He understood her better as well. She had apologized again for lying about Carl. She explained she was desperate to be accepted onto the wagon train and knew she had to protect the futures of Claudine and Daniel. A desperate woman seeking her own destiny.

They married a day after the wagon train arrived in Willamette Valley. Preacher Crawford officiated, and the whole congregation attended the outdoor wedding. A celebratory bonfire, feast, and dancing followed.

They both had disturbing histories which needed to be put to rest but first had to be lanced for the healing to take place. It didn't matter where either of them had been before. She had to let go of her shame from being abandoned and her struggles without the help and love of a man. Andrew's pained mind, haunted by the men he had killed and horrors of war that still dwelled there. And worst of all for him was his loss of Elizabeth.

For both of them, it would take months of good things and good feelings to compensate for the years of bad. But they would make it. They were making it.

At the site of the new house, Andrew raised an axe and brought it down onto an oak log. Wood chips flew right and left with repeated blows until the log gave way—the final piece to fit into the walls of the cabin.

Rachel had approved his rough sketch two months ago: a large main room with space for a fireplace, new stove, and a dining table and two bedrooms. It would do for now. He could add more rooms later or get friends to finish a proper stick-built home. She too was tired of living in a cramped cabin and winter was coming.

Daniel filled the space between logs with a mix of mud, horsehair, and straw. His new father showed his new son how to make the mix and use a trowel.

The boy had watched his mother's belly swell during their first year as a family. He thought about his new sister or brother on the way, but it was still a mystery to him what would happen.

During spring and summer, they put up jars of vegetables and fruits for the months ahead and stored potatoes, onions, squash and carrots in a root cellar. Andrew liked the coming of autumn with the leaves turning red and yellow and the summer growing season coming to a close. It was time to pick apples and pumpkins. Andrew's timber business was underway and his livestock had multiplied. He wanted to have the cabin finished before Rachel delivered their baby.

Frenchie rode up. "I got men splittin' shingles, *mon ami*. Wagon's on the way. The cattle driver paid for grazin' with a cow and her calf. Ray's workin' with the horses and we got plenty of hay put up."

"I'm glad you're here," Andrew said. "Help me with this last log, please. I'm about wore out."

"You need to take a day off. You ain't stopped workin' since we got here."

"Or you. What's for lunch?"

"Bread, cheese, and meat."

"Should I ask what kind of meat?"

"Does it matter?"

"Probably not."

Andrew left the axe stuck in a stump. Frenchie spread a blanket in a corner of the cabin's main room. Daniel stopped mudding and poured three mugs of milk and the three ate lunch.

Frenchie said, "I s'pect we'll have the roof done before sundown, what with three or four of us doing the nailin'."

They sat cross-legged on the blanket. Frenchie passed around sandwiches. Then he opened a clay crock. "Rachel made you all a surprise this morning. Potato salad with boiled eggs, nuts, and taters. She put some mustard in there. Here's a spoon."

After his last bite of food, Andrew stepped out of the cabin to enjoy the view. He looked across his land. It rolled across a green valley, past a meadow full of tall grass and wildflowers. It jumped a full stream and climbed into the hills. He watched a bald eagle soar into the sky then dive toward the stream. The bird plucked a shining fish out of the splashing waters.

Andrew felt like he had found a new destiny and learned from the turning points in his life, after they happened. He still dreamed of Elizabeth and war, but less often. Other dreams pushed those aside. He dreamed of hearth and home, of love and warmth, and Rachel.

He smelled the clear air and didn't miss the dust of the Oregon Trail at all. He saw his new life rolling out toward the mountains. Andrew thought he was content with 360 acres and saw years of work ahead. That's what he wanted. He would put his hands and heart to work. But it dawned on him that now he had a wife, he could add 360 more free acres.

Ray galloped up to the cabin hooting and hollering. "It's happening, Andrew. Baby's on the way. Rachel said to come get you. Emily and Claudine and Billy are there, but Rachel's calling for you and Daniel."

Frenchie said, "Go on, *mon ami.* I'll get this roof up and be there as soon as I can."

Riding Noah and Paint, new father and new son raced across the meadow.

Meet Art Williams

Art Williams is retired from a sales and management career in advertising and marketing. He worked with hundreds of clients to design, write, and produce award-winning, multimedia advertising. He also taught advertising courses at local universities. Combining that experience with a degree in English and an MBA, he is pursuing his interests writing fiction and non-fiction in various genres. He's been a member of writing groups since 2018. Art lives in North Carolina with his brilliant bibliophile wife, Carol, and barking dog, Ellie.

Acknowledgments

Turning Points, my first novel, could not have happened without the support of fellow writers, family, and Wings ePress Inc., a traditional publishing firm which originally published the book. A special thanks to my beta readers, mentors, and fellow authors: Agnes Alexander, Karen McCullough, Chet Meisner, and Dr. Hope Hodgkins.

Many thanks to publisher Linda Voth for her invaluable assistance as I made the change to self-publishing.

Dear reader,

I hope you've enjoyed reading this story of
early exploration and settlement of the West.
Your opinion is valuable to other
readers like you,

who may be looking for books like mine.
Please consider taking a few minutes to post a
review, however brief,

on the site where you purchased this book.
You may also want to visit my author page
at: www.artwilliams3.com

Thank you!

Art Williams

www.ingramcontent.com/pod-product-compliance
Lightning Source LLC
Chambersburg PA
CBHW071536110726
47908CB00007B/1899